'Mears has done for post-apocaly[...] Shardlake did for historical fiction [...] against a backdrop every bit as c[...] Robert Harris' *Second Sleep*. The st[...] the characters draw the reader int[...] climax that is both satisfying and le[...] you wanting more... I am already eagerly awaiting the next instalment.'
Rev Dr Simon Woodman, author of The Book of Revelation *(SCM Core Text)*

'*A Sock Full of Bones* is a glorious mix of Victorian detective investigators, tangled web of plot, characters both nasty and do-good, and a spine-chilling dose of the supernatural.

'Banyard and Mingle's relationship is a complex mix of well-meant intentions, completely ridiculous ideas, serious detecting skills and a beautiful, mutual friendship that brings a warm touch to every interaction. The supporting characters – including the gawpers – are vivid, and the settings that surround them are evocatively eerie. The story itself is both fun and serious, with social ideals and interactions mixed into the investigation of fraud, deceit and murder.

'If you like your Sherlock Holmes with a heap more supernatural, a dash more social conscience and a Watson who proposes the worst ideas, this is the book for you.'
Kate Coe, Writing & Coe, fantasy author and editor

'Although we are transported to a highly imaginative and intriguing world, this is still a classic thriller with a hero born from the finest traditions of doing whatever it takes to solve the case. Whatever your preferences are in a murder mystery or fantasy novel, Ben Mears delivers it, and you suspect this is just the tip of the iceberg for Banyard and Mingle. I for one can't wait for the next adventure.'
*Simon Lupton, Executive Producer (*Red Dwarf, Henry IX, Marley's Ghosts, Zapped *– and many more)*

A
Banyard & Mingle
Mystery

A SOCK FULL OF BONES

B J Mears

£1.50

30.10.21

instant apostle

First published in Great Britain in 2020

Instant Apostle
The Barn
1 Watford House Lane
Watford
Herts
WD17 1BJ

British Library Cataloguing-in-Publication Data

A catalogue record for this book is available from the British Library.

This book and all other Instant Apostle books are available from Instant Apostle:

Website: www.instantapostle.com

Email: info@instantapostle.com

ISBN 978-1-912726-25-7

Printed in Great Britain.

Thanks

Special thanks to Keith Munro, Edward Field, Alison Hull,
Kate Coe, Revd Dr Simon Woodman, Dan Sefton,
Simon Lupton, Henna Mears, Matt Cooper, Dr Alistair Sims,
Chloe Smirk, Chris and Sarah Lugg, Pete and Kate
Worthington, Joy Mears, Daniel Sibthorpe, Martin and Jo
Jones, Sam Curtis, Salvatore Catania, Rodger Scott, Rob Creer,
Nicki Copeland and the fantastic team at Instant Apostle.

Contents

Camdon City and Surrounding Areas

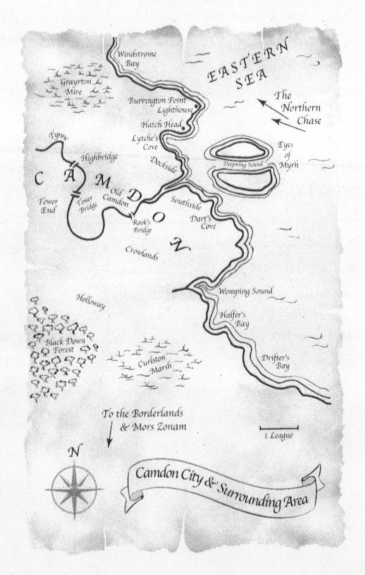

The Eleven Months of the Earthorian Year

1st: Tithemoon

2nd: Doblemoon

3rd: Trimoon

4th: Quartersmoon

5th: Thripplemoon

6th: Sixthmoon

7th: Fipplemoon

8th: Hexmoon

9th: Honourmoon

10th: Twinemoon

11th: Elventide

The threaders thread the silk.

The silkers wear the silk.

Prologue

Of all the cases that linger in my mind from those early years it is, perhaps, this one that looms largest. I was still studying my trade, one demanding trial by fire or, to put it another way, learning on the job. My father taught me what he could, of course, before passing over, but there is simply no substitute for experience, whatever your elders say.

Truly, it is not one case but many, each one complex and diverse. They rumble together like bones in a sock, a picture we shall revisit before my account is through.

My story concerns a widow, some bad men, a handful of gawpers, a philanthropist – that's me – and a violent storm. It begins on the twelfth night of Honourmoon, in the Eastern Sea. I was absent, being tucked up in bed, asleep and serenely oblivious to the drama, though others *were* there. For a few desperate and fleeting moments.

Tossed like a branch in a highland stream, the *Dollinger* rolled in thunderous waves, hull groaning under strain. The bosun pointed into the rain-lashed night and roared amid the pummelling elements.

'It's Burrington Point Lighthouse. Rocks ahead!' He slipped and slid to the ship's bell and rang it urgently. 'Turn the ship! Starboard, full rudder!'

The storm pounded at the stern, flooding the top deck, raking barrels and mariners into oblivion with its greedy reach. Through the maelstrom, Anders also glimpsed the light. He saw it swing and bellowed back across the deck as lightning flashed.

'That's a false light. A false light, I say!'

The bosun shoved him aside. 'Man the rudder! Turn the ship!'

'The ship is cursed!' shouted the mariner, Flinders. 'The sprites are coming for us!'

Deckhands grasped at rigging, at the masts, at anything fixed as the furious ocean swallowed all those who lost hold. The first mate heaved the wheel and, incredibly, the galleon turned. Slowly. Yet it turned.

'There now. What did I say? We'll ride out this storm yet!'

Anders could barely hear the bosun's words over the deafening crash of the waves. Running to the bow, he gripped the gunwale and gaped wide-eyed as the swell ahead yawned apart to reveal the glistening rocks beneath. The ship struck, splintered and pitched portside, its wound mortal. In a matter of moments the ocean swallowed it, bow and stern, welcoming timber, sail and crew down into the hideous black.

1

A Threader Client

In which Michael Banyard and Josiah Mingle fail to attain
employment

17th Twinemoon

The numbers in our case book cannot conceal the truth. My secret philanthropy is fiscally challenged.

Josiah Mingle enters 81 Bunson Street – the office of *Banyard and Mingle, Mysteries Solved* – and closes the door. Tall and broad for his years, he must stoop or hit the lintel. He is taller than me, although – and I quote him here – he has *a face like the sliced end of a turnip*. Not entirely accurate, but eloquent enough. I'll say this much, he looks like a thug. In contrast, I have the distinctive high brow and raven hair of the Banyard line and a nose that is somewhat longer than I should like. All the same, I'm told I'm handsome, though Josiah has on one occasion, rather annoyingly, referred to me as *pretty*.

The doorbell is silent, the quietness a reminder to me that it needs to be replaced.

On the desk lies a scatter of old copies of the *Camdon Herald*, the uppermost paper showing a headline in thick black lettering.

THIRTY-THREE DROWNED IN DOLLINGER WRECK

For a moment, Josiah turns and stares at the glass of the front windows. Not *through*, you understand, as though watching the bustling street outside, but *at*.

'What is it, Joe?'

He continues his study.

'What are you looking at?' Losing interest, I gaze back at the case book open on the desk before me.

'It's fascinating, how glass is solid and yet see-through. How can it be so?'

I smile. 'The word is transparent.'

'See-through, transparent, whatever. Do you think it was the same for the Old People, before the cataclysm?'

'Yes. I'm fairly sure glass has always been glass. It is only melted sand, after all.' The moment is drowned by the rising troubles in my mind. 'Well, if you can tear yourself away from the wonders of the universe for a moment, I have something important to discuss.'

'Oh! Is that Penelope Danton?' Now he *is* looking *through*. He points keenly at a trail of pedestrians passing shopfronts across the road.

My head jerks up and I'm searching from the window when I catch his wicked grin and realise I've been duped.

'This is serious, Josiah. We're out of work.'

'Out of work?' At last he forgets the window and crosses the room to the other side of the desk, grinning no more.

'It's not looking good. If we don't get a client soon we'll have to rob a bank or something.' I snort at the notion.

Josiah stares in silence while he mulls this over, his pronounced eyebrows rising together like small mountains.

'What about the Trevinky case?'

'Done, dusted, paid. And spent.'

'The Swineyards?'

'Pulled out before signing the contract. Gave the job to Stagnut and Brambles across town.'

'Why?'

'Apparently, we're not a big enough outfit.'

'The Bleakdon case?'

'They found their missing cash box. Mystery solved. Case closed before it ever opened.'

More silence follows while my faithful assistant dredges his brain for other potentials. Finding none, he allows his frame to collapse into the visitor's chair, like a physical expression of our impending financial downfall.

He says, 'Maybe we *should* rob a bank.'

I offer a tight-lipped smile and a noise that doesn't quite form a laugh and say, 'That was a joke, not a very funny one, but a joke, nonetheless.'

'But why not?'

'I'm sorry, Joe. Did you just say "Why not?"? As in: *Why not rob a bank?* Have you lost your mind?'

'I'm serious. *Why not?*'

'Because it's lunacy! It would be immoral. For one thing, people would get hurt or even die. Robberies generally involve some form of violence, which I'm strictly against, as you well know.'

'You're a strange kind of silker, all right. But what if they didn't?'

I frown. He explains.

'What if there was a way to do it without endangering a soul? Who else would suffer? I mean, who would it hit financially?'

'I'm not entirely sure. The individuals whose money was stolen, probably. Perhaps the bank, although I suppose they're likely insured against such calamities. To be honest, I wasn't seriously considering...' I stop midsentence because Josiah has that look about him again, a self-congratulatory expression that heralds doom as surely as a gawper's gaze. He parts his rubbery lips to expel the inevitable words I've heard so many times before.

'Mr Banyard, I have an excellent idea.'

'Come on, then. Let's hear it.' With a sense of dread I lean back in my chair, interlace my fingers behind my head and cross my ankles upon the desk. The explanation of Josiah's idea could be lengthy but today there is little else to do.

It begins.

'On my way in this morning I stopped for a cup of black soup. Mantrice Borrington's – you know it. Serves the best black soup this side of Druit's Lane. Old Mantrice were yacking with a lanky fellow, talking about the bank on Quaffer's Row. I heard him saying that bank will soon receive a royal visitor into its vaults.'

'Oh?' Though perplexed as to where this is going, my interest rises. 'Who's the royal visitor? Not King Lychling, surely.'

'Not Lychling.' Josiah leans closer and drops his voice. '*This* royal visitor is *dead*.'

A bent old woman pushes open the door, interrupting him. She wobbles in.

I'm surprised by the appearance of this potential client because the faded sign stretching the length of the building is drab and in need of repair. There's a temporary board crudely nailed over the surname of my father's previous partner, Shrud, and the lower corner of the 'd' can still be seen protruding beneath. The painted letters were once a golden hue and Mingle's name is notably a different shade. In any case, the sign has done its job and guided a needful soul to our lacklustre premises once more. I am privately grateful; perhaps Josiah's train of thought will be lost and his half-explained idea forgotten. I slip my feet from the desk and straighten up.

The woman approaches, tapping her cane across the floor. She's a threader, though better dressed than most. Threaders are forbidden to wear silk, but her cotton clothes are clean and serviceable. She's one of the few who have managed to survive well against the odds. When her eyes find mine, I detect a keen intelligence hiding behind the greyness of age and a hint of colour that tells me they were once a beguiling shade of turquoise. She was beautiful in her youth and a little of that beauty lingers still.

I clear my throat. 'Good day, madam. I am Michael Banyard and my associate here is Josiah Mingle. How may we assist you?'

She views Josiah and frowns, perhaps discerning that something about him is not quite right, yet unable to pinpoint the flaw.

'I'm a threader.' With a croaky voice, she floats the words into the air and lets them drift, watching for our reaction.

For a moment I wonder if I've been rumbled. I fear she has heard about Josiah's escape from oppressive servitude and has come seeking the same. I cannot save everyone.

'Yes. You are. What of it?'

'Bet you've never had a threader client in here before.' She narrows those eyes at me, a look somewhat close to an accusation. Peering at Josiah and me from beneath her lace-fringed bonnet, she slaps a palm full of dull coins onto the desk.

'There. That's everything I have. The rest has been taken by a murderous thief.'

I make a concerted effort not to count the coins and allow myself only a cursory glance. It's not much, not even enough for a day's pay, though it could buy a new bell and that would be something.

Josiah is gawking at her as though she is a newly discovered species. I glare at him and clear my throat again. Gaining his attention, I nod to my right. He takes the hint and relinquishes the visitor's chair.

I rise briefly to gesture. 'Would you care to sit, madam?'

'Thank you.' She sits, folding her frail hands on her lap. Her fingers are narrow, her skin almost translucent and mapped with raised veins and freckles.

'Will you take a cup of black soup? Josiah here can bring some.'

'No. Thank you.'

'*Who* is this murderous thief you speak of?'

'That silker rogue named Jacob Cullins. He's lawfully stolen every penny my dear old Jonty and I saved.'

'Jonty?' asks Josiah. At least he is paying attention.

'My husband. Died last year.'

'Was it much, your savings?' I ask.

With great effort, she drags the grand Wexford chair an inch closer to the desk and glances towards the door before continuing.

'You'd be surprised, sir. Between you and me, my Jonty did all right. He worked hard. He was lucky with his silker master – rubbed along well, they did, had a friendship of sorts. His master was one of the kinder ones. The sum of which I speak – the sum recently taken from me – was six thousand guineas.'

Josiah whistles and drops his jaw. I throw him a disapproving look. He snaps his mouth shut. Six thousand guineas *is* a considerable sum, even for most silkers to have saved. I forget the paltry pennies on the desk. If Jonty's life's savings were reclaimed, a proper payment for our services might be forthcoming.

'And, may I ask, how did this theft take place? You say *lawfully*?'

'Aye, lawfully, for by the silkers' law a bankrupt business cannot be forced to pay its debts.'

'So, what? You invested in a business that went bankrupt?'

'No, Cullins invested on my behalf, for as you know, 'tis forbidden for threaders to do business in that way. I was a fool to trust the old crook. Six thousand he invested in Golden Shores Imports and not a month later they sunk so deep they may as well be at the bottom of the Devil's Drop. A long list of disasters befell them: first a terrible shipwreck, then thefts, fires and the like. Sightings of gawpers have been reported down by the docks and men have died. 'Tis all in the claims report. I have a copy.' She places a folded document next to the pennies.

'How did you come by this?'

'I may be old and frail, Master Banyard, but I know a trick or two.'

'Wait. I don't understand the connection. What has the demise of Golden Shores Imports to do with Mr Cullins, other than your investment? You seem to think he has conned you somehow.'

'I suspect he owns it.'

'Really? Then why sabotage it? That's what you're suggesting, is it not?'

'Indeed, I am, though I cannot prove it. I believe he has stripped it of all assets and laid it to waste. He has bankrupted one of his own businesses and in the process stolen my money, along with other investments, no doubt.'

'I still don't see why someone would bankrupt their own business.'

'Cullins is rich. 'Tis merely one of many he owns. Perhaps the shipwreck was genuine and set him thinking. Tax evasion, insurance pay-outs, trading games, politics – I don't know why – but he did it and gained my savings to boot!'

I lean forward and drum my fingers on the desk, digesting her words.

'What, precisely, is it you wish us to do, Mrs...'

'*Widow* Blewett. Is that not obvious, Master Banyard? I wish you to investigate the matter, find evidence to prove my accusations. Without my savings I have no means to live. I appreciate I have not long to go in any case, but I'm not ready for the grave just yet. Prove Cullins has conned me and have my money returned to me.'

'Widow Blewett, it would take considerably more than...' Unhappily I sweep the coins from the desk into my palm and count. 'Nine pence alone. Regrettably, I cannot take your case.'

With a baleful look, she holds out her hand. 'Very well.'

I let the coins trickle back to her and she leaves without another word.

This is perhaps an appropriate point to explain a few things about Josiah and me. My father died five years ago and my mother and I fought valiantly to keep his private detective business afloat. When she became frailer we realised we needed help and, six months ago, employed Josiah to assist. Now my mother mostly remains at home.

Josiah is, or *was*, a threader. That is to say, he was an unfortunate of the lower class, trapped in a cruel world of bondage. Threaders work hard and receive little in return. Frequently they receive nothing. If a threader makes a mistake, he – or she – is ruthlessly punished. Because of their generally poor finances, the punishments mostly take a physical form, a beating, a shaved head or an arm branded with a T to remind them of their place. If the individual has already taken a brand, another T is added to the line, and so on.

If the error or crime is bad enough, a threader may be executed outright. Death also awaits any who talks back to a silker, but only after a grievously prolonged and contrived trial. This they simply call a *threader's doom*, a term meaning a prejudiced jury and certain death. If a threader so much as lays a hand on a silker, the killing is more imminent and may be lawfully performed by the offended silker in a manner of his or her choosing.

When guilty of a more serious offence, a quick death is deemed too lenient. The condemned threader is cast out of civilisation beyond the Borderlands, into Mors Zonam, where nothing grows beneath the irrepressible glare of the desert sun and where unnamed beasts lurk among the rocks and caves. No one ever goes there, not by choice, anyway. It is an inhospitable place, damaged by the ancient cataclysm that turned Earth into Earthoria. In Mors Zonam the hapless threader will die a long and painful death, ultimately suffocating in the hot toxic air.

There exist but two classes: the threaders and the silkers. The threaders are little more than slaves and work all manner of jobs from an early age. The silkers are born nobility. It is thought these terms derived from two distinguishable traits.

The threaders *make* the silk.
The silkers *wear* the silk.

The words are carved into the stone over the entrance of every threader courthouse in Londaland.

There is no lawful way for a threader to rise into silker ranks. Where do the gawpers fit in? You may ask. Gawpers are different, creatures somewhere between myth and legend. No one knows what they are. Those who have encountered them believe in their existence. Many, who have not, do not. They slink out from the moon shadows after dark. They climb from the fog in the small hours while we sleep. They come and go like the autumn mists. They are the stuff of a child's nightmare.

You will know when you see one. A ragged shape will rise from the gloom before you and a pair of glowing white eyes will gawp, two cold points of light that bore through to your soul and steal your breath.

Traditions abound: old wives' tales, superstitions, preventative measures in chants and charms, doom-saying and bedtime stories. The list goes on. The gawpers are harbingers of death. If you fail to die during an encounter, somebody close to you will soon perish instead. If no one dies, another kind of doom will befall you or those you love. I never gave much heed to all the talk, though I know two things for certain.

Fact one, gawpers are real because I've seen them.

Secondly, each time I've seen them, a most unsettling phenomenon occurs: I sweat blood.

I'm aware this is odd but it's also terribly inconvenient.

Now, the silkers in general are a merciless lot, cruel and oppressing. I have several friends among them who are not as bad as others, but mostly we're a ghastly bunch. I like to believe I am different. I try, at least. I help threaders where I can. Indeed, through clandestine means I have helped Josiah and now he is a silker, though I shall pay with my life should the deed ever come to light.

'Sit up straight,' I tell him, for fear he will give himself away. Dressing him in silks and setting him up with a position is one thing, but shaking his threader habits is proving to be quite another. He straightens his back and flashes an uncertain smile across our barren case book. Despite all his base attributes, I have a soft spot for Joe.

I watch silkers pass the windows and worry they may pause to scrutinise him. If they did, they might notice the knot of his scarf is too tight and yet the scarf worn too loosely around his neck. They may see he is so well muscled from lugging barrels in his previous threader employment that I have struggled to purchase a silk shirt that fits. Indeed, he has a neck like a bull's. Here and there, the shirt clings tightly to his bulges. They could ask why a silker has such weather-tanned skin. And if they heard him speak? Well, that might be the end of it!

To me, he looks awkward, *out of water*, as my silker friends would say, though I do not pretend to understand the origin of this archaic phrase. I'm sure it is only a surviving element of some ancient saying. When the cataclysm struck, much was lost.

2

The Encounter

In which Banyard talks to his hat

With Widow Blewett gone, Josiah confronts me.

'What did you do that for?'

'Excuse me?'

'That was a case. We need work. Why turn it down?' His face registers a mild anger that has nowhere to run.

'Widow Blewett has lost her money to a treacherous silker and cannot pay us. We do not work for free. Surely even you can do the arithmetic.'

'Yet, I'm sure she would pay if her money was returned.'

'*If* pays neither rent nor wage.'

'But she needs our help.'

'Ah! And did I say we would *not* help her? No, I did not.'

'You said you wouldn't take the case.'

'Indeed.'

Josiah spots the claims report still on the table.

'She's left her papers.'

In my distracted state I've overlooked the report. I snatch it up and run after her. Outside, crowds swamp the cobbles. Steam trucks belch fog and a din is rising. The Threaders' Rights Movement are protesting today and have just kicked off. The widow is lost among a riotous throng. A wave of campaigners floods the street, projecting a cacophony of mantras, heading for Rook's Bridge and Old Camdon.

'Threaders for justice!'

'Threaders' rights. Join the fight!'

'Justice in the Threaders' Court!'

'Out with the threaders' doom!'

'Threaders' rights! Threaders' rights!'

I duck back inside to avoid the tide, feeling a twinge of guilt. I should be leading the charge but that would be unsubtle and I might be arrested by the Drakers, our beloved silker watchmen. It's not that I'm a coward, but I wouldn't be much help to anyone imprisoned or hung for treachery.

Back in the office I take a cursory glance at the claims report. It is long and detailed.

'So, what are we going to do? I mean, how will we help the widow?' asks Josiah.

'I'm working on it.'

I help him out by reminding him of our previous unfinished conversation because I need time to think about the widow's case, and his present preoccupation is addling the process. 'You were explaining your idea, something about the bank on Quaffer's Row and an impending royal visitor. I'm curious to know who.'

He reclaims the visitor's chair and thinks hard. I can always tell when he's thinking hard because his face wrinkles like a prune with the effort.

'Great King Doon.'

I stare. The name is renowned, the king as legendary as one might be.

'Great King Doon, *the* Great King Doon, is visiting the bank? He's two thousand years dead.'

'Ay. His remains are to be kept in the vault under the strictest security. They're in a jar. Nothing left but a bit of ash and a few burned bones.'

'Urn.'

'Sorry?'

'You said jar but you meant urn.'

'Jar, urn, what's the difference?'

'If you're a legendary dead king, the difference may be significant.'

He shrugs. 'Anyway, I was thinking it might create an opportunity. Everyone will be focused on it. There'll be a ceremony, speeches and crowds. It'll be a proper big event. The bank guards will be all over that urn. They won't be thinking about the money down in the vaults.'

I smile wistfully. He's amusing if nothing else. 'I wonder where Mr Cullins banks.'

'Oh, he banks at Yorkson's.'

'You know Mr Cullins?'

'I know of him, aye. A threader friend of mine used to serve him. Nasty piece of work is Cullins.'

'Wait a minute. Yorkson's is the bank on Quaffer's Row.'

Until now I have been listening to Josiah's ramblings as a sort of kindness, but this latest nugget of information actually has me considering his ridiculous plan.

I shake myself. *Don't be absurd. You're not going to rob a bank. And yet...*

The protest outside is growing rowdy. Shouts volley and bodies crush against our building. Carbine blasts demand our attention and ducking low we head over to the glass and peer.

In the street, Drakers are clubbing and assaulting the threader crowd. No one has been shot yet, but the longer the stand-off rages, the higher the risk. We all know it. Drakers beat at the front line of threaders, bludgeoning several to the ground. People scatter at further shots and a couple of unfortunates are pinned in our doorway, unable to escape. The Drakers are killing now. The blood of threaders will pool between the cobbles of the street and no one will wash it away: It is threader blood and does not matter. Further down the street, threaders fall with staccato booms that resonate against the shopfronts. I open the door and drag the two protesters inside by their scruffs.

'The back room, now!'

They stare at me, untrustingly.

'*If* you want to live,' I add.

They run into our case room and Josiah shuts the door. He drags a chair across and placing it before the door, sits.

The protesters have gone, darting their separate ways like weevils into flour, along with the Draker force, an altogether darker form of beetle. The two threaders who hid in our case room are alive, grateful and released, flitting away with an eye for any lingering watchmen.

I glance at my favourite, though unfashionable, hat, feeling a need to get out of the office for a while because the air of unemployment in here is stifling. The tricorn was my father's and I won't be parted from it.

'What would you have done? Would you have taken the widow's case?'

In the distant recesses of my mind, I hear my father's voice. 'Yes. It's not about money or status. It never was.' The hat stares sightlessly back at me from the hat stand.

'But we're broke,' I argue.

'You have clothes on your back, a roof over your head. It could be worse: You could be a threader.'

I grab my hat and walk out into Bunson Street, taking in the shops and business fronts, occasionally nodding a greeting to people I know, all the while mulling over the widow's tale. Other silker pedestrians are wearing bonnets, the men, silky top hats in black or brown. I feel different from them, set apart. There is no silk on my tricorn and I couldn't give two hoots.

The Museum of Unnatural History is a large building not far on the far side of Rook's Bridge. I climb its steps to take a stroll around the exhibits and pause before a glass case displaying a range of small but interesting finds. Among them are the collected remains of an object, or objects, the purpose of which remains a mystery. It seems that a complete example, for none such have survived, might have been a small tablet of polished glass that would fit comfortably in your hand. One fragment shows a precise symbol that modern science has no means of replicating in such perfect clarity. It is without question a representation of an apple with a bite taken from one side. I think it is my favourite exhibit.

There are other bits and pieces, remnants of the Old People. Many are made of a material we do not know. It has been tested and can be heated and remoulded and yet it is not metal but something lighter and softer. For want of a better term, we call it moulded ware. One display case contains a line of transparent bottles formed from the stuff and it is believed the Old People carried drinking water in them. There are moulded ware casings with glass fronts in all shapes and sizes, some wide and flat, some thought to be older that are smaller and deeper – all damaged, of course, and no example is complete. We do not know what they were for, but several have the remnants of their interiors: wires joining various elements and boards with mysterious green or silver markings. There are panels of moulded ware bearing little square buttons, each with a letter or number. It is believed these were from the Old People's typographer machines. Another case holds a few fragile pages from an ancient sacred book. A portion of each page is charred from some long-forgotten fire. Curiously, no weapons have ever been found that are associated with the Old People, though I imagine they must have had them. They seem a rather sophisticated society, advanced in their industries. I wonder what went wrong?

Outside, I pause to buy a newspaper from a scruffy street vendor. The front headline confirms the recent gawper sightings with melodramatic panache.

GAWPERS PLAGUE DOCKSIDE!

Autumn is upon us again and as my feet rustle through rusting fallen leaves, I'm reminded of my first encounter with a gawper, which happened when I was eight, only a few steps from here at the junction where Bunson Street meets Brittling Street.

I still shiver to recall it, one of my earliest memories.

My overworked father was working late on that breezy autumn evening, stewing on a case about which I knew nothing. My mother, concerned by his recent decline in health, found me playing marbles in the parlour at the back of our house.

'Take this to your dadda at the office. Be quick, Micky.' She ruffled my hair – the colour of damp straw – and shoved a linen-wrapped bundle into my hands. It's my remembrance of those days that nearly everyone I met ruffled my hair, but that can't be accurate, surely.

The sandwiches smelled delicious, even through the cloth covering.

My mother, a slender, gentle woman, made the best sandwiches in the City of Camdon and thought it safe enough to send me down the street alone. There hadn't been a gawper sighting reported in Crowlands for over ten years and in that time the possibility of one making an appearance, and the accompanying fear, had cooled in local minds.

Except for that of the ever-vigilant and rather neurotic Jinkers.

I took the bundle and ran outside only to be waylaid by him, younger then, of course, though no less barmy. He shot like lightning from the neighbouring door to grab my arm.

'Micky, you can't go out like that!' he warned. 'Have a care! The gawpers will take you. Here, take my willow stick. Everyone knows they can't abide a strip o'willow. Did you say the verse and dance the nine steps? Did you make the godly sign? Lace your boots thrice?'

I stared at the once-tied laces of my mud-spattered boots. Did he really believe in all those tales?

Bonkers.

I didn't, not even back then.

Towering over me, Jinkers made the godly sign and continued. 'Really, Banyard, it's a wonder you're alive. Take it! What are you waiting for?' He wagged the staff at me and rolled his watery eyes in that uncommon way of his.

Tucking the sandwiches under one arm, I took the stick, if only to placate him.

'Yes, Master Jinkers.'

'Good.' Jinkers pensively rubbed at his chin where a fuzz of adolescent facial hair encroached. 'Now, I have two dozen frogs. How many can I put you down for?'

I shook my head.

'No, er, frogs. Thank you.'

'They're good'ens…' Jinkers was having none of it.

'No. Really.'

Why would I want frogs? Why would *anybody* want frogs, or consider parting with money for them? For one thing, they were easy enough to fish out of the pond down by the weir and every youngster for miles around knew it. I was aware that certain threader families were in the habit of frying them to suck their leg bones clean of flesh.

But I was a silker.

Silkers. Don't. Eat. Frogs.

I left Jinkers prattling on about the girth of his horrid frog collection and padded off.

The mid-year heat had passed and the days were cooling, the trees down Bunson Street shedding leaves faster than the westerlies could bear them away. This late in the evening most of the steam trucks were gone, leaving the road empty beneath a horizon darkening from a fiery glow. I peered its length, checking for… What? I'm not sure. Threats, perhaps. Threats of any description, though what could be worse than Jinkers?

The office was not far, a matter of twelve houses away. Arriving, I flung the door open and entered, calling for my father.

'Dadda, are you there? I brought food. Dadda?'

Sweat beaded on my forehead. I whipped a grubby handkerchief from a pocket of my shorts and dabbed, saw bloody smears on the cotton cloth and thought, *That's odd.*

I slipped through the reception room and into my father's

workspace, the case room. He noticed me at last and peering from an open ledger, smiled.

'Michael, my boy. Thank you. I could eat a Micklesworth pony. These smell fine!' Taking the sandwiches, he ruffled my hair.

You see? I'm surprised I had any left by the age of nine.

'Will you be very late tonight?'

'Yes, unfortunately, I shall. Now hurry back to your ma. Give her a kiss from me and don't tarry on the streets.'

Obediently, I turned for home. I had no need to tarry, nor the mind. I'd heard the stories. Listened to the tales. Why would any eight-year-old ever linger on the streets after that? With hindsight, it was akin to my father asking, 'Michael, are you an idiot?' Yet my father was kind and would never venture the like, even if he suspected it. With a nod and a wink, he sent me on my way.

I had another reason not to linger. If I had wanted to encounter a gawper, waiting would have been unnecessary. Not that people *want* to see them. To the contrary, most do their utmost to avoid such circumstances and the ensuing misfortune or horrendous death – that kind of thing.

In any case, a gawper I saw.

The lamplighter had made his rounds and the blue, glass-encased flames of the watch-lamps punctuated the street every thirty of my little paces. I walked the cobbles from welcome glow to petering shadow and on to the next gas-fuelled orb of blueness, each time glad of the guttering lamplight.

Not halfway home, I froze, speechless. The eyes struck me first, glowing and white, piercing and strange. Partially silhouetted against the gas lamps of the adjacent street, it stood, a tall humanoid figure in the junction, watching me. I remember thinking that, if it were not for those eyes, it might have been a man, like any other only very tall. Perhaps if I had approached its back, I would have thought nothing of it and passed by, but seeing those points of cold brightness peering back at me – *gawping*, if you like – I knew at once what it was, realised its excessive height and felt an urgent need to flee.

Ditching Jinkers' staff, I tried to run but found my legs had turned to marble. It had me in its dreadful gaze and, petrified, I stared back, mouth gaping. Turning fully towards me, the gawper neared, drifting over the cobbles. At first it approached slowly, its *gawp* deepening until I felt as though my mind was laid bare, as though those bright points of light were seeping through my eyes, reaching deep down inside and drawing out my thoughts. At that moment I knew nothing but tumultuous fear. Closing on me, it speeded faster and I toppled backwards to the ground to scramble an awkward retreat, unable to look away. In a blink it was there, peering down, overshadowing me and I knew that any attempt at escape was futile.

Closer and closer it loomed until our faces almost touched. I say faces, but all I could see of it was the burning gaze and its form, dark against the night sky. I heard my own voice cry out, sounding strangely distant and, just when I thought my short life was over, the gawper turned and receded into the dusk.

I bolted, glancing over my shoulder periodically and soon had an encounter entirely different in nature. I ran headlong into a person who stepped from the shadows into my path. A girl. A very pretty girl with fiery hair.

Penelope Danton. Penney, for short, though I had yet to hear her name.

Struck dumb for the second time that night, I stared down at her where she had fallen. I stammered the beginnings of an apology but, remembering the gawper, stopped and looked back. The street behind me was empty, the gawper gone. I offered my hand and pulled Penney to her feet.

'Sorry about that. There was a...' I checked again, not trusting my eyes. It seemed suddenly ridiculous. 'Never mind.'

'There was a what?'

'Nothing important. Are you hurt?'

'No, but thanks for asking.'

Penney was a mere two years older than me and yet she may as well have been from another planet. Those two small years came with a sophistication beyond reach, an intrigue that made her presence too great to bear.

I forced awkward words from my mouth. 'I… I have to go. Sorry. Goodbye.'

And fled in terror, this time not daring to look back.

A gust of cool wind reels a flotilla of leaves around the toes of my riding boots. Returning to my newspaper I skim an article on the technological advancements of modern travel. The Volts Steam Truck factory across town is closing due to the emergence of Clansly Haulage on to the market. Clansly are producing bigger, faster steam trucks that can haul more tonnage. More importantly, Gear and Cog have released their latest clockwork car, a long-awaited and spectacular vehicle that I would buy because of its looks alone.

If I had the funds.

The Old People had cars, though of a different nature – we know that much. We have yet to fully understand the few twisted remains that survived the cataclysm.

The Thripple Heart boasts a full sixty miles on one winding, thanks to the patented Gear and Cog Thripple Return Spring Relay Mechanism. A work of genius.

Shares in Hinkley Air have rocketed. A movement overhead causes me to glance skyward. Right on cue, a Hinkley Air ship drifts by, its distant turbines whirring.

I stop turning the pages when I read a headline on page six.

YORKSON'S TO STORE DOON'S BONES

So, it's true. Reading details, I learn that the historic shrine of Doon is in need of vital repair and, for the duration of the work, the royal remains are to be housed in the Yorkson's vault due to its impenetrable nature and flawless security. The last five words banish any lingering temptation I've harboured to dwell on Josiah's notion.

The Yorkson's representatives deem the bank to be the most secure location in Londaland and proudly state that they need no insurance against robbery as that eventuality is simply impossible. I feel instantly lighter on my feet and smile at those I pass. Perhaps one of them will be my next client and is, this very minute, hurrying to Banyard and Mingle.

Back at the office I stop outside. There is a new, rather badly written sign in the window.

RECEPTIONIST NEEDED
APLY WITHIN

I scowl and enter.

3
The Toll

In which Banyard and Mingle investigate the widow's case

Inside I find Josiah in my chair sitting opposite an extremely attractive young lady. Her hair is blonde and tied up neatly in a bun atop her head. Her face and figure are shapely and exquisite, and Joe has yet to notice my arrival, perhaps because our bell is broken but more likely because his senses are so acutely trained upon our guest.

'Elizabeth Fairweather. Pleased to make your acquaintance.' She extends a white-gloved hand which he smothers in his massive grasp, choosing to shake it rather than the more refined kiss. Threaders don't do the hand-kissing thing.

'Josiah Mingle, at your service.'

Glancing at the sign and Elizabeth, I approach to interrupt.

'Mr Mingle, may I have a word?'

He notices me at last.

'Can it wait? I'm interviewing.'

'No, it cannot. Please accompany me to the case room.'

Reluctantly he rises. Once in the case room I look back to offer Elizabeth a polite smile before drawing the door closed between us.

'What do you think you're doing? Honestly! I leave the office for ten minutes…'

'I'm interviewing a potential receptionist. We'll need one if we're to help the widow.'

'What?'

'You said we were going to help the widow.'

'No. I said I didn't say we would not help her. There's a difference.'

That's done it. He's squinting and as confused as can be. With a shake of his head, he gives up trying to figure it out.

'If we *are* going to help her, we'll need someone to watch the shop,' he says. 'You and I will be busy investigating. You know what it was like last time. We were barely here and you said we were losing custom with the shop unattended. You said next time we would employ a receptionist to free us up.'

It's true. I did say that, back when we had clients.

'We can't pay her. We're broke.'

He shrugs with a *not my problem* look on his face. I fold.

'All right. Let's see what may be done.'

We reconvene in reception, Josiah dragging a third chair over to the desk while I take my rightful place.

'My apologies, Miss Fairweather. Just ironing out a few details. My name is Michael Banyard. I'm the proprietor of Mysteries Solved. The role we are offering requires a confident and pleasant manner with all clients, whatever their background. You will frequently be the first face a client sees when they come through that door. Are you an experienced receptionist?'

'I am. My résumé.' She hands me a paper that I unfold and scan while Josiah gawks at her. She is amused by his interest and fighting back a smile. I flash him a warning glance and, amazingly, he takes the hint, breaking his gaze to peer out into the street, or perhaps he's contemplating the miraculous properties of glass again. I cannot tell which. Elizabeth continues. 'Two years at Minker and Sons. Six months with Drattmire.'

'Six months only. What happened?'

'The manager's wandering hands. I moved on.'

Take note, Josiah. I almost say it out loud.

'I'm only twenty-one, so I'm as experienced as can be expected.'

She seems forthright in nature, stating the facts concisely.

'Very well. And how did you learn of the vacancy?' I stall for time. This whole thing has me off guard and ill-prepared, but the more I think about it, the more I see the need to hire.

'I was walking by and saw the sign. Incidentally, apply has two ps, not one. I have another interview across town within the hour.'

'Hmmm. A client enters in a fury. Neither Mr Mingle nor myself are in attendance. The client approaches you rudely and, incandescent with rage, complains about the service he has been given. What do you do?'

She replies without pause.

'I invite him to take a chair and wait for your imminent arrival. I offer him black bean soup and send a runner for you. Later, when you have placated him, I have words with you because clearly something has gone awry and it is certainly not my fault, which means it's yours or Mr Mingle's.' She leans across to place a reassuring hand upon Josiah's arm and smiles apologetically. He giggles like a schoolboy. 'I reconsider my terms of employment and negotiate a higher wage.'

'Josiah, please,' says Joe.

For this I throw him another warning glance. He continues to smile at her. I've had enough of him for one day. As for the feisty Miss Fairweather...

'You didn't consider the possibility that the client is perhaps being unfair or is of unsound mind?'

'Ah, you did not specify otherwise, therefore I assumed he was a reasonable and sober gentleman.'

'Never assume, Miss Fairweather.'

'Please, call me Lizzy.' She skilfully breaks the tension by presenting her hand, leaving me no choice but to shake it. Or kiss it. Now I'm not sure which I should choose. I shake it.

'If we offer you the post, it would be on a trial basis and for the first two days you would work without pay. After that we would pay you fifteen pence a day for the first month before a further assessment. Would you be available to start tomorrow?'

'One day without pay and we will reassess in a fortnight's time.'

She has the right kind of nerve and command for the job. I decide she will be good for us.

'Do we have a deal?'

We shake hands again.

'Indeed, we do.'

Elizabeth leaves contentedly and, wondering how I'm to pay her, I turn my attention back to the claims report while Josiah presses his nose against the window to watch her walk down the street.

The first portion of the report details a shipwreck.

The *Dollinger* was the flagship of Golden Shores Imports, a considerable merchant galleon with a capacity unmatched by most on the Eastern Sea. Upon her homeward voyage on the twelfth night of Honourmoon last month, fully loaded with barrels of fine wine, gunpowder and black soup beans from Urthia, she struck rocks south of Windstrome Bay. The report tells me the cargo spilled into the sea. Casks were swept out never to be seen again while others washed ashore and were quickly scavenged by local rascals. A total of three casks were later reclaimed by Golden Shores. Thirty-three souls were lost to the waves. Only Geofferson and Anders survived to give account.

I recall reading something about the wreck in the *Camdon Herald*.

'Get your coat, Joe. I have an errand for you.'

He turns from the window. Elizabeth is long gone but my voice breaks the trance she has left on him like a fog.

'An errand?'

'Go to the docks and ask around. We must find two ship hands from the *Dollinger* wreck, the two survivors.' I scribble their names on a scrap of paper in case he forgets. He takes the note with a frown.

'I'll try.'

'You'll do fine, Joe. There's nothing to it. Oh, and Joe, try to keep a low profile.' Easier said than done for a man the size of an aurochs.

He nods and leaves. I read on.

Geofferson's and Anders' words are not recorded but a summation of their account is.

It was dark when they approached the shore, gone one in the morning according to the ship's clock. The storm had blown them home as though the sea was violently keen to be rid of them. When it quickened to roll the ship in a rage, the first mate roused the crew from their bunks with several shrill blasts from his whistle, his lantern swinging to dispel the pitch black of the night.

Lightning shocked the sky, flashing over the vessel. The bosun spotted a point of light across the water and raised the alarm: Burrington Point Lighthouse, which meant rocks. The crew rallied to rig and turn the ship while white water pummelled the deck and flooded the quarters. Soon after, a series of tall waves drove the ship onto rocks. A terrible sound was heard as the hull splintered. Water gushed in as she leaned and lowered. Men were washed overboard while the captain shouted orders. He, too, was lost to the depths as the ship keeled over. Mariners manning the only lifeboat hit the water when the boat was tipped and the galleon sank.

At daybreak, bodies on the beach at Lytche's Cove alerted fishermen to the disaster and they reported to the justice who raised a party to search for survivors and, later, the three casks were recovered further south at Dart's Cove.

It seems a reasonable and believable account and yet, the widow's words about Cullins and Golden Shores haunt me.

… *he has stripped it of all assets and laid it to waste.*

Has he? Bad luck can befall any soul, good or bad. In my experience, chance shows no favour.

I scan the remaining document. The widow spoke the truth when listing the calamities that followed. They are detailed here.

I close my eyes. This is not *a* case. It is seven. The wreck is only the first, followed three days later by a break-in and theft at the Golden Shores warehouse in Dockside. A second theft took place in the form of a mugging during which a company cash box was stolen. Soon after, in a separate incident, the company treasurer died unexpectedly, the coroner's report stating heart failure as the cause. The warehouse fire broke out sometime in the small hours of the same night. Unattended and unnoticed, the place burned for two hours before the cry was raised. When the flames were eventually out, the building was razed to the ground.

The sixth event took place in the Far East around the same time, the capture of the *Ingleford* – a small galleon, or galley, carrying gold and eastern silks – by Urthian pirates.

Lastly, another fire sent the *Parrot* to the bottom of the sea out in Deepning Sound, a stretch of deep water lying between two isles, a league from Dockside. The *Parrot* was reportedly the oldest ship in Cullins' merchant fleet and perhaps no great loss, but its extensive cargo of port and whisky was.

And there they are. Seven strokes of fate that stripped Golden Shores Imports to the bone. If the accounts are all valid, Cullins is the most unfortunate individual I have ever encountered. If they are fraudulent, he is likely a swindler and a murderer. I calculate the death toll: thirty-three drowned; five killed by pirates; with the treasurer's heart failure, thirty-nine in all.

Even accounting for the storm, which seems incontrovertible, that's a lot of dead people.

When Josiah returns later that afternoon, he's looking pleased with himself.

'I found Geofferson.' He passes the same note I gave him earlier except now it has an address hastily scrawled across the back.

I squint at his childish handwriting. '13 Monteroy Avenue. Good work, Joe. It sounds rather grand.'

'It's a dump.' He hangs his topper on the hat stand and begins to shrug off his coat.

'Keep it on.' I grab his hat and put it back on his head, crookedly. 'We're leaving.'

'But – '

'Come on, Joe. No time to lose!'

Number 13 Monteroy Avenue is a rundown shack in Dockside, one of the nearest dwellings to Cullins' burned warehouse. Most of the dwellings around here are occupied by mariners and so many are empty for much of the time. I knock on the weather-beaten door and wait until a thin man with a grey bush of a beard answers. His skin is like old leather, deeply carved with the weight of hard years and a troubled mind.

'Good day to you, ship hand Geofferson.' I offer my hand. Geofferson shakes it warily, his eyes fixed upon me. 'My name is Michael Banyard and this is my associate, Josiah Mingle. We're investigating the wreck of the *Dollinger*. May we step inside?'

Briefly, I think he may decline but he grunts and nods accommodatingly, opening the door wide. Inside, the room is basic, everything roughly hewn, the walls bare without a hint of decor. 'Do you live alone, Mr Geofferson?'

'Aye.'

The plaster has cracks and patches missing. The furniture looks like driftwood. After a closer look, I'm convinced it *is*. On the wave-worn table sits a small brown loaf of bread missing one slice, and a depleted ham – more bone than meat – hangs from a rafter in the smoke above the fire.

Without invitation, Josiah occupies a rickety stool at the table. It creaks under his weight.

'What do you want to know about that cursed ship?' asks Geofferson, clearly keen to be shot of us.

'Cursed?' says Josiah.

'Aye, cursed. Always voices, even in the dead of night. Voices from beyond. Haunting sounds and the like. As though the souls of the drowned was trapped in the very clinkers.'

'Interesting.'

I think Geofferson would be intimidated by Josiah's size and bearing if it weren't for his face, which is currently holding a vacant expression. Instead, Geofferson merely watches him with mild fascination.

'I'm afraid I can't offer you no refreshment. Can't afford to since the *Dollinger*. Unemployed…'

'Understood. We'd like to hear your account of the shipwreck. You *were* on the *Dollinger* when it struck?'

He nods. 'It were dark.'

'Yes?'

'We was sleepin' in our bunks when the call went up. It were chaos. The storm were already high by the time I reached the deck. Men was dashed senseless by them waves. Some was swallowed by the sea. I don't know who. 'Twas hard to see what was happening in the mortal rain, the wind and them daemon waves.'

'There was certainly a storm, then.'

'Oh, there were a storm, all right. A storm sent straight from the Underworld.'

'Were you aware of the ship's location at this point? Had anyone taken bearings?'

'The navigator will have taken bearings before the storm set in, though it could have driven us for leagues. I glimpsed cliffs and the bosun thought he recognised Burrington Point. That's when he saw the lighthouse and rang the ship's bell. He did all he could to turn us about. We worked hard, sirs, while all around us men was lost to the black.'

'I'm sure you fought most valiantly.'

Josiah asks, 'How come you survived when all those others didn't?'

'In truth, sir, I do not know. Sheer blind luck, I suppose. I near drowned. Was washed up and left for dead by the searchers. 'Twas only later they saw I were breathing and carried me up town. There were another who made it, a young'en called

Anders. He'll tell you how it were.' Geofferson scowled at the memory.

'Was he there when the bosun saw the lighthouse?' I ask.

'Aye. Though he argued it weren't no lighthouse on account of the fact he'd seen it move and – as you know – lighthouses don't move, but the bosun wouldn't listen. We turned that ship, I swear, but hit rocks nonetheless. She went down just off Hatch Head.'

'Hatch Head? But that's almost a league south of Burrington Point, is it not? Do you have a chart?'

Geofferson nods curtly and fetches a map, unravelling it on the table.

'As you say, Master Banyard. A rat's tooth shy of a league.'

'Why is that important?' asks Josiah.

Geofferson is keen to explain. 'Because we wasn't where the bosun thought we was.'

I study the area of the map around Burrington Point. 'Ah, wait. What if you were here?' With a finger I mark a point in the Eastern Sea midway between the lighthouse and Hatch Head. 'You'd have been less than half a league from the lighthouse. You'd have seen it even in the storm and turned, but the storm might have driven you a quarter league south, onto the rocks at Hatch Head.'

Geofferson throws me this look that tells me I'm a fool.

'I beg to differ, master. If you'd sailed these waters as long as I, you'd know the Northern Chase would've dragged us north, not south. We'd have hit Burrington Point head-on or washed through to Windstrome Bay. No. We was further south and that was no lighthouse.'

Joe frowns. 'You mean someone set a false light to turn the ship onto the rocks?'

Good old Joe. Got there in the end.

Geofferson nods. 'That's exactly what they did.'

Digging out a coin, I place it in his palm.

'For your trouble. Where is Anders now?' I ask. 'It's imperative we find him.'

4

Mr Kaylock

In which Jinkers talks to a cat

Anders' shack is empty. At least, no one is answering the door.
I send Josiah around to the back to try the other door but he
returns a minute later.

'Nothing. There's a window with no shutter, though. No one
home.'

I consider breaking in, but daylight is fading and I've had
enough for one day. 'We'll return tomorrow.'

A horse-drawn coach carries us home. Josiah accompanies
me because he currently resides in one of our spare rooms, a
temporary arrangement until I source alternative lodgings. For
now, it's convenient and perhaps safer as I can keep a close
watch on him. The coachman brings the horses to a halt and we
step down onto the cobbles outside 96 Bunson Street. Before
we can reach the door, Jinkers steals out from the shadows.

'Micky, I've been waiting for you. Why are you so late? What
have you been up to at such an hour?'

He stands between us and the door, leaving us no option but
to reply. He has become increasingly furtive and suspicious over
the years since his parents passed away.

'It's not *that* late and I'm not aware of any curfew. We were
working. You should try it sometime. It might do you good.'

He's clutching his cat – a hostile wretch – and cowers at the mention of work.

'We don't need any nasty *work*, do we, Mr Kaylock?' He strokes the cat, who rumbles a low growl. The cat is mottled grey with black tiger stripes. 'Mr Kaylock says we won't ever work.'

'Very well – '

'Mr Kaylock tells me there'll be a storm tomorrow. A big one!'

'I'll be sure to dress appropriately.' I doff my hat and try to step around Jinkers but he adjusts his position to block me, all the while watching Josiah distrustfully. It's the only way he's ever regarded Josiah.

'I saw a red-eyed gawper. Nine feet tall, it was!'

This again. Gawpers. His favourite topic. I'm not sure what to say, so I listen.

'Out on the ridge last night. It came up from the weir. Drifted, it did, riding the mist. What says you to that?'

Not much. I doubt he saw anything. He's obsessed, neurotic and paranoid.

'Hunting frogs, were we?'

'Never you mind. Did *you* ever see a red-eyed gawper?'

'No.' So which is to blame this time? Obsession, neurosis or paranoia? Ah! This could be jealousy. Jinkers hates that I have seen gawpers more often than he.

The cat hisses, bearing two rows of small but lethal teeth at Josiah and me.

'Mr Kaylock tells me old red-eye is the gawper king.'

'Interesting.'

Josiah is growing bored. 'Mr Banyard, we should go in.'

'Quite. If you'll excuse us, Jinkers. We'll bid you goodnight.'

'He also says the price of frogs is set to rise. You should stock up, man.'

He sidesteps enough for us to squeeze past.

'We have all the frogs we need, thank you.'

Which is none.

There is a detail here I must explain. Before I first introduced Josiah to Mother, I greeted her with a kiss on the cheek. Bewildered by his new circumstances and in a deep state of cultural shock, Josiah mimicked my actions, also bending to kiss Mother. An odd precedent was set and has become standard procedure whenever we arrive or leave the house. In her grace, mother has accepted this unquestioningly.

She doesn't venture out much these days. Her knees give her pain and her back aches from the years of stooping over casefiles. She has a kind face, an intolerance of nonsense and an incredible propensity to smile through whatever life throws her way.

I kiss her now and, like a dutiful adopted son, Josiah follows suit. I'll never get used to this arrangement but it's far too late to change it and, anyway, I think in a way Mother is enjoying the attention.

Her name is Sarah.

'Dinner's cooking. How's business?'

'Fine. We have a new client.' I throw Josiah a warning glance because he's opened his mouth and is about to expand upon my statement. A while ago I decided not to burden Mother with work issues for fear she would worry herself to death. Reminded of the rule, Josiah closes his mouth.

'She's a threader,' I add, meaning that to be an end of the subject.

'Michael, be sure she can pay. You're no charity.'

'Indeed. She's a wealthy threader. Wealthier than any threader I've known before.'

'A wealthy threader? Who'd have thought.'

'Indeed.'

'There's a little port left in the cellar.'

Mother knows me well. I'm partial to a nip after work and tonight Josiah joins me in the green room.

Our house is not grand but neither is it a hovel. It's somewhere in between, although at some point in history, in its prime, it was probably considered august.

A grandfather clock stands in the hallway leading to the green room, which is the one we use to sit and relax in late into the evenings. It has olive-green walls, the lower third panelled with dark oak so old that we oil them each spring to prevent them from cracking in the summer warmth. It also has a wonderfully broad fireplace that heats the room spectacularly well.

'What do you make of the claims report?' Josiah asks while we are alone.

'I've a feeling each account is fraudulent. The wreck is certainly suspicious.'

'That's *good*, right?'

I smile. 'Not for Cullins but yes, for us, very good.'

'What's the plan?'

'Tomorrow we'll continue our investigation into the wreck and we'll look at the other claims, each one in turn, if time permits.'

I pour the port and hand Josiah a goblet.

'Here's to a prosperous new client who isn't a client.'

He's looking confused again.

'What then? What if all the insurance claims are false?'

'If they prove false, we'll need to find the widow and lay out our findings. She can take Cullins to court and sue for repayment of her investment.'

'No, she can't. She's a threader.'

'Ah. You're right. She'd need a willing silker to present her case for her.'

'Who would do a thing like that? What about you?'

'Me? No. I don't think so.'

'Why not? You'd be perfect. You'd know the case better than anyone.'

'We're getting ahead of ourselves. Let's focus on the investigation for now.'

Josiah gazes into his goblet. 'Why is it red?'

'The port? I don't know. Why is anything the colour it is?'

'Oh! Good question, Mr Banyard.' He scans the room as though everything has changed, has been born anew in this notion. 'A *very* good question.'

18th Twinemoon

The next morning, Jinkers leaps at me as I leave the house.

'Ah! Micky, I was hoping to catch you. Have you seen Mr Kaylock? He's gone missing.' He is agitated, constantly fiddling with his hands, his clothes.

'He's a cat, Jinkers. That's what they do. They're free spirits. He'll return.'

'I'm not so sure. There was a flock of crowlings over Rook's Bridge yesterday at noon.'

'What has that to do with Mr Kaylock?'

'Why, it's an omen, of course! Don't you know anything?'

Jinkers and his superstitions.

'I must go. I'll look out for Mr Kaylock.'

Mr Kaylock is a miserable creature. If I *do* see him, I'll avoid him at all cost.

'Beware the gawper king, Micky!' Jinkers calls after me.

'Thank you, Jinkers. I shall.'

I'm not sure what I did to deserve Jinkers as my neighbour, but it must have been bad.

Josiah brings the horses down the alley from the stables at the back of the house. Today we ride because we have much ground to cover and the carriage prices are high. I fantasise I own a Thripple Heart but keep it to myself as Blink trots stoically beneath me, black and sleek, and more handsome than any machine.

Steam trucks rattle by and clockwork cars dash, but we're not the only riders on the road. There are horse-drawn carriages and loaded pack mules driven by threaders. Some are forced to use the beasts through a lack of finance or a master's preference. Others choose horse power, lovers of the old ways.

Josiah's horse is dappled grey and is strong, a recent purchase that all but emptied my purse. He's named the mare Willow after a girl he used to know back in Loncaster and his voice softens each time he speaks the name. He's not half the brute he looks.

A few yards from the office I rein Blink to a halt because Penelope Danton is walking towards us, smiling. She has no idea how resplendent she looks and I think that is what I like about her the most. Her hair is up beneath a modest hat, but enough of it is escaping to fall in auburn ringlets about her face, which is exquisite, as always. Her figure is shapely.

'Good day, Penney.' I doff my hat and she curtsies, poising the skirts of her emerald-green dress, the one that matches her eyes.

'Good day, Mr Banyard. How is business?'

'It's Michael and business could be better, though it seems we have an interesting new case.'

'*It seems*? Surely you either have a new case or you do not.'

'Hmmm. It's complicated. Confidential, you understand.'

'Understood.'

An idea strikes me. I'm full of ideas when Penney's around. 'Though perhaps you could help.'

'Oh?'

'Dine with us tonight at eight and I shall explain.'

She smirks, suspicious of me. My thing for her is no secret.

'Are you sure this is about work?'

'It *is* work *and* I would very much like the pleasure of your company. Will you attend?'

'I shall see you at eight.'

I hide my delight behind a controlled smile as we part.

Our new secretary is waiting for us at the door with a pinched look on her face. She's particularly smart this morning, primped in a grey silk skirt and a black fitted bodice over a white blouse. Her hat, a matching grey, is the squat topper style embellished with black lace as is the trend. Her hair is pinned up and businesslike. Josiah is already stupefied, unable even to offer a proper greeting, but he accomplishes a small nod and manages not to drool on his shirt.

'You're late,' says Elizabeth.

We are. I'm not used to having much of a reason to be punctual in the mornings unless I've arranged a meeting with a client. The accusation is most unwelcome but it's far too early for confrontations. At the very least I need a pick-me-up first.

I unlock the door and open it.

'After you.'

She nods and enters.

I hang my tricorn on the corner stand as she runs a finger through the dust on the end of the desk, leaving a clean line.

'The petty cash box is under my desk in the case room.'

'And why would I want the petty cash box?' she asks, brushing her hands.

'Because your first job is to fetch two cups of black soup. Three if you want one.'

She disappears into the case room, returning a moment later with a frown.

'Your cash box is empty.'

Of course. We're broke. I pluck several coins from the dwindling supply in my purse and drop them into her palm. She leaves and it feels like a bad start to the day.

'Never mind, Mr Banyard. Things'll pick up.'

'They'd better or we'll be forced to *sell* up.'

'It could be worse. You could have even less coins.'

'Less money. Fewer coins.'

'What's the difference?'

'The difference will be considerable if a silker hears you speaking like a threader. You need to learn these things or you'll get us killed.'

He nods. 'Less money. Fewer coins.'

'That's right. It's the same with any substance. Less of a substance. It's different with items. We say *fewer* items.'

'Got it.'

'Good.'

In the case room I take a new file from the shelf, dip a quill into the inkpot and scrawl *Widow Blewett* along the spine, case number – I check the registry – 2364.

I slide the claims report from my pocket to unfold it on the desk, planning the day. Firstly, we will revisit Anders' shack and if he's in, hear his account of the shipwreck.

After the wreck came the warehouse break-in, the same warehouse that later burned. The address is listed in the report. It's close to Anders' place so it makes sense to visit there next. That's as much of a plan as we need. I want the claims report with me so for now the casefile will remain empty. Elizabeth can copy the report later.

When she returns with the black soup, we all sit around the reception desk and Josiah and I bring her up to date on Widow Blewett's story.

'If the widow calls again be sure to take her address,' I say. 'She left in rather a hurry. You may also inform her we are exploring her case.'

'Certainly.'

'We'll be at Dockside investigating. Mind the desk and familiarise yourself with the place while we're gone.'

'I can't just sit here all day doing nothing.'

'Fine. Do some cleaning, learn our filing system but, most importantly, keep a lookout for the widow. We must speak with her.'

On our ride to Dockside I warn the smitten Mr Mingle as subtly as I know how.

'I'll dismiss Miss Fairweather if you persist in gawking all the time.'

'Sorry, Mr Banyard. I understand.'

He's working on his silker accent again and I nod approvingly. 'Better, but you're still rolling your Rs too heavily.'

'I shall endeavour to rein in my Rs and my eyes. You have to admit she's a fine-looking lass.'

'That may be so, but if she addles your brain, the pair of you make for a poor investment, one I can ill afford. Anyway, in my experience, looks aren't everything.'

'Yes, Mr Banyard.' At some point he'll need to stop calling me that. I'd prefer *Micky*, or *Michael* at least.

'This is Anders' shack.' We dismount and Josiah holds the reins while I knock. There's no sign of life.

Further towards the seafront a rag 'n' bone man clicks his tongue and flicks the reins. 'Move on. Move on.' His bony nag draws the rattling cart closer. A monstrous aurochs' skull is mounted upon the front of the cart. 'Bring out y'rags. Bring out y'bones.'

There's no reply from Anders. I knock again.

Nothing.

The man repeats his call.

I'm about to suggest we search the perimeter and am considering breaking in, when the cart draws up.

The man leans his craggy face down from the driver's seat. 'He ain't in. Ain't been home for weeks.'

The cart reeks of mouldering bones and stale decay.

'Do you know where he is?' asks Josiah.

'It is imperative that we speak with him,' I add.

'He's a sailor, masters. He's likely at sea.'

Of course. 'Thank you.'

'You're welcome, masters.' He clicks again and with a flick of the reins the nag walks on.

Surely with this unmistakable stink there is no need to announce his presence.

When he's driven his cart down the next lane, I stir. 'Now, let's see what we can find.' The front door is locked. We circle the house, testing windows. At the rear we navigate a battered collection of maritime bric-a-brac: ropes, nets, planks, casks, crates and a badly made ladder that is propped against the wall. It's only then I realise the entire shack is built from salvage. Even the windows are reclaimed portholes, ripped from the lower decks of a broken ship. The bleak morning light reveals a few tools scattered about, amid half a dozen wooden roof shingles. Anders left halfway through a repair job. The back door, however, remains locked.

Josiah points. 'The window.'

A high, shutterless porthole invites. Josiah is tall enough to see in but I have to drag a casket over and climb up, steadying myself with a hand on his shoulder. The shack is barren within: a table, a stool, a fireplace and a low cot in the corner. If Anders has other possessions, he has taken them with him. It is almost certainly not worth breaking in but I decide to do it anyway, just to be sure we're not missing something.

'Tether the horses and keep watch, Joe.'

I am no Draker and so what I'm about to do is illegal.

'Right.' He turns, scanning while sea larks reel and shriek in the sky overhead.

As long as he's silent I know we are safe. I pick the simple lock of Anders' back door – more a latch than a real mechanism. Opening it, I nod for Josiah to enter and follow him in, closing the door behind us.

'Check under the bed. Check the walls for hiding holes.'

While Josiah works, I busy myself examining the ash in the fireplace, which has not seen flame for several days, perhaps weeks. It is not light and crumbly like fresh ash but flattened, damp and condensed. I pluck out an unburned corner of a page and slip it into my pocket notebook for later inspection.

It rained last night and across the room a damp patch glistens on the floor. Anders was fixing his roof when something called him away.

The furniture holds nothing, tells of nothing. The floor is next. He could have gone with a dirt floor or laid stones, but Anders' is consistent: salvaged wood, everywhere I turn. The floorboards – gnarled ships' planks – are nailed firmly and arranged so that no two lengths end in line.

Except for a spot beneath the table, that is, where three boards, shorter than the rest, run in a perfect row.

'Anything?'

Josiah shakes his head. 'Nothing but cobwebs and dirt.' He leaves the bed and starts tapping his way around the walls.

I drag the table aside and kneel to lift the three planks, unsurprised to find they are nailed together to form the lid of a cubby hole. Leaning in, I huff and stare at its emptiness.

5

The Fickle Tide

In which Banyard and Mingle take a boat out

Today the air is clear and, looking north from the docks, Burrington Point is visible projecting into the sea beyond Hatch Head. We stand at the edge of the Cogg, an extensive hook built of giant stones that stretches out into the ocean. At our toes the sea wall plummets thirty feet to the water.

The fickle tide is low and calm, a cold shade of dark turquoise, lapping gently against the shell-speckled mortar and limey, barnacle-encrusted rock. It threatens nothing and no one. Galleons and steam ships coast in the safe harbour. Boats bob contentedly. Strollers parade the foamy edge hand in hand, while sailors stow cargo and fishermen come and go.

John Ferris is one of them, a grafter recently returned from fishing the Deepning Sound. He's a reasonable man and for half-a-crown he readily agrees to loan us his rowboat for an hour. My personal coin reserve is depleted further.

'You're welcome to her, masters. I'll be sorting for a goodly while, anyhow. Take care of her and rope her up back here when you're done.'

'You have my word,' I promise as he slips the coin from his calloused hand into a pocket and turns back to his full crates. Several fish twist and dance on their slippery pile, unaware the sea is now forever beyond reach. 'There was a shipwreck near here a month ago, the *Dollinger*. I don't suppose you know where she lies.'

Ferris turns and points to the rocks beyond the port, further up the coast. 'She lies yonder, submerged at high tide.'

'But visible now?'

'She protrudes at low tide, if that's what you mean. Whether you'll see her or no is another matter.' He points out to sea where a dirty green fog drifts in.

'I'm much obliged.' I turn to Josiah. 'We'll have to hurry if we're to reach her before the fog.'

The rowboat sits beneath a corroding iron ladder set into the wall and we descend to board. Josiah stands in the middle, wobbling and threatening to capsize us. He flings his arms out to his sides attempting to balance.

'Sit down, man! Haven't you been in a boat before?'

Clumsily, he sits on the aft thwart and shakes his head. 'No, and I wish I wasn't now.'

I soften. He has the wrong physique to man a small boat: tall and top-heavy with muscle. Despite his size he reminds me of a child.

'We'll be all right. Just stay there.' I take the oars. He grips the edge of the boat on either side. 'I'll take the first turn. Watch and learn how it's done.'

I row us out from the Cogg and turn north towards Hatch Head, the rowlocks squeaking with every pull. I want to see for myself the location of the wreck and understand how it happened. Only by doing so do we stand a chance of proving it was no accident. Anxiously and with due diligence, Josiah watches.

'Can you swim?' I know the answer before he confirms it. Each second he is imagining what would follow if he errs and spills us into the drink.

'No.' He doesn't shake his head this time. Doesn't want to risk even the smallest movement.

'Relax. If the boat turns over, keep hold of it. The chances are it will stay afloat.'

He forces a dubious smile as I pause to point.

'The headland there is Hatch Head. The next is Burrington Point. See the lighthouse?'

'Aye.'

Halfway to our destination, we precariously swap seats and he takes a turn rowing. To be fair, once he's settled down, he's not half-bad. A few strokes in, he masters the art and with his superior upper body strength we're cutting fast. It's a good job because the fog is crawling closer to land with each second, low and dense like a greedy smothering blanket.

'You're good at this, Joe.' I check our position, estimating we are approaching midway between Hatch Head and the lighthouse and equidistant from shore. 'Take a break. We've arrived.' Was this the *Dollinger's* position when the storm turned bad? From somewhere around here the bosun glimpsed a light and, believing it to be the lighthouse, turned the ship northwards. With the Northern Chase currents drawing them up the coast, this bearing would send them into open water, providing they could clear the rocks at Burrington Point. It might be viewed as a risky strategy but pounded by the storm from the east, I don't suppose they would have had much choice.

At night and in a storm it would be different. Was the real lighthouse visible? Hard to say. In the chaos of the tempest could anyone know for sure that the source of a light was stationary or moving? Surrounded by chaos, their deck was heaving, their vision blurred by a torrent of wind and rain. I close my eyes and picture the scene. The ship pitches with each wave and sailors dash about, derigging as ordered. Cargo breaks loose and slides freely, dangerously. A man goes overboard and billows threaten to overturn the ship. All are fearful and panic-stricken. Someone calls *Lighthouse*! I open my eyes.

'What do you think, Joe? Your ship is in trouble. You see a light that could be the lighthouse. You think you're heading for rocks.'

'I'd turn the ship quick smart.'

'Which way?'

'I'd head for open water. That way.' He points towards the rolling fog.

There is only one quarter of the compass that is open sea from here. The mainland coast, running roughly north to south, takes up 180 degrees of our present view. Behind us to the south-east, the Eyes of Myrh tower from the ocean.

'I concur. It's the only logical reaction. So why, when they turned the rudder, did they run directly onto the rocks?'

'Maybe the storm…' he ventures.

'You're right. In a real storm their efforts may have been futile.' I had the foresight to bring my telescope. I pull if from my coat pocket and extend the brass rings. Scanning the coast, I trace a line from Dockside northwards through Lytche's Cove and Hatch Head, ending on Burrington Point. The lighthouse is a tall tower, topped with windows that shelter an enormous carcynine lamp.

Josiah follows my gaze. 'The lighthouse is high, unlikely to be mistaken for a ship's lamp.'

'Indeed.' I turn towards the Eyes of Myrh and focus on the twin islands' coasts. Their purple shores climb steeply from the sea, forming two rounded peaks like loaves, both higher than the mainland.

'Are there no lighthouses on the Eyes?' Josiah asks.

'Not to my knowledge. Not on the harbour side.' I search for anything that could be mistaken for a lighthouse.

'But on the night of the storm…'

'On the night of the storm, who knows what happened upon the Eyes?'

'So, where's the *Dollinger*?'

I sweep the rocky shoreline at the base of the cliffs below Hatch Head and find the broken masts and a battered portion of the *Dollinger's* gunwale protruding from the deceitfully calm water.

'It's there. Take us over, Joe.'

As the green fog fingers closer to our position, he rows us towards the rocks until I raise a hand, in fear that we, too, may strike stone and sink. From above the water I can see nothing that helps, except that it is the bow of the galleon that juts from the sea and it is facing landward.

'They were steering towards the rocks when they struck, but if we're to make a proper examination we'll have to go down there.'

Josiah looks horrified. 'Go down... *There?*' He nods towards the submerged wreck.

A steam-tug smokes across the water to us from Lytche's Cove, scuttling my thoughts.

'Hello. Who's this?'

We grip the gunwale, rocking in the tug's waves. It bears Camdon City's official crest, a three-headed lion wielding a lance, all set upon a black shield. A figure at the stern adjusts a lever and, with a bout of filth from its rear funnel, the tug quietens and drifts to an uncertain stop at our port side. As he approaches, I recognise Inculus Legge, our *endearing* harbour master.

'Good day, Master Legge. I trust we are in no trouble.'

'You're not in trouble. Yet.'

'Then, how may we help you this fine day?'

'You can't, most likely. Just a friendly routine visit to see what you're up to out here.'

He's not friendly. In fact, he's distinctly unfriendly and his features remind me of the craggy rocks at the base of the cliffs.

'What we're up to?'

'Aye. So, why *are* you and your friend out here, Mr Banyard?'

'We're... Investigating. I couldn't possibly confide anything about the case, I'm afraid. It's confidential. I'm sure you understand.' He has chugged all the way out from the harbour solely to check on us. He's cantankerous and wants to know *exactly* why we're here.

'Be that as it may, I'm ordering you to land. You're sitting between a shipping lane and the rocks. There are currents. The fog is heading in and if you're not careful the Noosely Swells will drag your little boat out to sea. Whatever you're investigating, stop it.'

'Are there rocks near here that would snag us?' asks Josiah. Good thinking! Legge might help us without even knowing.

'Who's asking?'

'Apologies. This is my business partner, Mr Josiah Mingle. Joe, our friend here is the diligent Harbour Master, Inculus Legge.'

'Josiah Mingle, eh? You're not from round 'ere, are you?'

'No, Master Legge. I'm from Borrington in the north.'

'Borrington. Never heard of the place,' says Legge.

Neither have I, but I'm pleased Josiah had the nous to avoid leaving a trail back to Loncaster, his real home town. Legge continues. 'No matter. There are hidden rocks betwixt here and the shore. Why, just last month, there was a wreck not a spit from here.'

'Ah, you must mean the *Dollinger* over there. Where did the ship hit rocks exactly?' My attempt to sound casual and uneducated about the matter is met with a suspicious scowl.

'What do you know of the *Dollinger*?' Legge growls.

'Oh, nothing, really. It was in the papers, wasn't it?'

'You forget about the *Dollinger* and the rocks. You've no business being out here. Now, to shore with you!'

Between the harbour and the Golden Shores warehouse rests the maritime deadfield. In passing, it feels apt to pause and view the thirty-three recently added graves, their headstones running in orderly rows of which any captain would be proud.

'Thirty-three.'

It trips from my tongue in a trice, but the graves cover an entire corner of the field and it seems an unreasonable number of needlessly dead men.

Crowlings stab for worms in the grave fills where grass has yet to regrow. They are wretched birds that would happily pluck out the eyes of a dying man.

'If only they could rise up from the dead, Mr Banyard.'

I frown.

'I mean, then they could tell us what was done to them, couldn't they?'

'Oh, I see. Quite.'

We quieten as a small, scruffy girl with long, mousy hair timidly enters the deadfield and kneels to place a fistful of dandyblooms and hedge flowers in the shadow of a headstone. We are close enough to hear her sobs. Her father, no doubt, is six feet below. In that moment I forget about the widow's claim and our potential reward. If the *Dollinger* was purposefully wrecked I want to bring Cullins down for each and every orphan and widow he's created. In that instant I only wish to see him punished.

'Come, Joe. It's not good to linger in deadfields. That's what they say, isn't it?'

'It is, indeed.' We dig heels and turn our mounts away, the echoing clip-clop of hooves on the cobbled street the only sound. 'What does the report say about the warehouse?'

'The theft occurred three days after the shipwreck. Another day passed before a clerk named Markle Odson was mugged for the company cash box. Two days later the treasurer died of heart failure, apparently, and later the same day the warehouse burned down.'

'Good timing for a cover-up.'

'That's what I was thinking. It would take a few days for word to reach the insurers and for the authorities to process the paperwork. What would *you* do if you heard someone was coming to investigate the theft and it was you who'd arranged it?'

'I'd be nervous, Mr Banyard. I'd worry I might have left clues behind. I'd probably send someone down there – quick smart – with brushwood and a packet of Sulphurs.'

'Indeed.'

The sour smell of wet ash reaches us long before we round a shipyard and see the charred remains. The warehouse plot is substantial, covering an area the size of six town houses, now nothing but burned ruins. A blackened ribcage of uprights and roof beams is all that stands above our knees. The timbers reach up high, starkly silhouetted against a bleak sky.

I dismount and, with the toe of my boot, turn a semi-charred sign laying in the muck near what used to be an entrance. The words are still visible, though much of the paint is blistered.

Golden Shores Imports

To my left, Dockside sprawls towards the city. On my right, a stone walkway drops down to a slipway and docking points with iron mooring posts at the water's edge. It is prime real estate for any shipping business. Here merchant galleons can comfortably berth in the deep harbour, their loads to be transferred from or to the capacious warehouse a matter of yards away.

Josiah secures the horses and joins me, poking around in the ashes. There are fragments of wood, burned and smashed roofing tiles, several sets of iron wheels remaining from some kind of box-haulers and a scatter of iron hoops, presumably from wine barrels. Everything is burned and blackened.

'What would you say was the contents of this place before it went up?' I ask Josiah.

'I wouldn't say. I couldn't. That's the point, isn't it? After this, no one would be able to tell what was here or what had been taken. What did you say they were importing at the time?'

'The *Dollinger* was reportedly carrying barrels of fine wine, gunpowder and black soup beans from Urthia. The claims report lists a detailed inventory including more of the same plus a fortune in bottled whisky, rum and Eastern silks.'

'Gunpowder and spirits. How fortuitous, if the warehouse contained more of the same...'

I nod. 'The silks and beans would burn away without trace and the chances are if anything else was to remain, the spirits and gunpowder would obliterate it all.'

Except...

'Make a search, Joe. You take that half.' I wave towards the far end of the ruins.

'What am I looking for, Mr Banyard?'

'Cullins claims he was storing two thousand bottles of whisky and rum here at the time of the fire; a considerable amount, if the inventory is correct. The molten glass from the bottles will have flowed to the floor. Search every inch beneath the ash.'

It's a dirty, stinking job and takes us the rest of the morning, but it's worth it. Around noon we meet at the centre, caked with clammy ash up to our elbows.

'Anything?' I ask.

'Nothing. Not one drop of melted glass.'

6

The Dancing Dead

In which Banyard and Mingle encounter an unfamiliar smell

Outside the office we scrape the worst of the ash from our leather riding boots and, to Elizabeth's disgust, enter. Her nose wrinkles and she narrows her eyes.

'You can't come in here like that.'

'I think you'll find we just did.' I hang my hat.

'Oh, you're filthy and you stink. I've spent hours cleaning this grimy dump. Look! Look what you've traipsed in!'

We all look at the smudgy trail of ash on the floor. 'And what makes you think I'm happy to be cleaner and soup fetcher? We've discussed no such aspects of my role. And another thing, I've been bored to death with nothing to do for most of the day. This simply will not do.'

'Good afternoon, Miss Fairweather. I take it we've had few customers, then. No widow?'

'Not one. Not the widow. Not anyone. Mr Banyard, if you're going to employ me, *employ me*!'

I drop the claims report on the desk before her. 'Make a copy of this. Should keep you busy for a while. I need it back within the hour.' At a tilt of my head, Josiah follows me sheepishly into the case room, trying not to drop more ash, and I close the door, glad to have a barrier between Elizabeth and me.

'I'll have to let her go, Joe. It's clearly not working.'

'Give it a chance, Mr Banyard. Please. She's feisty but she'll be a good worker. I know it.'

'I'm not sure. I don't enjoy the tension. Let's clean up and get back out. We've plenty of folk to interview, Sergeant Goffings, for starters.' A horrid man to deal with but I suppose I should face the inevitable. 'He's in charge of the Dockside Drakers and was undoubtedly the one called when the fire was discovered and the cry raised. No, wait. First things first. Have our dear Miss Fairweather fetch us black soup and pork buns. We deserve a break and something to eat.'

Josiah throws me a questioning look, his eyebrows raised, his gaze darting periodically to the door beyond which Elizabeth sits in a venomous haze.

'Or fetch it yourself,' I add. 'I don't care which.'

He leaves the room and a moment later I hear the outer door open and shut. He's collecting our victuals himself and I don't blame him.

I'm left in an unusual situation, for a few precious moments, alone in my case room. No one is bothering me. It is one of my favourite places to be. With a moment's study, a wallchart shows me tomorrow morning there will be a low tide at nine. Good. We will dive the wreck then. I've already arranged to borrow the gear we need.

Above and to the side of my desk sit our casefiles, usually roughly ordered: I don't always have time to find the appropriate slot when returning a file to the shelves, but today they are in perfect numerical order.

Our new secretary *has* been busy and I'm pleased. It's good to know they are properly arranged. It feels, somehow, more professional. I notice other details then. The cobwebs in the corners have gone. The room is clean, the table waxed. Running a fingertip along its surface produces a squeak rather than the usual line of absence. In fact, the entire room is spick and span. It smells fresher, too. I draw a long, deep breath through my nose.

The inkpot on my desk has been refilled, the quill and spares newly sharpened and arranged neatly in the little pot. The small window overlooking the back street is polished and allowing considerably more light in than usual. The bin beneath my desk is abnormally empty.

Perhaps I'm wrong about Elizabeth. I'll give her another day, although it may cost me the last of my pennies.

One of the casefiles catches my eye. It often does, because it is five times thicker than any other. It has no case number but a single word scribed down its fat spine in my father's hand, the ink faded.

Gawpers

It is a file I revisit regularly, the one containing every account concerning gawpers that's been collected over the last fifty-seven years. I draw the file lovingly from the shelf as the widow's words return to me.

'Sightings of gawpers have been reported down by the docks and men have died. 'Tis all in the claims report...'

Gawpers down by the docks. I don't recall anything about gawpers in the claims report and make a mental note to check through it again when Elizabeth has finished copying it.

My next ten minutes are spent reviewing every recorded account of gawpers in Dockside, twenty-three in total. They range from vague, unsubstantiated glimpses of tall figures loitering in the shadows – sometimes noted to have eyes like white fire – to encounters by multiple witnesses and group sightings. The most notable of these is an instance during which six gawpers were supposedly seen drifting at the sea's edge. The witnesses, five shipbuilders of Dorsons and Kribbs – the shipwrights along from the Golden Shores warehouse – could not say if the figures were hovering over the sea or the shore, on account of the high tide and a thick green mist that was covering everything at the time. The sighting took place at dusk on the third day of Thripplemoon some twenty-two years ago. There is mention of a shipwreck later that same eve in which twelve men drowned.

I shudder. Are the events connected? Perhaps we'll never know. In any case, I must enquire to learn if any of the recent gawper sightings occurred in association with the *Dollinger* wreck. I dip a quill and make notes on our findings so far, to add to the widow's file. I also write the following:

> *Are gawpers mentioned in the widow's claims report?*
> *Were gawpers sighted on the night of the wreck?*

Another thought hits me. Did the widow mean that men had died during recent gawper encounters? Did the gawpers attack and kill? I add another line.

> *Reported gawper encounters resulting in death?*

Hurriedly I search files for examples where deaths have, rightly or wrongly, been ascribed to gawper appearances.

Josiah returns, interrupting my flow.

'Black soup and one pork bun.' He plonks the copper cup and a newspaper-wrapped bun on the desk and takes a seat. 'What's that smell?'

He's noticed, too. Beeswax and something lemony.

'That, my friend, it the scent of cleanliness. Miss Fairweather has cleaned up.'

'Ah. It smells… *Better*!'

'Hmmm…' I can't bring myself to be overly enthused but I force a nod.

Sergeant Goffings is a rough sort. He *has* to be; Dockside is a brutal place. A hard place. Scowling, he meets us in the lobby of the Dockside Draker Headquarters and jerks his thumb towards his office door.

'In.'

He knows me well enough and it's as much a welcome as we can expect to get, although, ominously, a nod of his head has two officers escort us. Inside, he bids us to sit while he takes his seat behind his desk and the officers guard the doorway.

'Now, what's all this about?'

I explain. 'We've come to question you about a potential case we're considering. It's regarding possible criminal activity surrounding Golden Shores Imports.'

'I thought as much.'

Through the open doorway I glimpse Harbour Master Inculus Legge talking with another Draker. Legge pauses to give Goffings a curt nod.

I open my mouth to speak but Goffings cuts in.

'You've overstepped the mark this time, Banyard. You and your friend will be held in custody while I look into the matter.'

'*The matter?* What *matter?*'

'The matter of you poking your nose around where it's not welcome. You'd stay away from Dockside if you had half a mind between you.'

'Why?' I ask, as Goffings flicks a hand and the officers close on Josiah and me. 'Under what charge are you holding us?' Podgy fingers clamp our shoulders.

Goffings stares, enraged, mostly because he has no real answer. 'Meddling!'

I'm stunned by the nerve of the man. Yes, I broke into a ship hand's shack but *he* doesn't know that, surely. Beyond that, we're innocent… ish.

'I demand to know why we're being held! This is an outrage!' My cries are ignored as Goffings calls more of his men. Josiah struggles and catches my eye. If he fights, people will die and our position will only worsen. I shake my head and he allows them to take him by the arms. We are manhandled out of the room and dragged down to the cells.

Condensation descends the stone walls in tiny rivulets. Drips repeatedly fall from the ceiling to splash on the filthy ground near our manacled feet. A puddle slowly grows.

'Could be worse, Mr Banyard.'

'Yes, Joe. It could.' I say no more about how it could be worse because my position does not afford a view down the hallway and so I don't know who's listening beyond the iron bars of our cell door. But he's right. It would be worse if we'd truly been discovered, a lot worse. They could have found out that my cousin Mardon and I rescued Silus Garroway from the noose by posing as gawpers and that he's here in Camdon, posing as a silker. They could have discovered a multitude of my other sins against this hideous society, each one a private rebellion that – somewhere, somehow – helped a threader to survive another day or better their circumstances. I close my eyes and recall the events of the rescue:

The rotary-pressed letters of the Loncaster Chronicle*'s headline slowly form cohesive words.*

GAWPERS SIGHTED ON GALLOWS HILL

I'm struggling to focus because across the street a silker is bludgeoning his bedraggled servant with a stick. The threader is bleeding from the head and from his hands where he raises them in defence. He's in his late teens, the same as Mardon and I.

Pedestrians ignore the scene, or worse, cross the road to avoid it. They dodge the steam trucks and clockwork cars that rattle past, spraying an oily slick up from the gutters. They brave this filthy spatter rather than acknowledge the outrage that is the norm.

I am different. In this moment that is all I know.

Folding the newspaper, I tuck it under my arm and approach a greasy-haired street vendor selling black soup.

'Two cups, if you will.'

A Hinkley Air ship cleaves the distant cloud and for a moment I wish I was on board. Closing my eyes, I imagine it. Briefly, I am away from this grounded reality.

The vendor dips a ladle into his cauldron that bubbles and steams over an open fire. He pours black soup into a copper cup and takes my money with a smile that thinly veils his hatred of my kind. It's nothing personal.

He reserves the same for every silker customer.

The second cup is for my cousin Mardon, a fine fellow, a surgeon and a gentleman.

The silker across the street thrashes the brass knob of his cane against his servant's head. Why so angry? The threader's blood weeps from his hair to the cobbles in strings. His face is a mess.

I sip. The black soup is hot and strong. The vendor probably spat in it, but I drink anyway.

'Who is that?' I ask Mardon because, other than Aunt Myrtle, he is the only person I know in Loncaster.

'Bartholomew Corston.' He cradles the cup to warm his hands. 'The threader he's pounding is Silus Garroway.'

Another blow stuns Silus who drops to the ground like a sack of meat. His hands are manacled, and a Draker escort — two armed officers — hang back to watch, with no intention of intervening.

'Get up, dog-scum! Wretched bile-snipe!' Corston's outrage reaches us across the road. He kicks Silus hard in the ribs and, when his servant fails to respond, boots him in the face for good measure. There is an audible crunch and I swallow uncomfortably.

I sometimes wonder if I'm from another place, another island or planet, perhaps. Why is it that others can saunter about their business, top hats and bonnets bobbing, untroubled by such outlandish cruelty? Why does it not appal them as it does me? Indeed, I must be different. Perhaps it was my father who made me so. Lifting my tricorn hat to brush hair from my brow I'm reminded I am also unfashionable.

Mardon glances at it and shakes his head, mildly amused.

I fight the urge to cross the road and strike Corston. One good punch would do it. He's fat, slow and unfit. He continues his assault — the exertion causing him to sweat like a threader in a courthouse — although his servant is now unconscious. My intervention would not do, however. It is lawful for silkers to beat their threaders. It is unlawful for a silker to harm a fellow silker.

For a moment I ponder again the terms deemed to have originated from a single industry.

The threaders make the silk.

73

The silkers wear the silk.

I remind myself. There is no lawful way a threader may enter silker society. Such a crime would end in the swift execution of all involved, if it were ever known.

Mardon paces at my side as we leave the town centre to head back to Aunt Myrtle's. Dressed from head to foot in the latest silk fashion, he looks wealthier than he is and a little garish. Before long we leave the town houses behind to climb a rise they call Gallows Hill where, at the peak, a line of five gibbets hang from gallows, each occupied by an unfortunate threader who has seen better days. A cool wind blows in from the hills beyond, caressing the corpses and setting them swaying with its gentle touch.

'Poor blighters,' Mardon mutters. He's not completely unsympathetic. He points to the central corpse, the most putrid of all. 'I see old Fangles Hingleson is turning to soup.'

Fangles drips from the gibbet. The death stench wafts my way and I gag. I hold a handkerchief over my nose and turn my back on the line while clearing my throat.

'What was his crime?'

'He wore a battered silk topper he found in the gutter. It was in the news.'

'They hanged him for wearing a hat?'

'A silk hat.'

'All the same, it's a bit harsh, wouldn't you say?'

Mardon shrugs, his face remarkably indifferent as he checks his pocket watch. 'Dinner will be ready soon. Come on. Let's get out of this wind.'

I wrap my long coat more tightly about me. Glancing back, I find the place eerie even in the late afternoon light. Picturing it in darkness, I see gawpers creeping to the feet of the dancing dead and shiver.

7

Mardon's Special Mix

In which Banyard is inspired

After dinner, Hobbs – a grey-haired threader in mid-life – brings extra candles to the smoking room where my cousin and I lounge in grand Wexford chairs of green leather. Only the best for the Loncaster Banyards. Mardon lights his pipe. The oak panels of the walls have imbibed the smell, giving the room a permanent taint like a ghost that refuses to leave. Strangely, I enjoy the smoky scent but have never partaken. A glass of my cousin's finest port, on the other hand, is most welcome. I quaff it and wave for Hobbs to refill, all the while trying not to think of Silus Garroway's blood as the port flows.

'What more do you know about this Garroway fellow, and why was his master beating him so severely?'

Mardon blows smoke rings and flicks his fingers to dismiss Hobbs.

'Two nights back he stole a loaf of bread from the bakers on Whitegate. When we saw them in town this afternoon they were returning from the courthouse. They must have been heading for the threader gaol. I don't suppose the verdict was good news. He'll most likely hang at dawn.'

'So Corston is angry at losing a servant to the noose.' When I blink, I see Garroway's bloodied face behind the gibbet bars. I straighten in my chair, unnerved. 'Then his sentence will be listed in the Evening Witness.'

Mardon gives me a searching look and tuts, but calls Hobbs back into the room.

'Hobbs, be a good fellow and fetch a copy of the late news.' He tosses a coin into the air which Hobbs rushes to catch.

'Right away, Master Banyard.' Hobbs leaves, polishing the penny on his shirt. He's enjoying holding it while he can.

'Why would he steal bread? Is Corston the sort to be tight on rations?'

'Not by the looks of his belly, but who knows? There's no law that says you have to feed them properly.'

'Perhaps there should be.'

For several minutes we sit in an awkward silence until Hobbs returns, breathless and mopping his brow with his sleeve. He presents a folded copy of the Evening Witness to Mardon.

'Excellent work, Hobbs. Quick. Very quick.'

Hobbs' haggard features brighten. He bows his head and leaves.

Mardon flings the paper across to me and I open it hungrily, breathing the pungent ink. I hunt down the article and read aloud.

'Threader Silus Garroway to hang for theft, promptly at dawn upon the twelfth day of Quartersmoon. That's tomorrow.'

Mardon raises his eyebrows dismissively and sucks on his pipe. 'Told you so.'

'It says here he pleaded for mercy on the grounds that the stolen bread was not for himself but for a threader family of six hungry children, recently bereaved of their father and so their income.'

'Ah, yes. That will be his brother's lot, no doubt.'

'So, it's true. He only stole to help others.'

Mardon's had enough. He fixes a heavy gaze upon me. 'Why he did it is immaterial. That fact is he's guilty.'

He's right, of course. The facts are the facts. All the same it irks me and for an hour after he's retired I pace the floor, unable to shake the image of six malnourished children and their overburdened mother from my head. At last I can bear it no more. Dangling a lantern before me to light the way I climb the stairs to Mardon's room. The old house creaks with every footstep and is dark because Aunt Myrtle refuses to have gas lights installed. She's never liked them and says the gas is a danger.

At Mardon's door I knock tentatively. I listen to the resulting shuffle and a moment later it opens and Mardon squints, frowning through the gap.

'Can I help you?'

I smile apologetically. 'Possibly.'

'With what?'

'This Garroway fellow, he'll be locked in the threader gaol adjoining the silker courthouse, will he not?'

'He will. What of it?'

'I was wondering if I might borrow a little gunpowder, your special mix.'

He rolls his eyes and tries to close the door. 'Go to bed, Micky.'

My foot finds its way between the door and the jamb. Mardon pushes but the door is wedged.

'You can't break him out of gaol,' he says. 'That would be a crime.'

'Who said anything about breaking anyone out of gaol?'

He glares, considering my request. I see his thoughts like ink on a parchment: Perhaps if I give him what he wants he'll go away.

'How much gunpowder?'

'Half a cup should do it.'

'Then you'll leave me be?'

I nod.

Opening the door fully he commandeers my lantern and leads me down the hall and the grand stairway to a finely veneered writing desk on the lower landing. He lifts a key from a drawer and crosses to the gun cabinet. Unlocking it he takes a powder magazine and pauses. 'A pistol?'

'Two would be better.'

He shakes his head. 'What are you planning, exactly?' He hands me the flintlocks but I only take one.

'The other's for you.' I receive a dark look.

'I'll not be coming with you.'

'My odds would improve if you did.'

'I agreed to the gunpowder. You can take the pistols and I'll hold my tongue, but that's it.'

'Actually, we'll also need some old clothes. I expect Hobbs will have some tucked away. No silks, obviously. I suppose our guest might be rather encumbered after his mistreatment this afternoon and so we'll also need your horse and carriage. Your Double Heart would be far too loud.' The Double Heart is a model of clockwork car by Gear and Cog, a fine machine, but unsuitable for our impending task.

Mardon shakes his head in disbelief and starts for the stairs.

'Oh, come on, Mardon. It'll be an adventure. What do you say?'

'I say it's late and I'm tired. You're a madman for chancing this. I'm going to bed now. Goodnight.'

I step after him. 'All right, just the clothes, then. Help me with those and I'll take my own horse, leave you alone.'

I know him. I know he'll turn. His nature demands it. He can't help himself.

He's almost at the top of the stairs when it happens. 'All right. The old clothes, but that's it.'

You've got to love Mardon. We've played this game before, but never to this extent. He fetches worn clothes from Hobbs' cupboard and before he can turn away, I remove my neck scarf and shirt.

'You really mean to do this? What will you do with the man? You'll have to take him with you. Hide him. Feed him. He'll be a burden to you. You don't even know him.'

I open my mouth to speak but he cuts in.

'Ridiculous! And what will you have achieved? The world is full of Garroways. You can't save them all.'

'One would be a start.' I slip Hobbs' clothes on. 'Shoes? I can't wear mine. Far too new.'

He digs out a tatty pair of Hobbs' shoes and I squeeze my feet into them, turning for his inspection.

'What do you think?'

'Rub some dirt on your face and you just might be mistaken for a threader. Slouch, man. You've a back like a plank.'

I oblige and, approving of my posture if nothing else, Mardon sees me off. 'Would serve you right if you got shot.'

I grin. 'Sleep well, cousin.'

Blink plods steadily beneath me, his black mane and flanks silky in the moonlight. He's an old rogue of a horse, though steady enough on the road.

Over Gallows Hill the moon sits high upon a bed of silver-trimmed cloud. I watch for gawpers as I pass the swinging gibbets and dab expectantly at my brow. No blood, but I was right. It is eerie here at night. Doubly so when alone. Of course, I have Blink, but he's as big a coward as you might find in a stables. An alert companion with a loaded musket and a cudgel on his belt would be better.

The forecourt between the gaol and the adjacent courthouse is deserted. Blink clops me across the cobbles and I steer him down a side street where I dismount to hitch his reins to an iron ring set into a tavern wall. He'll be safe enough here. I take a short rope from a saddlebag.

Back at the gaol I slip the powder magazine from my long coat pocket and remove its stopper. The dim street is silent and unoccupied to my left and right. Tucking the muzzle snuggly into the keyhole of the door, I tip powder into the lock and remove the flask to peer in. It's too dark to see much, even with the blue glow of the gas lamps. No wiser, I tip more of the powder in until the keyhole overflows, a trace spilling to the ground. Too much. I do not wish to kill the turnkey. I lean in and blow a little out of the hole.

Perfect.

Further on, a path leads to the guardhouse, little more than a cell in which the turnkey sits, eats, rolls dice and, tonight, naps. I consider leaving him be, but he'll need to be dealt with sooner or later and I'd rather it was sooner. Stooping outside the open arch I rub my fingers on the ground and smear a little dirt around my face to complete my transformation.

'Guards! Guards, awake!' I run in and shake him violently by the shoulders. For this to work he has to still be half-asleep by the time he reaches the primed lock. 'Hurry! Wake up!' He reels, dropping the musket that was resting on his lap and losing his cap. Rousing, he scrambles for them in the gloom and I lift him to his feet and briskly guide him out with an arm around his shoulder.

'What? What is it? What's the big hurry?'

'The captain sent me. There's a riot in the threader gaol! They're murdering each other in there! Hurry, man!' My attempt at a threader accent is dubious at best but he's too stunned and sleepy to notice.

'The captain was here? Where is he?' A hint of fear colours his voice.

'Gone to fetch reinforcements, boss.' Nearing the door. 'Quickly, boss! The key!'

He fumbles with a ring of keys on his belt and shoves the largest into the lock. Stepping away, I close my eyes as he gives the key a firm turn to the right.

Boom! The powder ignites with a flash of blinding white light and I marvel at the properties of Mardon's special mix.

The explosion blows the lock apart, throwing the turnkey onto his back. I check his face, his body and arms. No blood.

Good.

He's too dazed to rise.

Also good.

'Don't worry. The blindness is temporary. Now listen carefully. You're going to need a believable story if you're to keep your job. Tell them a band of five — no, make it ten — threaders fell upon you at once. Say they were armed with muskets and blunderbusses. There was nothing you could do. Here, put your arms behind your back.' Helping him to sit up, I glance quickly around before tying his hands with the rope. He doesn't bother to fight but shouts.

'Call the Drakers! Help! Help me! Call the guards. Call the Justice!' He continues with his theme.

'Now, believe me,' I say, slapping him firmly across the cheek. I have his attention. 'I'm utterly against any sort of violence so this is going to hurt me far more than it is you. Well, actually that's not true, but I'm afraid it's necessary or they'll think you didn't put up a fight.' My right hook meets his jaw, knocking him out cold. I'm mildly surprised at my own strength. I grab the gaol keys from the ground where they've fallen.

A light flickers to life in a window across the way. My time is short.

The gaol door leans open, smoke wafting from its charred lock hole. I rush inside clutching the keys, but which key do I need? Separated by a narrow path, two rows of cells greet me. Silus is awake among a dozen other prisoners and watching with interest through the bars. I know him only by his bloodied and misshapen face as he attempts what I assume is supposed to be a smile. The rust-worn keys are not numbered or marked in any way. I curse. I suppose the guards here are never in a rush to use them, yet picturing them painstakingly trying key after key each time they need to open a door doesn't help my predicament. Surely there's a system to it.

Ah-ha! A key fits!

Alas, it won't turn.

I try another and another, a total of eight, before footfalls alert me to approaching reinforcements. Time to go. I sprint from the gaol and turn for *the alley while shouting men give chase.*

'Oy, you there! Halt and desist!'

I think not. Blast the keys. I flee.

Behind me, a musket shot streaks the night with smoke. The lead ball whistles past my ear. I reach Blink and, leaping into the saddle, yank his tether free, lash his reins and dig heels. Already startled by the shot, he launches into a gallop, bearing me away as another shot sends hot lead deep into my upper arm.

My saviour, the night, swallows me whole.

Understandably, Mardon is displeased to see me bleeding at his bedroom door.

'I'd be terribly obliged if you'd spare me a minute.'

In his long, pale nightshirt he peers, bleary-eyed, and tips back his head to squint at my wound.

'Well now, Micky. You've got yourself shot.'

'Yes. Though, before you say it, I'm doing my best not to bleed on the carpet.'

'Musket ball?'

'No, thanks, I'm pretty sure I already have one, lodged in my flesh.'

'Wait there.' Despairingly he leaves, returning moments later in a silk dressing gown and slippers. 'To the lab. I'll need some decent light if I'm to extract it and stitch you.'

In Mardon's laboratory I take a seat at his invitation and he hands me a splint of wood to bite on. Ducking at his work station, he fishes out the strangest pair of glasses I've ever seen. Either side of the three-layered lenses are mounted small tubes of clear glass with silvered ends.

'Lithorium. The secret ingredient to my special mix,' he explains, tucking a small strip of shiny metal into each tube and clipping their lids closed. He strikes a carcynine match and heats each tube in turn until the metal strips burst into bright white flames. 'When trapped in these cylinders it's starved of oxygen and forced to combust at a hugely reduced rate. There's enough in here to burn for a good ten minutes or so.' He dons the spectacles and, everywhere he turns, the brilliant light illuminates.

'Exceptional.'

'No threader in tow, I see. I assume you failed.'

'Indeed.' I consider commenting about his absence in the escapade to invoke guilt but think better of it. For one thing, he's now probing at my wound with a scalpel and tweezers and I'm biting hard on the wood. Not the wisest moment to rile your personal surgeon.

We'll soon have this out and then we'll cauterise the wound with a little gunpowder.'

'I can't wait.'

The lithorium lights are blinding me, burning points on my retinas like a gawper's eyes. And that's when it hits me. This is how we will rescue Silus Garroway from the noose!

8

Gallows Hill

In which Banyard concludes his account of Josiah's rescue

Dawn approaches out on the hill, bringing with it a hazy mist that rises, ghostlike, to cloud the air.

Mardon and I crouch in the foliage of the low-grown trees that fringe one side of the mound. We've been waiting for over an hour and our feet are like ice.

'This Garroway fellow better be worth it,' says Mardon.

While he is probably still wondering how I managed to talk him into this, I think ultimately it was the idea that captured his attention. That and a pinch of jealousy because, as he had slept, I had ridden into adventure. A disastrous one, granted, but an adventure nonetheless.

What self-respecting surgeon would be found without a spare set of lithorium spectacles?

Certainly not my cousin.

Armed with a pair each, we wove headgear from wicker that extended up from our shoulders by a good two feet. Into each one we fixed a pair of the spectacles and trialled them for effectiveness. In the deep night they worked perfectly, each appearing as a pair of glowing eyes issuing from a tall, rag-knotted head. We made matching clothes with more strips of rag, further depleting poor Hobbs' humble wardrobe.

On the far side of the woods around Gallows Hill, Mardon's Double Heart nestles beneath trees, fully wound and ready to go. And so, the scene is set. *All we need now is the execution party to arrive with the doomed man. If he's to hang at dawn, they'll need to get here before the sun shows.* I gaze intently at the dim horizon segmented by silhouetted branches and echo Mardon's thoughts.

Be worth it.

I will Silus Garroway to strive, to prove himself a worthy man, someone worth rescuing but, then again, my old conviction strikes: silker or threader, he is surely a man like any other.

Isn't he? Isn't this entire awful system wrong? How can it be right? And why am I the only one to see it?

They come, the rattle of the cart giving them away moments before it rolls into view along the track, Garroway's battered frame shackled to its back boards. He's forced to stand so that any who so wish can freely lob filth and rotten food at him as he passes. This morning there are no takers. Perhaps it's too early for them, or perhaps Garroway is well liked. I don't know which as I'm not from Loncaster.

We watch. They prepare in the light of their storm lamps. Without thinking I scrutinise each man for weapons. Between the small party there are five cudgels, three muskets and four rapiers. The hangman wears a black hood and has a blunderbuss slung across his back. *Let's hope this doesn't get ugly.* Mardon and I have one pistol each and our rapiers, hidden beneath our rags.

Guiding the cart up the mound, the Justice halts the nag with a word and a tug of the bridle. The hangman ties the noose, throws the rope over the gallows and lashes it to the post. When satisfied it's secured, he lifts a stool down from the cart and places it directly beneath the noose. *This will be a simple affair.*

The neighbouring gibbets swing softly, one bearing a mouldering corpse while the other awaits Garroway's hapless body.

My heart thumps like an overwound clock. *Tick, tock.*

At a word from the Justice, men guide Garroway to the gallows.

Tick, tock.

The hangman places the noose around Garroway's neck and tightens the knot.

Tick, tock. The pulse hammers in my skull.

They beat him again to force him precariously up onto the stool.

Tick, tock!

The hangman adjusts the rope to remove the slack and all is ready. The sun is rushing to rise. I feel its approaching heat even here in the shade, stifling, sweltering, burning its way ever closer. Briefly removing our headgear, we ignite the lithorium.

Time to act or forever comply with insanity. Tugging at Mardon I step forth.

A cry arises.

'Gawpers! Gawpers in the trees!'

It's working. I'm shaking but it's working. I watch through the wicker weave of my disguise and catch quick movements in the lamplight: men fleeing. A lamp crashes to the ground. The nag stamps and bolts back towards town, dragging the cart in a wild ride.

'Gawpers!'

'Run!'

'What about…?'

'Leave him or we'll all die!'

I'm wishing I could see Mardon, watch him work. He's somewhere to my left. Is he walking with me or are we diverging? I cannot tell. Who cares? It's working! The gawpers of Gallows Hill are back to reap souls from the night.

The tallest of the runners speaks. 'Wait.' The running stops, at least, some of it. 'Are you sure they're gawpers?'

'Look like gawpers to me!'

Yes, we're gawpers! What else would we be? We're gawpers all right! I think it but no one says it.

The tall man continues. 'They ain't gawpers, I tell you! I seen gawpers with my own two eyes and these ain't them!'

This is bad. There is uncertainty in his voice but the hangman has not run. He remains with Garroway at the gallows, only now he's reaching for his blunderbuss and taking aim. At me.

I'm sweating. A wet trickle drips to my lips and I taste warm blood.

Boom! He blasts the gun; a warning shot, sent between Mardon and me, meant to ward us off, perhaps. Beneath my costume, I struggle to draw my pistol while the hangman hurries to prime and reload, his hands shaking. His gun is a single-shot weapon and more for show than anything *else. Useless in a battle.*

A short distance to my right Mardon appears in my periphery, his tall fake frame imposing, lithorium eyes blazing away. Behind him the first golden streak of sunlight mounts the horizon. But no, Mardon's on my left! I step back and it's confirmed. There's a gawper to my left and another to my right. So who's this second figure? A fellow imposter? A gate crasher?

A gawper...?

The hangman shrieks and fires his second shot at the newcomer.

'Save your souls! Run!' He kicks the stool away. Garroway drops to hang by the neck, eyes bulging.

Unaffected by the blast, the gawper neither recoils nor bleeds.

I rush forward. For a moment everyone runs: the hangman, the nag, the Justice and his men.

I reach Garroway and wrap my arms around his juddering legs to support him. Across the track the gawper gawps as though trying to figure me out.

What are you? What are you trying to achieve?

I could ask it the same!

The hangman has not finished causing problems. He slows, stops and turns while the others flee. I'll never know why. He strides back to the gallows and clubs me in the gut with the butt of his gun. I fold and glimpse Mardon rushing in to take Garroway's weight. The hangman prepares a similar blow for my cousin but the gawper moves.

Silencing us all. The. Gawper. Moves.

It appears to slide across the ground, an effortless and unexplained motion. It has no legs that I can see but is a hulking shape, extending and widening to the leaf-littered ground. I catch a hint of its mouth, wide and narrow-lipped, its skin the colour of ashes beneath a ragged fringe of... what? Straggled hair? Strips of rag? A shaggy coat?

It reaches the hangman swiftly. If by a stride, it is long and quick. In a breath it meets him and, with a flick of an arm, hurls him away into the gloom of the lower slopes. His cry distances with his fall and that is the last we see of the hangman. With one last gawp at Mardon and me, the gawper slinks after the retreating party.

Garroway is sucking breath through a constricted throat. His wrists are bound at his back, preventing him from tugging at the tightened noose. I right the stool and direct his feet to it. He stands, the bulbous whites of his eyes rolling. Mardon draws his rapier and saws the rope free from the post, allowing Garroway to topple to the ground where I loosen and remove his noose. Mardon and I ditch our headgear.

Blood has soaked my mouth and chin and seeps through the upper portion of my shirt, but it's forgotten. Garroway is breathing. Rescued, freed and breathing. I'm amazed his neck didn't snap with the drop but, now he's towering over me, I see he's built like a bull with barely any neck to break.

We watch the gawper dissolve into the dawn towards the town while Mardon, Garroway and I are left alone on the hill, bathed in a glorious golden light.

Rubbing at his throat, Garroway nods and grunts in a low rumble.

'I'm much obliged, masters.'

Looking him up and down, I say, 'You're going to need a new identity. From now on you are Josiah Mingle. Remember that name.'

Josiah Mingle and I ride in Mardon's luxurious carriage, exhausted from the previous morning's escapades. Our journey to Camdon City will take most of the day. Joe is snoring deeply, his noise louder than the trotting of the horses and the clatter of the wheels on the hollow way below.

I unfold this morning's Loncaster Chronicle, purchased before we set out, and read the headline.

GAWPERS SNATCH THREADER CORPSE FROM NOOSE

I smile.

He's grateful to be alive and has, at last, stopped crawling at my feet with vows of eternal servitude. We'll have to do something about that if he's ever to pass as a silker. He'll need a new wardrobe, of course. That's going to cost. And falsified papers. That's seriously going to cost. I examine the contents of my coin pouch.

Oh dear.

And then there's his accent, his vocabulary and his mannerisms – pure threader, through and through. This won't be easy.

Perusing the pages, a name leaps at me from the obituaries.

Bartholomew Corston suffered a heart attack and died soon after dawn, yesterday morning. I wonder. Did the gawper pay him a visit while in town?

A wind traverses the gaol chilling our bones. I open my eyes and I'm back in the now. Josiah and I are manacled in a damp Draker cell.

'Do you think they'll keep us long?' asks Josiah and, for once, our thoughts are in sync. How long *will* they keep us? What trumped-up charges are Goffings and Legge fabricating this very minute?

'*That*, Mr Mingle, is a very good question.'

We watch the pale light slowly arc through the window bars, dim shadows sweeping as night approaches and soon it is dark. Our effects, including my brass pocket watch, were taken from us before we were locked up.

I call out. 'Guard, guard, what time is it?'

A thick-necked thug – one I doubt they let onto the streets – lumbers down the hallway to us and appears at the bars.

'What do you maggots want?'

'I simply asked for the time. Do you know it?' He frowns at me as though I've asked him to calculate the next lunar eclipse. 'Do you have a watch, or is there, perchance, a clock nearby? This is a Draker station. Surely you have a clock.'

His next words confound me. Not because of their meaning but because they come from *him*.

'Time is an abstract concept established by the rational intercepts of the human mind.'

I'd pinch myself but I know I'm not dreaming. The cold and discomfort are far too real. Clearly *his* mind was not the origin of this statement and yet he must have a brain somewhere in his thick skull to have memorised the words. I persist.

'What is the time, please?'

'I don't know. I don't have a watch.' He stomps away and I won't bother calling again.

'What do you think, Joe? Six? Seven?' We look at the

darkness on the other side of the window.

'Hmmm. Six-thirty, perhaps.'

'We have to be out of here within the hour. Penney's coming to dinner.'

'Oh, yes. Are we going to break out?'

'If need be.'

'How?'

'I don't know. Yet.'

For a while we sit silently in the lightless cell, thinking.

A blue glow arises outside, although we can only see a faint trace as our position allows us to see mostly sky. All the same, it's enough to tell us the lamps are being lit.

'Lamplighters. It must be seven o'clock.'

'We'll need an hour to ride home and get cleaned up for dinner,' says Josiah. 'We'd best be going.'

'If only it were that easy.' I've had enough. Goffings has made his point. Now it's time to release us.

'Guard! Guard! I demand to see the sergeant!'

Thick Neck's heavy footsteps echo to us after a short pause. He's in no hurry.

'What do you maggots want?' This, his standard line.

'I demand to see the sergeant.'

'Oh, you demands, does you?'

I nod. 'I demand to see the sergeant. Demand in the singular.'

'What sergeant?'

'Sergeant Goffings, of course.'

'He's gone home.'

'Then whoever is in charge. I demand you bring them to me. Or me to them. I don't mind which.'

He sighs, undecided. *Can I be bothered to walk all the way to the superintendent's office?* I see him think it.

'By law we have the right to a consultation with the supervising officer of the station in which we are being detained. It's in the book. See for yourself. We also have the right to each send one letter or a runner with a message. That's also in the book. Have you read it?'

The mention of the law and my rights has him baffled. Clearly out of his depth, he leaves promptly. By the time the superintendent arrives around half an hour later, rain has begun to fall outside our window.

'What do you maggots want?'

Really? Him as well?

'We're being held on false pretences. Release us this very minute or I shall have you investigated by Internal Affairs and you'll be sacked.' He takes a moment to digest my words. 'Do you want that to happen?'

'No. Goffings said to hold you for a goodly time.'

I check the stripes on his shoulder. 'And you take your orders from Goffings, do you, Superintendent?'

'No.'

'So tell me, for what crime are we being detained?'

'He didn't say exactly. Something about taking a boat into restricted waters.'

'Restricted waters? Nonsense!'

'Anyway, I dare say you've been here a goodly while. I suppose you can go.'

Snatching our effects, we mount up at the back of the station.

'What was all that about?' asks Josiah when we're alone.

'A warning from Legge and Goffings. Nothing more or we'd still be shackled. Someone doesn't want us poking around the *Dollinger* wreck.' My pocket watch displays gone eight. Of all the nights for Goffings to mess with my life... Honestly! 'Come, Joe. We've a dinner to attend.'

9

Fish Stew

In which Banyard learns the appalling truth and Mingle has another excellent idea

Like vengeful wraiths we streak through Dockside in the rain to thunder across Rook's Bridge into Crowlands, slowing as we approach 96 Bunson Street. Jinkers is asleep, or else eating or otherwise engaged. Whatever the reason, he's mercifully slow in accosting us tonight and we hurry down the side alley to stable the horses and use the back door.

Mother hears us and finds us in the porch, dripping and still stinking of stale ashes.

'There you are, Michael.' We proceed with the usual and slightly uncomfortable kisses. 'Why are you so late?' She drops her voice. 'You might have warned me we were expecting company. Penney has been here for over half an hour already. She's delightful but I might have worn a better frock and polished the woodwork. And I had no meat in the house.'

'I'm sorry, Mother. It's a long and involved tale, but we're here now.'

'Well you'd better run up and change, both of you. You can't dine like that.'

We go, quickly change into dry, clean clothes and re-emerge in the green room where Mother and Penney are seated in mid-conversation. Penney is in the same green dress, which pleases me because it's my favourite.

'Good evening, Michael, Josiah.' Her formidable smile hits us like a Toral wind and I swear she has no clue of its impact.

'Good evening, Miss Danton,' we chorus.

'I'm sorry we're late. A complication down at the Dockside Station. Unfortunate business.'

'The Drakers?'

'Regrettably.'

'I'm sorry to hear it. Mrs Banyard was just telling me dinner is almost ready.'

'I do hope you don't mind,' Mother says. 'It's only Ullensian fish stew. I had nothing else in.'

Penney smiles again and firelight dances in her eyes. 'It sounds wonderful.'

'Shall we?' Mother collects a candle and rises, leading the way to the dining room where she has hastily set the table with our best silver and shellware. We take our places and Mother fetches her finest serving bowl, heavy with steaming-hot stew, while I bring extra candles. We shall fill the room with light for our honoured guest.

'Cut the bread would you, Michael?' Mother's words are not so much a question as an order. I obey and proceed to float the platter of slices around the table. It's all going incredibly smoothly considering that an hour ago Joe and I were incarcerated. Mother ladles stew skilfully into bowls and passes them out until we're all served. We eat and the stew *is* wonderful. Mother is a great cook. I don't even like fish but I've always enjoyed Ullensian fish stew. The flavour is somewhere between cod and chicken, which I know sounds awful, but you have to taste it to understand. Penney likes it, too, I'm pleased to see. She butters her bread and dips it before doubt washes over her face. She's wondering if she has broken a house rule. Quickly, I dip my bread and raise it as though making a toast.

'To Mother, the finest cook in Crowlands.'

We eat.

'Oh, I quite forgot,' says Mother. 'There's a little wine left in the kitchen. I put a drop in the stew. Be a dear and fetch it would you, Michael?'

'Certainly.' Happily, I rise and hurry to the kitchen, elated to have Penney in my house, to have the chance to invite her into our latest investigation and thereby bring her closer to me. I might be penniless but I'm thrilled to be out of the gaol and Goffings' miserable clutches and all is well with the world. That is, until I enter the kitchen.

There, a scene greets me that I shall never forget. It is clear. My mother is the frog butcherer of Crowlands. The evidence is strewn around the kitchen: frog skins, frog bones, the upper bodies of frogs, their entrails hanging, their cold, dead eyes bulging at me. And the truth rises like a gawper fog, to drown me there and then. Ullensian fish? No. Not unless Ullensian fish is another term for...

Without my knowing, Mother has fed me frogs since I can remember. And tonight, of all nights, she has chosen to feed my beloved Penney frog stew! My world is collapsing in upon me. My only consolation is the possibility that Penney may not yet know. There's a chance it can be kept from her and I grab at it with both hands.

I take a bowl and collect every last fragment of frog before scraping it all into the bin. I do what I can to compose myself and carry the wine, less smiling now, to the dining room. Before entering I swig from the bottle to bolster my fractured nerves, and take a deep breath. With a bracing grin, I turn into the room and offer Penney wine, filling her glass while eyeing the offending stew.

'Michael, are you all right, dear? Why, you've gone quite pale.'

'I'm fine, Mother, absolutely fine.' My voice has become squeaky, my throat dry.

Penney gives me a strange look. She knows something's not right but is too polite to ask. Instead she revisits the reason for our dinner meeting.

'This morning you said something about a new case.'

'Yes. Joe, perhaps you could tell Penney about the case so far.' Turning to Penney, I add, 'Though you'll have to swear to keep this secret.'

She flashes a reserved smile.

'Very well. I promise.'

Josiah nods and launches into the story and, in fairness, he makes a reasonable job of it. He's practising his silker accent, refining his pronunciation. I can tell because I know him better than anyone else. While he talks, I grudgingly force down a few mouthfuls of frog stew which will never taste the same again and, when he's done, I explain my proposal.

'So, you see, Penney, we've a lot to investigate and it's a very local case. Too many of the individuals involved might well know our faces. I wondered if you might lend a hand and make a few subtle enquiries on our behalf. We need a silker we can trust.'

'Don't you involve her in anything dangerous, Michael,' says Mother.

'I wouldn't dream of it.' I adopt my most innocent face.

'I'd be delighted to assist,' says Penney after a thoughtful pause. She is a kept woman, wanting for nothing but a little excitement. Mother's mention of danger has only helped.

'Excellent.'

'Though, I do have one question.'

'Fire away.'

'If there's no guaranteed payment from the good widow, how are you to pay for my time?'

'Ah, yes. You would be working speculatively, the same as Josiah and me.'

That's done it. Her entire demeanour has changed, her subtle smile gone. She looks me in the eyes, choosing her weapons; the words that will scythe me to the ground.

'And the pay would be?'

I'm staggered. She's still considering it. 'Twelve shillings for every day you give us.'

'On condition that I get nothing should we be unsuccessful with the case.'

'Yes, although I'm confident we shall win back the widow's savings and be paid in full.'

'But you haven't seen the widow since she first visited your premises. You don't even know where she resides.'

'And that, my dear lady, will be your very first task. I'd be much obliged if you would start tomorrow.'

'I shall.'

'Very well. Be at the office for eight o'clock, sharp.'

An air of contentment settles throughout the room. We are fed, business has been attended to and there is even a little wine left in the bottle.

Mother collects empty bowls and grills me with a glower when I pass her mine, which is still half-full. I decide I must lend a hand – after all, there are no threaders here – and rise to gather cutlery and the serving bowl. In the kitchen, I place the bowl down and turn to her.

'Frog meat, Mother! What were you thinking? And why is it only now that I discover my childhood favourite stew is made with frogs?'

'Ullensian fish stew has always been made with frogs. I thought you'd worked *that* out long ago. 'Ullensian fish' is what the northern folk call frogs.'

'But silkers don't eat frogs!' I compress my voice to stop it from reaching the entire household.

'The poor ones do, the ones who use all their hard-earned money to rescue threaders, to bribe corrupt silker masters, to pay for forged papers and food for the half-starved. Your father was the same and his father before him. You're the same and I dare say your children will be the same, if you ever have any. Which at this rate – '

This again. 'Mother, I'm only nineteen years old.'

'Well, I can't wait forever.'

'But where did you get the frogs? You said we had no meat in the house.'

'Michael Banyard, call yourself a detective?'

'Ah,' I mumble. 'Jinkers…'

Penney has gone. In the green room I sit to one side of the fireplace, seriously doubting my powers of deduction. I may not be the world's greatest detective but I know this: Cullins is conspiring with Legge and Goffings, and I've never even met the man. That's something I'll soon remedy.

Warming myself in the glow of burning logs, I reread the claims report which I pocketed before leaving the office. If there are mentions of gawpers, I will find them. Over the mantel, a scatter of candle flames waver to throw a delicate blush across the creamy pages.

The gawpers do not feature until page fifteen. Here I learn of an eyewitness who purportedly saw several tall, shady figures loitering in the alley where, several hours later, the treasurer's untimely heart failure occurred. The report has no actual mention of gawpers per se, although those too superstitious to name them do use these other terms, *tall ones* and *shade men*. The phrase 'tall, shady figures' is therefore notable and I deduce the witness might well have specifically meant gawpers and not men at all.

Likewise, the only other mention of gawpers in the report is small: a single, short line only.

Gawpers on the foreshore.

It's written at the end of an account from a resident of Dockside, one Mr Fisher, who apparently watched from his cottage through the lashing storm across Lytche's Cove as the *Dollinger* splintered upon the rocks.

I'm struck by one fact alone. The gawper sightings in this report coincide with times when men have died.

That night I dream vivid dreams: I am the worst detective the world has ever seen. Find missing people? I can't even find my hat! Penney hates me and makes this abundantly clear. My stomach growls and frogs leap from my plate whenever I try to eat. And Mr Kaylock is always growling in my face and speaking to me in a grating cat-voice. 'They're coming for you, Micky! The gawpers are going to get you!'

19th Twinemoon

I'm at my door the next morning when Jinkers appears like a reoccurring nightmare.

'Micky. I'm glad I caught you. Would you do me a favour and drop this into Glint and Sons? It's on your way, isn't it?'

Glint and Sons is Jinkers' bank, which reminds me of my unfortunate financial situation and prompts an idea. Jinkers is loaded. All of it inherited. For all his penny-pinching and diet of frogs, squirrels and probably the odd morgue rat, it's obvious: *he* could lend me money. I snatch the letter from his hand.

'Jinkers, I'd be delighted to drop this into the bank for you. I also have a small favour to ask in return.'

'Oh?' His face transforms in a flash, his features narrowing, eyes darkly glazing. He retreats towards his door as though becoming a creature somewhere between a wizened miser and a hermit crab.

I should have thought of this before!

I continue. 'Yes, I'm in a real squeeze. I wondered if you might loan me a small sum to tide me over.'

'Oh… Oh…' He turns purple and makes a strange gurgling sound as if he has swallowed his tongue. When he finally speaks, he stutters. 'S-s-sorry, Micky. G-g-got to go. I think I hear M-M-M-Mr Kaylock.' He closes his door faster and tighter than a shellfish at low tide.

Josiah and I ride to the office, greet Elizabeth and install ourselves comfortably in the case room.

'The problem is we need to get a decent look at that wreck but, with Legge on our case, how are we to do so?' I say. 'John Ferris may have procured the diving gear, but…'

'If we knew Legge's movements, there might be a way.'

'All I know is he drinks at The Ship Keepers most nights before retiring.'

Josiah has that smile again, the one that means he's pleased with himself. 'Mr Banyard, I have an excellent idea, though we'd need to visit the apothecary before – '

Elizabeth sticks her head through the doorway to scowl, interrupting Josiah. 'Mr Banyard, Miss Danton is waiting. Should I go out for black soup?'

This is more like it. 'Yes! Yes, please! A cup for everyone. And send Miss Danton in, would you?'

I pass Elizabeth some coins for the soup.

Josiah taps the side of his nose, his way of saying: 'Later.' His *idea* is clearly odd or illegal, or he'd share it now.

Frowning, Elizabeth leaves. Penney stands in the doorway until I usher her in and pull up a chair for her. 'Good morning, Penney. Are you ready to begin?'

'As ready as I'll ever be. Where should I start – to look for the widow, I mean?'

'I have a notion she's from Southside – something in her accent – start there.'

'I'll take a carriage.'

'If you do, I'm afraid you'll have to pay for it yourself. I'm down to my last tuppence and the cash box is as barren as Mr Jinkers' charitable capacity.' Penney has met Jinkers once or twice and knows him well enough to smirk.

'Really? Why, you should have said. Would ten guineas help tide you over?' She fishes in her purse. Ten guineas could keep us afloat for another week if not more.

'No, really, I can't take money from you.' I wish I could but I can't. 'It wouldn't be right.'

'Why ever not?'

She's got me there. I rack my brains for an answer but find none that is not born of pride or stubbornness.

Josiah to the rescue. 'What Mr Banyard means to say is we really shouldn't take anything from you while you are in our employ but,' he speeds up, 'if you insist, ten guineas would be extremely useful right now.'

I offer a forbearing smile and give the smallest of affirming nods. He's right and, before I know it, a ten-guinea note is in my hand.

'Thank you,' is all I manage.

Elizabeth returns with black soup for all and I give her the note. 'Take this to the nearest bank and exchange it for useable currency. You'll need the cash box.'

'Right away, Mr Banyard.' She collects the cash box and leaves, closely followed by Penney on her way to Southside. Josiah and I return to our previous conversation.

'We'll have to visit the apothecary before closing time and then be sure our attendance at The Ship Keepers coincides with Legge's,' says Josiah, and we spend a while planning until Elizabeth returns. Taking the full cash box, I pay what is owed to Josiah for the last week's work and draw my own wage, smiling at the thought of the leg of lamb I shall buy for dinner tonight. No more frogs for me. Elizabeth is watching so I pay her an advance for her first week's work to ease the tension. The rest remains in the cash box, which I lock and secure in the old, iron wall-safe at the back of the case room.

'I've never dived before,' says Josiah.

'It's easy. You'll love it.'

'You do remember I can't swim…'

'You don't need to swim. You only need to walk.'

'Is it dangerous?'

I can't lie. 'Yes, but we'll take every precaution possible and it's safer with two.'

Josiah nods and, just like that, a new case walks through the door. We see him firstly from the open doorway of the case room. Mr Barrows is a tall, gaunt raven of a man in black silk, the sort of man who gives children the chills when met on the street as they scurry by on their way to school. He is a dour but polite gent with a clean-shaven look that accentuates the hard lines of his pale, skull-like face. He leans over from above to introduce himself and I respond in kind, naming my associates and shaking the cold, clammy hand he offers.

'Please, take a seat. How may we assist you this fine day?' I gesture towards the visitor's chair in the corner of the front room. It's the most comfortable chair in the office, an old, battered grand Wexford, bound in brown leather with patches of wear on its arms and a seat deeply sunken by years of compression. Mr Barrows sits as Josiah and I bring other chairs.

'Will you take black soup?' I ask.

'No, thank you.' He removes his top hat and places it with precision upon his lap. There is something skeletal about his movements, a creepy manner that's hard to pinpoint. He is the Grim Reaper, but in a suit rather than the usual hooded robes. I'm not warming to the man.

'In all honesty, I'm not certain you *can* help me. Not at all,' he states.

'Oh?'

'You see,' he fixes those Reaper eyes of his on mine. 'Three moons ago, on the fifteenth of Fipplemoon, my son vanished without trace.'

10

The Vanished Son

In which Banyard and Mingle find employment

I gaze back at Barrows, intrigued. 'Vanished without a trace, you say?'

'Yes. Jonathon, my son, disappeared. He left our house that morning for work as always and hasn't been seen since. It is my belief that somebody has murdered him.'

Turning to Elizabeth, I prompt. 'Take notes, if you will, Miss Fairweather.'

She fetches a ledger, quill and ink from her desk and sits keenly, cross-legged, opposite Barrows. 'Do continue, Mr Barrows.'

He clears his throat and plucks a speck of dust from his lapel.

'What's your son's profession?' asks Josiah, before Barrows can speak.

'He was a watchmaker at Hunt and Slaker, in Highbridge.'

I recognise the brand name. My brass pocket watch is by Hunt and Slaker, and a very fine chronometer it is, too. Barrows continues while Elizabeth scribbles. 'I questioned his partner. He swears Jonathon never made it in to work that day.'

'His name?'

'Excuse me?'

'Your son's business partner.'

'Monkfield. One *Gerard* Monkfield, an accomplished craftsman who trained under the great Slaker, himself.'

Elizabeth scratches the name in the ledger, catches me observing her and scowls.

'Is there anyone you can think of who might wish your son harm?' I ask.

'Hardly. He was a quiet soul. He went about unnoticed most of the time. I don't see why anyone would even have disliked him. He didn't have an objectionable bone in his body.'

'You seem quite persuaded of his death. Why is that? Might he not have run off, left Camdon for a spell, or simply be visiting a friend in the north?'

'Without a word to his father, his neighbours, or his friends? With no baggage or possessions? No clothes other than those he left the house wearing? Even his money box remains untouched in his room.'

'Then what possible cause had anyone to kill him?'

'That is precisely what I want *you* to discover.'

'You say this happened some three moons ago. Pray tell, why has it taken you so long to seek help with the matter?'

'The Drakers convinced me they had everything in hand, that they were following leads and would soon return my son to me. I now fear they have failed.'

'I see. No body, no motive, no suspects, no evidence or proof of a crime of any sort. You present quite the conundrum, sir.'

'I have a recent imograph.' He passes a grainy black and white image of his son. In the picture, Jonathon stands formally, unsmiling, his hands resting on his lap, his gaze meeting the camera's. He is a handsome young man with a thin face and his father's hairline. 'I can pay you handsomely. Will you take the case?'

'We certainly will. We'll begin this very hour.'

'I'm much obliged.' Barrows rises and we shake hands again. We agree on a fixed sum paid weekly, thereby employing the agency for two weeks, and thereafter to reassess the situation.

Elizabeth takes his details and he leaves. There is still a week to survive before his first payment is due. Just as well we have a loan from Penney.

To work seven cases at once is challenging, but I feel like a line has been crossed. Eight cases are just too many, even with Penney and Elizabeth in tow. I'm tempted to drop the widow's cause but will not. Instead, I install myself at my desk and scratch out a hasty letter to cousin Mardon.

> *Dear Mardon,*
> *I trust this note finds you well.*
> *Due to an inundation of recent and most intriguing cases, I find myself once more in need of your assistance. Can your surgery spare you for a few days, I wonder? Will you come to Camdon City, post-haste? A room awaits you at 96 Bunson Street, as always. I would be truly grateful. Payment as usual.*
> *Warmest regards,*

I dip my quill for one last flourish: my signature. A sprinkle of sand mops the excess ink and I shake the page, fold it and seal it with a dollop of melted wax and my father's insignia, an image of Rook's Bridge with a crowling in mid-flight over the peak of the arch. I replace the ring on my finger before slotting the letter into Elizabeth's hand.

'Please take this to the post office immediately.'

'Yes, Mr Banyard.' She takes the letter and rises to fetch her coat and I allow myself a smile. Mardon's coming to visit. Mother will be pleased. I'm pretty sure he'll come because, although he'll undoubtedly whinge about the journey and make out that I'm thoroughly inconveniencing him, he can't help himself. He enjoys my vocation more than his own.

Josiah watches Elizabeth leave and I flip the door sign to read *Back Soon*. Returning to the case room, I press the hidden button at the end of the mantelpiece to open the secret door. The door swings away from me revealing a small hidden chamber in which stand racks of clothes hangers bearing garments of all descriptions. There is a mirror mounted upon the wall over a dresser, a variety or hair pieces, hats and other accessories, everything needed to disguise oneself. I open a drawer and take out glue, select a fake beard and spectacles, make-up and an old striped scarf. Josiah studies me for the next few minutes as I create a disguise that must fool Cullins. When I'm ready, I appropriate Josiah's topper to complete the look.

'Hey, that's *my* – '

'We're in for a busy time, Joe. Come on. Things are looking up!'

He mutters as he grabs his coat. 'Not for Jonathon Barrows, they're not.'

I send Josiah on a mission of his own, to investigate the treasurer's death. Armed with the dead man's name and address, he plods off, his broad shoulders lurching, and I marvel at the way he walks. He has a swagger that sends a message and, if I could interpret it, I believe it might say something like *I am untouchable*. Unfortunately for Josiah and me, it's not true. *I* know he is vulnerable. Oh, yes, he could take on five average men in a fight and come out the winner but, if we were found out, that would count for little.

Steeling myself for what's to come, I mount Blink, head out and cross the river into Highbridge. The office of Cullins and Co is on the second floor of a tall stately building, terraced, yet grand. Marble pillars frame the entrance from the roadside, each adorned with an intricately carved climbing dragon. The surrounding buildings are almost as impressive.

I knock on the office door and enter when I'm bid, 'Come.' Inside, a man sits behind an opulent desk of walnut veneer inlayed with ivory.

'Good day, sir.' I make my voice thin and high and I don't sound like myself. 'Am I correct in assuming you are Mr Cullins, proprietor of Cullins and Co?'

'Indeed you are, and the proprietor of a great many establishments. Who might you be? And what is your purpose here?'

'I do apologise for my unannounced arrival.' Feeling something close to disappointment because, so far, there is nothing obvious to dislike about him, I close the door. He is straight-talking and carries a *no-nonsense* air. His beard is shaven around his mouth and chin but otherwise thick. There is a hint of grey in his black, oiled hair, slicked back from his forehead, and green in his eyes, which regard me impartially. 'I, sir, am Stephen Paulter,' I say as we shake hands. 'I'm here to enquire about investment opportunities.'

Cullins' eyes alight with dull fire at the words, though his face remains impassive, and he leans forward in his chair. Behind him, in the back of the office, a clerk busies himself filing paperwork. Another man, tall and swarthy with a scarred face, enters from the rear door and Cullins introduces him as he joins us.

'Mr Paulter, this is an associate of mine, Nickolas Moor.'

I shake Moor's hand though he is slow to reciprocate and bears a fixed scowl.

'So, you wish to invest?' Cullins asks.

'I do. I have an inheritance of eight thousand guineas,' I say. 'Can you suggest a suitable enterprise? Something with promising expectations?'

Without pause, he lists six eligible businesses.

'And are these all under Cullins and Co?'

'They are, indeed.' Cullins proceeds to give a breakdown of each of his businesses, waffling on about details, finances, dates and forecasts. At last I find something to dislike. He's boring me to death. Perhaps he *is* the killer!

I make notes and, when he's finished, say, 'I'm curious: I was advised to strongly consider investing in a business named Golden Shores Imports, yet this is not among your recommendations.' My statement hangs in the air like a pregnant raincloud while he considers his response.

'I'm afraid Golden Shores Imports is no longer trading.'

It's obvious I've hit a nerve and, as the cloud overshadows his face, I withdraw.

'I see. Well, my thanks for your time. I shall consider your portfolio and return in due course with my decision. Good day, Mr Cullins, Mr Moor.' I tip my hat.

'Good day.' From his seat he watches me go, his eyes smouldering like coals while Moor simply holds his scowl.

Gerard Monkfield is next on my list. He doesn't know me and I see no need for a disguise here. I remove it in a side alley before entering Hunt and Slaker and introducing myself. The shop is run from a modest but tastefully furnished lower room on West Row, not far from Cullins' office. Gerard is alone, hunched over and squinting through a set of lenses at scattered pieces of a brass chronograph, the miniscule tools of his trade poised delicately in hand. I stride to his work bench.

'My name is Michael Banyard, of Banyard and Mingle, Mysteries Solved.'

'Gerard Monkfield, pleased to meet you,' he replies. Smiling, he offers a rather limp hand, that I shake firmly.

'I'm investigating the disappearance of your business partner, Jonathon Barrows.'

Gerard's smile evaporates and he places his tools on the bench. 'Yes. Yes, of course.' He is a timid young man with a bespectacled face, pointed and harmless. With rounded shoulders and a stooped back that is peculiar for his years, he reminds me of a mole. If first impressions are to be believed, Gerard is as innocent as a new-born. In fact, he strikes me as the socially challenged sort, one who struggles to hold a genial conversation, not through any sinister underlying but merely due to an analytical disposition of the mind. 'Please go ahead.' His eyes are like dark beads and yet, enlarged behind his thick spectacles, appear unbalanced against the rest of his mild features.

'When did you first realise Jonathon was missing?'

'I wondered what was wrong that day, when he failed to show up for work. On the odd occasion when he's sick, he sends a runner with a note but, that morning, no note arrived. The next day his father visited the shop asking after him and, well, what could I tell him? I knew nothing. I suppose that's when he went to the Drakers. I was shocked. Jonathon was – *is* – a friend. If he's gone for good, it's more than a business partner I've lost.'

'What share of the business does he own? How were things between you?'

'We own equal shares and things were well. We were content in our work. It's a peaceful pursuit, you know. You have to be meticulous, but it's a quiet life. We would often work for hours on end without sharing a single word – unless a customer arrived, of course.' He laughs but it's awkward and short-lived. 'Must talk to the customers.' He raises a finger for emphasis.

Clearly, Jonathon has invested time drumming this into his closeted associate.

'Did you notice anything unusual about Jonathon in the days leading up to his disappearance? Did anything go missing from the shop?'

'No. He was perfectly normal and nothing was missing.'

'You have checked the safe?'

'You'll excuse my suspicions, sir, but yes. It was one of the first things I did after Jonathon's father called. The safe was untouched and everything in its place.'

'Hmmm. May I see it?'

With a nod, Gerard leads the way to the back of the shop, through a door and into a small office where he unlocks and opens the safe. Inside there are bags of coin, notes and documents. It all looks orderly and mundane. We return to the main room.

'You're certain there was nothing different about Jonathon the last time you saw him?'

'There was one thing, I suppose, a small matter really. He seemed mildly distracted the afternoon before he vanished. His bench is over there by the window, with a decent view down the street.'

'This one here?' I cross the room and stand over Jonathon's old bench, studying the few scattered objects on its surface: a set of watchmaker's tools in an open leather roll, shop tickets stacked on a spike, a quill and inkpot, and a bronze paperweight in the shape of an oversized pocket watch. To one side sits a strange four-handed clock with a robust brass case. Around its outside is a dial etched with measurements.

'That's the one.'

'Is this how he left it?'

'Oh, yes. I haven't touched a thing. Anyway, it's a view that usually goes to waste as we spend most of our days straining over magnifying lenses – the view from his seat, I mean – but, that afternoon, I looked up several times and caught him staring pensively out. I only remember because it was most unlike him to be so… distracted.'

'Can you suggest what might have been the cause of his concern?'

'I'm afraid not. I wish I could, for it has troubled me ever since.'

'No matter. Who will inherit the business if Jonathon is dead?'

'There will be a tribunal if his body is ever discovered – heavens forbid – or if he fails to return alive within five years. You understand, I am not the only shareholder this situation impacts.'

'Oh?'

'No. Hunt and Slaker also have a stake.'

'Ah, yes.'

Gerard pauses and his eyes widen to fill his lenses. 'Oh, dear me. Am *I* a suspect?'

'No more or less than anyone else. Not at this stage in the investigation. What about lady friends?'

'Of Jonathon? There was one, a pretty slip of a girl, though I think it had finished by the time he disappeared. Jennie something or other. From Tower End.'

I make a note and place my card into his hand. 'Thank you. You've been most helpful. If you think of anything else, please contact me at this address.'

Returning to my office I'm surprised to find Penney and the widow seated in reception. Penney looks invigorated and has a triumphant smile while Widow Blewett cradles a cup of black soup and sniffs. She's aged in the short time since I last saw her. The lines of her face are deeper and darker. A look in her eyes hints at a soul who has suffered cruelly. She is frail, gaunt and pallid. I'm gladdened to see Penney has seen fit to seat her in the visitor's chair.

'I found her,' announces Penney. 'In the threaders' gaol. I paid her fine and brought her straight here. She's barely eaten for three days. I've sent a boy to fetch bread and stew.'

'The threaders' gaol? What were you doing in there?' I ask.

Widow Blewett trains her watery eyes on me. 'I was arrested soon after I left here. They threw me in there and wouldn't even tell me why. They took my last few pennies and said I had debts to pay. Lies. All lies. This poor girl has parted with good money to set me free, money I did not owe, nor can repay.'

Meeting Penney's gaze briefly, I impulsively speak for us both. 'My dear woman, forget about the money. Miss Danton and I will discuss the matter and see to it that the sum is covered, irrespective of our dealings. The important thing is that you are out of the gaol and safely in our midst. Miss Danton, can you shed any light on the matter? Someone must have lodged a complaint or made an accusation.'

An errand boy delivers the widow's food and she sits up to dip bread in hot stew and eat, savouring each mouthful as though it's the greatest thing she's ever tasted. She devours it with impressive speed while Penney draws me aside.

'There is a sergeant from Dockside, named Goffings. It was he who had her arrested and thrown into gaol but, Michael, she swears she has no debts. She is moneyless but debt-free. There is something improper here.'

'Goffings, again…' I mutter as Josiah bursts into the room, filling the doorway to proclaim:

'Doncley Maples was murdered!'

11

The Ship Keepers

In which Banyard and Mingle break the law — again

Josiah's announcement stills the room. Even the widow stops chewing.

'Care to explain yourself, Joe?'

He crosses the room in two strides and, throwing the widow a cursory nod, pulls up a chair.

'The treasurer of Golden Shores Imports, Doncley Maples, was murdered. I'm sure of it.'

'Why do you say this?' I ask.

'A neighbour heard raised voices and a scuffle in the moments before the treasurer was found.'

'But the coroner declared it *death due to heart failure.*'

'Yes, and he may have been right but, if so, it was heart failure brought on by an attack of some kind. Two men were seen running from his house, fleeing the scene.'

'Was any of this reported to the Drakers?'

He nods. 'According to the neighbour. She was questioned by the Drakers and gave full account – just as I said.'

'So, I suppose the matter was investigated.'

'Not as far as I can tell. We'd need to enquire at the Dockside Draker Headquarters.'

'I'm not going back there in a hurry,' I say.

'Me neither,' shrugs Joe.

Penney stands brightly and brushes her skirts. 'I'll go.'

On our way home I stop at the butchers to buy a cut of meat. There's a juicy leg of lamb in the window that looks perfect, has my name all over it.

The butcher is a hardworking threader whose master is a lazy and particularly cruel and unlikeable fellow, a silker called Maddox. I would use another shop but this one is on my way home and I'm tired. There's another reason I like to occasionally call: the butcher's assistant, a threader girl named Jemima Gunn, is a gentle, mistreated soul.

And I fear for her life.

She is curvaceous with dark skin, savagely beautiful and, unfortunately, a constant draw to grimy old Maddox. He gropes and prods her flesh on a regular basis and that's in front of the customers. I don't like to imagine what goes on beyond public view.

Today she enters from the back of the shop, flustered and ruffled, straightening a dress that's too small to properly cover her curves. Truly, it's indecent, though everyone knows it's not her fault. Maddox controls all. As she enters with a limp, she glowers at the wall until Maddox appears behind her and then she forces a straighter face because she will be beaten if he catches her scowling. Her left cheek is bruised and shining. Her dress is torn at her left thigh, which is also bruised.

'Ah, Mr Banyard, good day to you, sir,' Maddox chirps.

'Good day, Master Maddox.'

Awkward silence. My words dangle from an invisible noose. Unfortunately, it's not around Maddox's neck.

He seems to notice the uncomfortable air and, thankfully, withdraws. There's a customer ahead of me in the queue buying woodhog sausage and Jemima edges nearer while the others are busy.

'Are you all right, my dear?' I whisper across the meat counter, when she is close enough.

She nods, but she isn't. Her eyes radiate an inner torture of which she cannot speak. It's as though her soul has been torn. 'Though I shan't be if he sees my dress is ripped.'

'How did you tear your dress?'

'He did it.'

'Can you sew it?'

'Yes, though he'll notice the stitching and that won't be good enough.'

Delving into my purse, I produce a guinea and press it discreetly into her palm. 'Buy a new dress – one that covers you properly – and a shawl for your shoulders. Who knows? It may help keep him away.'

For a moment, her fearful eyes meet mine with a glimmer of hope before she glances at the coin and the hope dies. 'I can't. He'll know.'

'Tell him you were given a tip in the shop.'

'We're not allowed to keep tips.'

'Then hide it. Buy the same exact dress but one size bigger and if he says anything, tell him you've lost weight.' I wrap her hand around the coin. 'Take it. I insist.'

'Thank you, Master Banyard, sir. I –'

'You owe me nothing. It's the least I can do. Now look busy before he returns, and hide that coin.'

The leg of lamb must wait for another occasion. I find a cheap cut of pork and decide that will have to do instead. Oh, well. At least it's not frog.

The Ship Keepers is a sprawling, cavernous tavern as old as the quay and as pitted with niches and nooks as a deep-sea cave. Opening its iron-studded door, a smell greets us: stale beer and grime, four hundred years of dust and an iron tang from the spilled blood of bar fights. I debate whether the odour is pleasanter or fouler than the stink of putrid crab and fish that blights the docks outside, but remain undecided. Sea winds freshen the air when blowing from the east. The tavern is as *local* as it gets. Any strangers are scrutinised by sea hands who are forever suspicious and mean to intimidate.

In my pocket sits a small vial of Pinchley salts, a sleeping drug recently purloined from the apothecary. I would happily have paid for it but that would leave a trail leading directly to me if Legge decides to report he has been drugged, which he will soon be, if I have my way.

Josiah and I scour the various alcoves and far-reaching corners, pretending to seek a place to sit when, truly, we hunt for Legge.

But Legge is not here.

We order ale and occupy a spot across from the door where we'll be able to see him enter when he arrives. We're not waiting long. He marches in with great gusto and bullishly shoves his way through to the bar to demand a drink. He's amid a crowd of bawdy sailors and I deem it the perfect opportunity. He'll not notice an extra body slipping in among the others before quickly retreating and, if he happens to witness a hand tipping white powder into his tankard, he'll not be able to tell who is on the other end of it.

Fingers wrapped around the vial in my pocket, I rise with purpose but sit again as Sergeant Goffings bursts into the room, Thick Neck the gaoler in tow. So, they *do* let him out from time to time. Incredible! I turn away and hide my face as Josiah dips his head low and turns up the collar of his long coat.

Goffings is in a dreadful mood, cursing and stomping across the room. He grasps an old threader by the throat and lifts him from his stool at the bar, throwing him aside to make space for himself. The old man lands badly and hobbles away, powerless to protest or defy.

For a full hour, Josiah and I observe Legge and Goffings drinking and talking. Thick Neck eventually staggers out into the street, having swallowed his fill.

We continue to watch.

'I'm not sure how much longer I can nurse this pint,' says Josiah, swirling the dregs in the bottom of his tankard. It's not that he doesn't want another, but we still need to watch the pennies.

'Me neither. If Goffings doesn't go soon I'll have to buy us another Ruby's.'

''Twould be a terrible shame.'

I grin. Ruby's ale is good and has made my head pleasantly foggy.

Four pints later, I'm drooping on my stool when Goffings stands to leave. On his way to the door he bumps shoulders with a tall merchant who spills his drink, and takes offence. There's a tussle between Goffings and the merchant, starting with a shoving match that evolves into a fist fight. Josiah taps my arm and gestures for me to pass him the vial. I do so because I'm fairly convinced I'm now incapable of walking in a straight line, let alone surreptitiously slipping the powder into Legge's drink. Josiah, on the other hand, is there like a shot. Four pints of Ruby's strong ale appear to have had little impact on his massive frame.

Legge leaves his stool to watch the altercation, his pint forgotten on the bar. I can tell he's pondering the correct line of action: interfere, and he may receive the pointy end of Goffings' boot. Ignore Goffings' plight and – well – the same. Apparently deciding the sergeant can look after himself, Legge simply watches, his flabby lips curling in mild amusement.

While Legge and most of the other late drinkers are distracted, Josiah places his pint on the bar next to Legge's. With the vial wedged neatly between his first and second fingers, he reaches out to take his tankard, pausing only long enough to tip the powder into Legge's. Job done. He reclaims his pint and rejoins me opposite the exit. We drain our tankards and leave.

A few paces from the tavern I stagger and lean on Josiah, who throws a steadying arm around my shoulders.

'You do know you were only supposed to give him a pinch of the powder?'

He grins but forces a straight face. 'No, I didn't know. I'm sorry, Mr Banyard. It was an honest mistake. I do hope he don't suffer none.'

'Good grief, man. You may have killed him!' I slur.

'That would be a sore loss to humanity, sure enough.'

20th Twinemoon

Head pounding, I rise to check the cabinet clock on the mantel of my room. It's almost eight-thirty, the morning after, and much later than I meant to wake. The full weight of our actions last night falls on me like a wall. Legge drank a whole vial of Pinchley salts, possibly enough to knock him out for a week, if it doesn't kill him first. I attempt to convince myself the amount of beer he downed and the meal he surely consumed beforehand will have dampened the salts' potency. Mardon would have a better idea, but he's not here, yet.

I throw on clothes and tap briskly on Josiah's door on my way past.

'Rise and shine, Mr Mingle. We've work to do.'

A deep moan reverberates from the room.

Half an hour later, we're mounting our horses in the street when Jinkers draws a curtain and briefly narrows his eyes to peer out.

'Good morning, Mr Jinkers,' I call.

He sees us and snaps the drape back in place, presumably still in fear of a favour being asked.

We ride in haste, across town to Dockside and skirt Lytche's Cove to the northern end where the partially submerged *Dollinger* awaits near the base of Hatch Head's cliffs. Moderate waves lap the rocky shoreline. Nothing too big. Nothing to prevent our dive. Legge is nowhere to be seen. All is well.

John Ferris shares a lock-up with another man who does a spot of diving for giant lobster, crab and hallard eggs, a delicacy in these parts. For a price, he's cleared it for me to collect the diving apparatus and loaned me a key. The lock-up is little more than a cave carved out of the cliff base to the side of the cove and secured with an iron gate. Inside we wade through fishing nets, floats, rods, tools and a whole barrage of other fishing tackle before finding the bellows, tanks and diving suits, all piled in the deepest corner. It takes both of us to lift and carry the long coils of air hose out to the shore where exposed rocks lead down to the water's edge. A steam-powered generator hooks up to the bellows which, in turn, force air down the hoses to the dive suits at the end. Gone are the days when men had to work the pump. In five minutes, we connect all the pipes and hoses and have the generator running nicely and we're suiting up in rubberised fabric, lead boots and heavy brass helmets with glass portholes, the latest in deep-sea diving technology. We load our belts with lead diving weights before arming ourselves with submarine carcynine lamps and spear guns. Once submerged, the lamps will burn for a good half an hour before they run out of oxygen, unless there's a fault in the housing, in which case they'll die in a blink as they fill with water. They have hooks that also attach to our dive belts and it's a good job. We don't have enough hands. I also hitch a diving compass onto my belt.

Across the cove, boats leave the deeper harbour, heading for open sea. Workers load and unload cargo, converse and stroll. No one pays us any attention as we clamber through rock pools, across slimy seaweed-infested rocks and wade into the foaming surf, uncoiling hose as we go.

A strange sensation ascends my legs, a cold dry pressure. It mounts until I'm fully submerged and an eerie quietness settles over me. Beneath the waves is a heavy, slowed-down world. Josiah is at my side with a hand on my shoulder, doing well. My greatest fear is that, at a depth from which we cannot easily escape, he will panic and drown. There are various ways this might happen – a snagged air hose, a torn suit, or a malfunction with the generator or the bellows – to name a few. I carry a secondary fear into the water and wish I'd brought Penney along: while Josiah and I are under the waves, the air pump is open to sabotage. Too late, now. We descend.

Slippery rocks give way to sand, into which our heavy boots sink and suck uncomfortably, each laborious step throwing up clouds of silt. Periodically one of us stumbles when a rock, hidden in the churning tide, trips us and we reach out to clasp each other until we've regained balance.

After an arduous walk over the sand, we reach a depth and distance from the surf where visibility clears enough for us to see each other's hazy outlines and our close surroundings. Ahead, a vast shadow reaches from the seabed to the surface in the particle-strewn miasma: The *Dollinger* rests, broken and leaning at an angle. Above a high outcrop of jagged rocks, a gaping hole in her bow allows fish to swim freely through, silent visitors seeking shelter from gillings and other stealthy hunters of the deep. Several hallards claw at the seabed among the coral and tendrils of weed, their armoured shells red against surrounding blues and greens, their many limbs poised like gargantuan spider legs.

I check my compass and one thing is clear from our first glimpse of the wreck. The galleon *was* running towards the southern point of the headland and facing north when it struck, head-on, upon the rocks.

My senses are bombarded. The oily rubber from my suit produces an overpowering smell. The fluid sounds of water wafting all around and the bubbling of our lamps, press in. With the cold, the weight and compression of the deep, each movement is a concerted effort as we climb the rocks to reach the wreck, careful to steer the hoses clear of snags. The coils we carry over our shoulders have depleted, now stretched out behind us in fading lines, but what's left should be enough to see us into the broken ship.

Leaping from the peak of the rocks, our weighted boots drag us down into the void of the hull and we work our way into the deeper darkness of the tilting galleon's innards where splintered wood is a constant threat to our suits. This is the gun deck. Gun ports punctuate the sides, allowing a feeble liquid light to penetrate. A few of the heavier objects have remained in the lower decks but everything has shifted. Cannon, no doubt installed for protection against Urthian pirates, lie scattered across the boards, some still upright, others overturned, while barrels and cannonballs cluster on the lower side against the clinkers. A loop of rope hangs, suspended, from a hatch that leads up to the galley.

A creak from the timbers startles me and I realise I'm unsettled, on the edge of my nerves, muscles tensed, eyes and ears straining in the uncanny quiet of this cloudy otherworld as I sweep my lamp around. A fleet of greenish dabs darts past from further in and I recoil, almost dropping my lamp. I regain my composure as the fish flit from the ship in a tight shoal.

There is still a little excess hose, which is good, because I want to see as much of the ship as possible before turning for shore and this may prove our only chance.

Josiah prods my arm and points down at a breach in the planking. The impact of the bow hitting the rocks has parted the deck boards to open a gap. It's fortuitous because, although I can't see it from here, the closest hatch is further on, in the middle of the deck, most likely beyond our reach and the cleft means we can simply drop down onto the next level without leaving the ship and re-entering.

I shine my lamp in at the orlop deck – the level between us and the hold below – and shudder as the trapped corpse of a sailor, suspended, with hair adrift, catches in the pale light. It's enough to make me want to leave but I force myself to go on, hauling on the dangling rope until one end comes free, and guiding it down through the hole. The other end seems solidly fixed and takes my weight when I pull myself up on it. With an exit strategy in place, I edge to the gap and step off.

There are two bodies visible on this new level. Judging by the wisps of remaining grey hair, the one I glimpsed from above is an older man, his jerkin caught on the snapped end of a twisted plank. The body is floating a foot above the floor, partially skeletonised, a grisly sight. The other is an obscure figure haunting the distant reaches of the deck. I should probably try to investigate, but the hose is too short and it's taken us a good twenty minutes to get this far. Soon the lamps will burn out and we shall be plunged into near darkness.

Closer to the bow end, a corresponding tear in the planks lays open like a ragged, gaping mouth and again, we angle the beams of our lamps through to illuminate the unknown, only to be met by another grim face, this one picked clean of flesh and grinning up at us through a row of iron bars.

12

The Caged Man

In which conclusions are drawn and Mingle eats cake

Descending, we join the hapless individual. The skeleton is gripping the bars of its cage, head thrown back in mid-silent scream. It has a greenish-white hue that causes it to glow in the beams of our bubbling lamps but, other than that, there is little here to illuminate. For a moment, it appears the hold is empty and dark, but our lamps catch on more timber and out of the gloom a wall emerges. We must be in the hold, surely. I swing my lamp out behind me and glance at the broken end of the galleon. Yes, we are standing in what should be the hold, except it's not a deck but a small chamber, isolated from the rest of the level. The wall partitioning us from the main portion intrigues me as it's complete and undamaged yet appears to have no door. I close in to inspect. Josiah follows and, by his shrug, seems to understand my conundrum. Who caged this man in a sealed compartment at the bottom of the *Dollinger*?

And *why*?

For a time, we hunt across the timber surface before Josiah beckons me over. The carpentry work is admirable, the door so finely crafted into place that it's almost invisible. There is no knob, catch or handle on this side. Presumably, there is something on the other – a subtle lever or switch that opens the

120

latch.

My lamp splutters and belches a stream of bubbles. Our time is nearly up. With a nod to Josiah, I turn and head back to the rope.

The reek of rubber is still in my nostrils when we enter the Tower End office of Lord Bretling Draker, in the Draker City Headquarters. It's the snooty part of Camdon City, all silker dwellings and high-end businesses. The buildings are grander and taller here. Bretling Draker, as his name suggests, is the man behind the Drakers. We owe him for this wonderful institution that keeps our streets so safe. Unless you're a threader, that is, and then you don't owe him much and you'd better watch out. Or unless you happen to get on the Drakers' wrong side, or if it doesn't suit them to play fair with you.

Bretling, however, *is* a reasonable and intelligent man without an ounce of cruelty in his blood. He's also government, not local authority, which means he swings more weight. His only weakness is that he presumes all other men to be as reasonable and uncorrupted as himself.

He's not met Josiah before and the thought of him becoming suspicious gives me the shivers. Pausing in the doorway, I adjust Josiah's tie.

'Remember not to slouch and try not to say anything,' I say before knocking.

'How come the great Bretling Draker will see *you*?'

'Believe it or not, I've helped solve several crimes that were under investigation by Lord Bretling.'

'Oh, aren't we the shining star?'

I stab him with a sharp look as Bretling calls us in.

'Enter.'

Bretling sucks on a long curving pipe while studying a document as we approach his desk, the smoke plumes like extensions of his copious sideburns. The room is foggy with it and spotted with trophies from cracked felonies, official certificates, medals in display cases and watchman awards.

Hearing our footsteps, he looks up, his face dour.

'What do you want, young Banyard?'

He's preoccupied and has cut straight to business so, withdrawing my hand, I launch right in. 'My associate, Master Mingle, and I wish to report the discovery of a murder victim and several unrecovered bodies that remain trapped in the wreck of the *Dollinger*.'

That has his attention. He sets his document down and straightens.

'My clerk tells me you've refused to talk with any other officer in the building. Why is that?'

'The case we're investigating is sensitive. We've experienced some, er, interference from certain officials. We can't risk anyone else meddling or obstructing our work. I do hope you understand.'

'I see. The *Dollinger*, eh? Went down off Dockside, didn't it?'

'Hatch Head to be precise, a little over a month ago. We're investigating a case of fraud and embezzlement. I do not yet wish to reveal details, but I demand the remains of this murdered fellow be retrieved for study before further pertinent evidence is lost. It could have a marked bearing on our case. Of course, the other bodies should also be recovered for interment in the maritime deadfield, thus allowing the relatives to properly mourn.'

Bretling takes a long drag on his pipe while examining us. His gaze lingers longest on Josiah, but eventually ebbs back to me and he announces, 'You demand, eh?' He's mildly amused. 'All right, Banyard. I'll arrange a small team to visit the wreck and drag these remains onto dry land. Come with me.'

When Bretling has a mind, he can move fast. He marches through his headquarters at a spritely pace bellowing orders and, before he's passed from one end to the other, he's arranged equipment, a diving team and transport. Soon we are back on the shoreline watching as the divers rig their gear, much the same as the stuff we borrowed, before they trudge heavily into the waves.

122

'Someone with finances, is it?' Bretling asks while stuffing a fresh pinch of Old Beauty into the bowl of his pipe. The question takes me by surprise and I meant what I said. I don't want to share details. My silence prompts him to continue and he surprises me again with an astute observation. 'It's only the wealthy can afford the influence of officials.'

Perhaps he's not as naïve as I thought. I decide it tactful not to mention that at least one of the officials is a Draker and leave him guessing. 'You could be right. If it's not money then it's leverage of another kind.'

He raises a brow but changes the subject. 'So, do you have an idea who this murdered fellow is, Banyard, the one caged in the secret chamber?'

'At this stage I don't even know it's a fellow.'

'We'll soon see, I suppose. Did you know, I knew your father? He was a good man, a keen investigator.'

'I didn't know but, yes, he was.'

Down by the rocks, the bulbous tops of the divers' helmets submerge, small trails of bubbles on the water's surface charting their progress. The sea has calmed and it's good diving water. Glancing back, I scan Dockside and the cove for Legge, gladdened to see he's still absent, but Goffings is here. He squints with disdain at our operation and I give him a friendly wave and my broadest smile, which seems to tip the balance. With a scowl, he turns and stalks away.

While Bretling strides over to the officer stationed at the bellows, Josiah steps closer and we both watch, waiting for the moment when the divers bring out the skeletal remains. I don't suppose they will tell us much.

'Do you think it's him?' asks Josiah.

'Do you mean Jonathon Barrows or ship hand Anders?'

'I meant Jonathon, though now you mention it... But Anders was recorded in the claims report as a survivor of the wreck. How could he end up down there afterwards?'

'I don't know. It may be neither man, but at this point I'm ruling nothing out. My feeling is something unusual has happened here.'

After a long wait, the divers emerge with the first body, the old man I saw up close, I think. They lay him on the shore and return. Other bodies follow in slow succession, the whole process taking well over an hour with breaks for the divers to rest and refuel their lamps and the steam generator. At last, the skeleton rises from the surf, still caged, still articulated and looking like a grotesque display in a freak show.

We join Bretling at the water's edge as he stoops to study the slimy bones.

'Well, Banyard, it appears you were right again.'

It is obvious from the skull that the remains are of a man – a detail I could not discern in the murky depths – but the proud brow ridges are a giveaway. The age I cannot tell.

'You wish to examine him, I suppose,' says Bretling.

'Of course. This is highly pertinent to our investigation.'

Bretling huffs but checks his pocket watch and says, 'Headquarters. Two o'clock precisely. You'll get your chance.'

'But – '

'No buts, Banyard. Two o'clock. Take it or leave it.'

'Caged, you say?' Penney sits to one side of our reception desk opposite Elizabeth, a large sliced butter cake between them, three pieces gone.

Josiah nods and makes two white-knuckled fists. 'Still gripping the bars.'

We've reconvened at the office and brought everyone up to speed. The widow is still here because her hovel has been possessed by the authorities and she has nowhere to go. Tonight, she will take one of the spare rooms in Mother's house. She listens in, keenly, squinting every so often while straining to hear the details.

I check my pocket watch – another hour before we leave to examine the skeleton. 'Anything else to report?'

'I paid Dockside Station a visit,' says Penney. 'They wouldn't let me see Sergeant Goffings and the Draker on the desk sent me away.'

'Well, thanks for trying,' I mutter. There is too much to think about. Too many possibilities in my head. Where is Jonathon Barrows? Who is the caged man? What crime was Cullins involved in that led him to destroy his own company?

'I didn't give up.' Penney meets my gaze to regain my attention.

'Oh?'

'No. I went around to the back and sweet-talked one of the officers. He let me in and showed me the log book. A Draker named Sinnett brought Widow Blewett in around ten, soon after her first visit to you.'

'Sinnett, not Goffings?'

'Sinnett, acting under the direct orders of Goffings. Goffings surely had the widow followed even before she came here. It could be why he's had his eye on you from the start. I did some more digging, too. Goffings, Legge, Cullins – they're all on Camdon's Board of Associates. I took a copy of the roster.' Penney passes a scroll and I open it to scan the list of names, stopping when I recognise another of Cullins' crew.

'Nickolas Moor. I met him yesterday at Cullins and Co. Cullins himself introduced him. Talkative fellow. It says here Nickolas Moor is the foreman at Golden Shores Imports.'

'Obviously they need to update the roster,' says Elizabeth, examining her polished nails. 'Golden Shores is no more.'

I continue. 'But the point remains. All four are in the same club. They're in cahoots.'

'Others, too, most likely,' says Josiah. He reaches out for a second slice of cake and chomps into it like a machine.

'And between them, they wield considerable power,' says Elizabeth, taking notes.

Penney and I watch Josiah eat with mutual fascination. He notices and pauses, gawking back with his mouth full.

'What? It's good cake. You should have some.'

I think about the wrecking of the *Dollinger* and Cullins' probable motives. 'If these remains in the cage *are* those of a murdered man, the *Dollinger* may have been wrecked to cover it up.'

'It would have been quite a sacrifice – all to cover up the murder of just one man – and they made a poor job of it if that's the case,' says Elizabeth.

'Be that as it may. It could be true.'

'How?' asks Penney.

I give it my best shot. 'Say, for instance, the man was caged secretly in the hidden chamber – held captive for a reason we do not know. No one knew he was even on board except the chosen few, perhaps Cullins and Moor – who were ashore – the captain and one or two others, each sworn to secrecy. The caged man is gagged and left to starve to death, but someone else learns of it. Word gets out. Less than half a day later, every man aboard knows the secret.'

'Ship hand Geofferson spoke of hearing strange voices in the ship. That could have been the caged man.' Josiah is thinking hard, his forehead wrinkling again. 'But if the galleon was wrecked because of a false light, how did the wreckers ashore know what was happening on board? How can the two possibly be connected?'

Elizabeth chips in. 'There's a constant stream of vessels passing between Urthia and Camdon. A faster ship could have born a message home to Cullins or Moor, who then might have waited, watching closely for the *Dollinger's* return while planning to murder the entire crew.'

It all fits. 'And then fate gifted them the storm! What better way to silence the crew than to wreck the ship?'

13

Tobias

In which Banyard and Mingle visit the city morgue

The ways of humankind are frequently odd and unaccountable. Some things, however, do make a little sense. Here in Camdon City morgue there is a tradition that every nameless male cadaver be named Tobias, a logical enough outcome when you understand the reason. It's said that, decades ago, the assistants here were using a system of labels and numbers to keep track of the dead. This involved numbered toe badges and, frequently, the abbreviation TOE B. would be followed by a number beginning with a one, like so: TOE B 1.

And there it is, according to popular belief. TOE B1 became Toby or Tobias. Now it's synonymous with the unnameable dead.

Bretling, Josiah and I stand to one side as a battered and bloodstained gurney bears in the skeletal remains from the cage, the latest Tobias in a long, unfortunate line. Around us, a multitude of repulsive biological specimens are displayed in various bottles and jars on shelves. Parts of people float in etherlin, discoloured to sickly yellows and browns.

The coroner has manipulated the bones and the gristle of the surviving joints to straighten them out. Our Tobias is flat on his back, a putrid stink accompanying as the morgue assistant brings the gurney to a stop before us.

'Number 42780.' He turns away, leaving us with Coroner Myrah Orkney, a willowy woman in her late forties who, by her own admission, drinks too much but is experienced and reasonably good at her job. She strikes me as honest and has never given me a reason to think otherwise. Right now, she's sipping steaming-hot black bean soup.

She hands the death certificate to Bretling who takes a cursory glance before passing it to me. 'Male, between twenty and forty. Not much I can tell beyond that,' says Myrah.

I peruse the document. 'May I take an imograph of this?'

Bretling takes the pipe from his mouth and speaks with a long stream of smoke, each word a puff. 'Be my guest, but the original stays here.'

'Certainly. Can you say how long he's been dead?' Unpacking my camera and tripod from a bag, I set about taking imographs.

Myrah says, 'Between two weeks and two months, perhaps longer. That's my best guess, but it is only a guess. The corpse may have been kept on dry land for a time before entering the water, or he may have drowned when the *Dollinger* sank. Every fish in the Eastern Sea has taken a bite of him.'

'Are there no marks on the bones?' asks Josiah while I angle the camera towards the skeleton to take more imographs. 'No cuts or stab marks that might tell us how he died?'

'Sorry. Wish it were that easy. There is this, though.' Myrah points to a place several inches below the elbow on the left ulna.

'There's a lump on his bone,' says Josiah. 'Why the lump?'

'At some point, Tobias here broke his arm and the bone healed. When bones heal back together, they thicken to make the mend stronger.'

Josiah brightens. 'That's good, isn't it? It could help us identify him.'

Bretling snorts. *Some hope...*

'It might. It's something to work with. Estimated height?' Taking out a notebook and pencil, I make notes as Myrah reports.

'Around six two.'

I check my notes. Jonathon was just over six feet.

'Weight?'

'Twelve stones. Again, guesswork.'

'Any other distinguishing features from what you see? A gammy knee or a slumped shoulder?'

'None. He's just your average Tobias.'

'How long ago did he break the arm?'

'Anywhere between one and fifteen years, I'd say. Long enough for the bones to mend well.'

'Not much to go on. A man of average age, of average height and weight. Faceless but for a naked skull. Nameless. If it wasn't for the arm, it could be any one of a thousand missing people,' I conclude as she walks away.

She replies without breaking stride.

'It's just as well he broke his arm, then, isn't it?'

I take out the grainy imograph of Jonathon given to me by his father and hold it up to compare the face with the skeleton's. It fits well enough. 'What do you think, Joe?'

We're dismounting outside our house when a voice jumps us.

'Beware the red-eyed gawper!'

'Jinkers, you gave me a start.'

Josiah helps the widow down from his saddle and takes the reins of both our horses as Jinkers continues.

'Sorry, Micky. *You're* easily spooked. Must have a guilty conscience.'

'My conscience is better than most, thank you.'

'Pray, who is this with you? A guest?'

'This is the widow Blewett. She'll be staying with us for the near future.'

'Oh. Very well. Mr Kaylock is back.'

'So I see.'

The creature growls in Jinkers' arms as though understanding me perfectly well. We pass and turn to head down the side alley.

Deciding he's been snubbed, Jinkers scowls. 'I'll say goodnight, then. Goodnight to all three!'

I wave fleetingly. 'Goodnight, Jinkers. Perhaps you should put a lead on that pet of yours.'

'Old fleabag,' mutters Josiah and he doesn't mean the cat.

The widow, clearly a sound judge of character, says nothing. She is housed comfortably and strikes up an immediate friendship with Mother, who appears genuinely pleased to share in the female company of someone closer to her age. The widow is older than her, but no less spritely or astute. A distant chatter echoes down the hall from the kitchen where the women sit and I'm glad they have each other.

This evening I spend hours in silent contemplation, planning in the green room while Josiah snores in his chair across from me. I find the old newspaper I have kept and reread the article about Great King Doon's bones and Yorkson's Bank.

Maybe we should rob a bank…

Josiah's words echo in my mind.

It is this evening that I make an important decision about which you will hear more later in my tale but, for now, it will suffice to say I believe Cullins guilty and that he should not be allowed to get away with his crimes, even if he were to bribe the entire judicial system.

21st Twinemoon

The morning comes all too quickly. For some reason, I'm exhausted and in no mood for Jinkers' antics as we set out. Today he is back to his usual self but has managed to combine his two favourite obsessions, gawpers and frogs, which is quite an achievement.

'That's when I realised,' he says, as though he's solved the entirety of the world's problems in one genius strike. Mr Kaylock winds around his shins while he prattles on. 'The correlation between the increase of the frog population and the number of gawper sightings is directly proportionate. Do you understand what this means, Micky? The two are *integrally linked*!'

'Is that so?'

'It is! I have the proof! If you come around, I'll show you. I've been charting the statistics for some considerable time.'

'Oh.'

We leave him muttering about dates and figures and the various frog counts he's taken of late, and ride for the office. A twinge of guilt tugs at my gut. Despite Mr Kaylock, Jinkers is desperately alone. The problem in me remedying this is that it would take time – lots of my time. I'd have to visit him and socialise with him, take an interest in his craziness, which I simply can't do. Not right now, anyway. People don't give him time. It would help if he got out more, but even when he does, the sad truth is that they don't give him the time of day. He's strange. And people don't like strange people.

On the road ahead Elizabeth is in mid-conversation with a tall man and the sight initially cheers me. She is turning out to be a fine secretary and an asset to Mysteries Solved, never late, always well dressed and businesslike. Here she is again, as prompt as ever, except, as we ride closer, I recognise the one she is with.

Nickolas Moor. Cullins' right-hand man.

I put a finger to my lips and nod to my right where a horse-drawn carriage fills the road between Elizabeth and us. With an inquisitive expression, Josiah follows my lead and we coax our mounts in behind to conceal ourselves and slow the horses to a walk, allowing time to observe. Spying from around the side of the carriage, I watch Elizabeth and Moor converse. She hasn't seen us. I can't hear the words that pass between them but they seem at ease with one another and, what *is* that? A playful familiarity?

Is Elizabeth a spy, sent from Cullins? I must consider the possibility and yet, if so, would they truly choose to meet candidly right outside our office?

Surely not. I have it wrong. There must be an innocent

explanation, although the thought has me wary. I can ill afford to be outdone by Cullins and his crew.

Eventually they tip hats and part, Moor heading towards Rook's Bridge while Elizabeth crosses the road to unlock and enter the office.

I gave her a key!

She has access to all our files and to insider knowledge of the case. All this leaves me grossly unsettled and guarded about all I say in her presence. I'm prickly for the following hour as I further plan our course of action, that is, until a welcome arrival that gladdens my heart. It starts with the roaring approach of a Double Heart that parks loudly outside our windows.

Mardon climbs out to rap on the door with the gold knob of his cane before entering and hanging his hat and coat. He deposits his brown leather doctor's bag beneath the hat stand.

'Good day, cousin. I must say, the streets here about are a disgrace. Someone should have them cleaned up.'

'Mardon. You're here!'

'Indeed.' He looks down at himself, mocking me. 'Apparently, I am. Once more running to your aid, Micky. One of these days you'll learn to wipe your own backside.'

'Mardon, this is Elizabeth Fairweather, our secretary, and Penelope Danton, our latest recruit.'

'Pleased to meet you, I'm sure,' says Mardon. 'I can only spare a few days so be a good fellow and tell me all about these cases you're mixed up in. But, first, a drink. I'm parched.'

I throw Elizabeth a nod and she leaves to buy black bean soup, although Mardon's notably unimpressed when she returns.

'Don't you have anything stronger?'

'I'm afraid not, old boy. You'll have to wait until after work.'

'Oh, well.' He accepts the soup with a nod. 'Let's get to it, then.'

For now, Elizabeth is unwelcome in the case room and our briefing. 'Miss Fairweather, mind the front desk, if you will.' I lead into the case room and sit at my desk as the others draw chairs around so we can talk. Mardon collects his bag before settling. There is much to convey and for a moment I'm uncertain where to begin. I revisit the door to close it and retake my seat, resisting the temptation to spy through the keyhole to see if Elizabeth is listening on the other side.

'A widow came to us with a complaint,' I fill Mardon in on all the details, now and again allowing Josiah and Penney to chip in while Mardon leans back in his chair, hands tucked behind his head. We explain about Golden Shores Imports, its seven supposed disasters, about Cullins, Moor, Goffings and Legge and, because there is a possible link between the cases, about the missing man, Jonathon Barrows. When we've explained about the caged skeleton and the damage to the *Dollinger*, he closes his eyes to think in silence.

Josiah and Penney glance at me.

Mardon speaks. 'It seems to me there's an obvious and most vital part of your story missing.'

'Being?'

'Why, this ship hand's account of the *Dollinger* wreck, of course. We must find this Anders fellow and hear from him what happened in the last few moments of the voyage.'

He's right. I know it. I've been far too distracted by Goffings, by the Barrows case and everything else. Perhaps it's having Penney around. She's the biggest distraction, but I can't face losing her now, not in any sense of the word. In any case, I resolve to achieve a higher degree of focus. 'I agree. Anders must be found. It's a priority.'

'We did search his shack,' says Josiah. 'He hadn't been there for days.'

'And we enquired around Dockside. No one's seen him for weeks,' I add. 'There's a good chance he's on another voyage and beyond reach.'

Mardon leans forward in his chair, his expression remaining aloof. 'Dead or alive, he's somewhere. It's just a matter of finding the fellow.'

'Not necessarily,' says Josiah. 'What if Cullins has had him killed and burned his body. How are you going to find him, then?'

'Witnesses, evidence… Science. That's how. There's always a trail, old boy, whatever the story.'

'Good luck with that.' Something's bothering Josiah but I don't know what. He crosses his arms and stares at the door. Is it Mardon's arrival or Elizabeth's absence that's unsettled him? Or is he simply trying to figure out why wood is not 'see-through'?

I clear my throat. 'Well, now. We have much to do. Perhaps a fresh pair of eyes on Anders' trail is just what we need. Mardon, will you take on the search?'

'If I must.' He puffs on his pipe.

'Good. That's settled. We should examine the little evidence we have before moving on. Evidence is what the widow's case is about. Gather enough of the stuff and we can take Cullins to court and win back the widow's money. We have Geofferson's account of the *Dollinger* wreck, which may count for something.'

'There's the damage to the wreck, itself. That suggests it was facing the rocks when it struck,' says Josiah. 'It's further evidence of the ledged wrecking.'

'*Alleged.*'

'And, of course, the body in the cage,' says Penney. 'That can't help Cullins' case.'

I make notes in my book. 'It may break it, if we can name the man.'

'What about the bodies that washed up over the following days?' asks Mardon. 'Did anyone examine them?'

'Good question, although it would mean exhuming them all.' I kick myself. What's wrong with me? Why didn't I think of that? 'If Cullins motive was to murder the entire crew, he may have had survivors finished off as they came ashore.'

'Then why is Geofferson still alive?' asks Josiah. Another good question.

'I don't know. Perhaps they're still looking for him. Anders could be in hiding. We'd better find them both quickly and put them somewhere safe. Josiah and I will go for Geofferson directly after our meeting.'

'Really, Michael, you should have considered that before.'

Mardon's right and I realise he's probably a better detective than me, even though he's not a detective. That's annoying.

'There's the attack on Doncley Maples, the treasurer. Two witnesses who'll stand up in court.' Josiah has stopped tormenting the door. 'And then there's the fact that Sergeant Goffings and Inculus Legge have made it their business to obstruct us.'

'*And* the widow's unjustified incarceration. Although, these things will be hard to prove in court,' I say.

'There's the warehouse, Mr Banyard. An extinct lack of melted glass. There were no bottles in that warehouse when it burned, which proves Cullins claimed on false losses.'

Penney frowns, unaware that Josiah is from threader stock.

'You mean *distinct*, but yes, a valid point. Although, again, this will be contested in court. They will say the fire happened too long ago for the current state of the warehouse to be considered evidence. They'll suggest someone has since tampered with it, or they'll claim the glass vaporised in the extreme heat, which I suppose is possible but unlikely. Don't you think, Mardon?'

'I'd need to experiment before confirming it either way but it sounds reasonable. Molten glass would have run to the lowest possible points. It's likely that at least some of these areas would be cooler than the heart of the fire and so I would expect some glass to survive.'

'What about other lines of enquiry?' asks Penney.

I check the claims report. 'There's mention of a man who witnessed the *Dollinger* wreck, a resident of Dockside, one Mr Fisher. It may be worth tracking him down.' I flip through my notes and a small piece of burned paper falls out and flutters to the floor at my feet.

'What's that?' Penney asks.

It takes me a moment before I realise. 'It's the corner of a page I pulled from the hearth in Anders' shack. I'd forgotten all about it.' I pick it up as Mardon takes a complicated arrangement of laboratory lenses from his bag and crosses to me.

'May I?' He takes the fragment in a pair of tweezers and, placing it carefully on my desk, arranges the various interchangeable lenses set on pivots and retractable arms. He chooses a large lens and, from over his shoulder, I read the previously indistinguishable, partially carbonised text aloud – disjointed ends of lines written in a meticulous hand of ridiculously small letters.

'To warn you as it has… should take decisive… put an end to… Moor is… '

'Nicolas Moor?' wonders Josiah, matching my thoughts.

'It's part of a letter,' says Penney. 'But what does it mean?'

I take each segment and ponder. 'The first bit seems to suggest the author is writing with a warning of some sort. The next may be a suggestion – you should take decisive action – and so forth.'

'Whoever is writing is saying the recipient must end something,' says Penney.

'Agreed,' says Mardon. 'And this Moor fellow is something to do with it.'

'So, let's recap,' I say after a short pause when we have run dry of suggestions. 'Mardon, you're on Anders. Joe and I will follow up on Geofferson and then pay Mr Barrows a visit. I also want to meet this supposed girl Jonathon was keen on. That just leaves Penney.'

'I could go with Mardon.'

'Not to say you wouldn't look good on my arm, Miss Danton, but I prefer to work alone.'

'As you wish.'

Mildly relieved that she's not heading off with my cousin, I suggest, 'Penney, why don't you hunt down this Mr Fisher and hear his story? Perhaps he can add something to our knowledge of the wreck.'

Let's hope Mr Fisher is less threatening to my chances with Penney than my debonair cousin who, I'm sure, could whisk her away in a blink if he so desired.

14

Mr Barrows

In which Banyard and Mingle deliver ill news

Geofferson is gone. The day after we questioned him, he signed up on another crew and left the port at dusk on a halker (a ship, bigger than a sloop, smaller than a galleon) bound for Amorphia. Hopefully he's safe from Cullins and his men. I stand on the Cogg and look out to sea, wishing him fair winds. Perhaps by the time he returns we shall be ready to take Cullins to court.

'Why does it not run away?' asks Josiah, squinting at the sunlight bouncing off the waves.

I'm baffled. 'Why does *what* not run away?'

'The water. Water always runs away, but this water does not. Why?'

'It's the sea, Joe. This is where all the water runs *to*. This is where it stops running because it has nowhere else to go.'

He seems placated by this explanation, his frown dispelling into an open gaze that settles on the horizon. To me he can often appear childlike, or *simple*, but I have to constantly remind myself he has not had the privilege of a proper education, while I was schooled until breaking point. Is he less intelligent than me? All things considered, probably not, but if he is – and I'm aware I'm introducing a new and possibly larger topic here –

does that make it easier for him to be happy? I'm convinced overthinking is not good for you and yet, that is precisely what a good detective must do: think, re-examine, deliberate, ruminate and then think again. Whatever the truth of it, Josiah and I certainly think differently.

'Come on, Joe. We must find this girl Jonathon used to be keen on.'

'How are we gonna find her, Mr Banyard?'

'*Going to.* Jonathon's business partner says she's from Tower End, so we'll start there.'

Tower End, being on the western edge of Camdon and so a good distance from Dockside, is a well-to-do part of town. It takes us three hours of trawling the streets to track down five different Jennies living in the area who are of an age compatible with Jonathon's and, two hours after that, we find the Jennie we want, serving cakes in a fancy patisserie.

'Jennie Lowery.' Jennie is attractive in a dainty way.

'The Jennie who used to be with Jonathon Barrows?'

'Yes, that's me. Why do you ask?'

'Jonathon is missing. Did you not know?'

In turquoise silks, Jennie has a soft, oval face with a gentle look, although there is something hard about the line of her mouth. Concern blossoms around her eyes beneath her lustrous blonde curls, which are pinned high like a tier of honeyed cakes.

'Yes, I heard. Is there news of him?'

A flicker of hope dissolves with my next line. 'Nothing good, I'm afraid. His father remains convinced he's dead. We're investigating the matter. Perhaps you can help us.'

'I shall certainly try.'

'When did you last see Jonathon?'

'It was around the start of Fipplemoon. We parted after a quarrel – no – a misunderstanding.'

'So, this was a week or two before he disappeared?'

'It was. Though *I* deemed our misunderstanding a trivial matter, Jonathon turned cold and I barely saw him again.'

'Cold?' asks Josiah.

'Uncommunicative, reclusive. I thought it best to leave him alone for a time, give him space. It's happened before but he usually comes around in the end.'

'Only this time, he didn't,' says Josiah.

'No. He just vanished. You don't think it had anything to do with our disagreement, do you?'

'We're still investigating the circumstances of his disappearance. What was it about?'

'Oh, it was nothing much. He was acting possessive and a little jealous. I drew his attention to the fact and he didn't like it.'

'I see. Jealous because of attention you were attracting from another man?'

'Other men, certainly.' There is something enigmatic about Jennie's eyes. I scrutinise them briefly yet learn nothing. What secrets lay hidden beneath?

'Anyone in particular?'

'No. Only the looks men gave me when we were out walking together. That sort of thing.'

'So, he didn't trust you?' prompts Josiah.

'I suppose not.'

'Did he have reason?'

'No. None whatsoever. Are you able to tell me what you've learned so far? I'd like to know.'

'I'm afraid we're not at liberty to divulge any details at this point.'

The hardness returns to her lips. 'Oh, but *I* must tell *you* everything!'

'Perhaps as the case develops we'll be able to share more details,' I say quickly.

'Very well. If you've finished, I must get back to work.'

'Of course, Miss Lowery. Thank you for your help.'

When we arrive at the Barrows' residence, our horses breathless from the climb up Peak Street, Mr Barrows is leaving his front door. The door is glossy black, in keeping with his hat, his clothes and his cane. His property is grand and tall, rising in creamy stone and surrounded by black painted railings that are capped with diamond-headed spikes. He abruptly abandons his errand and, stern-faced, welcomes us through the door and into his study, a capacious room with quilted silk chairs and many wonderful, leather-bound books lining the walls. I resist the temptation to browse the shelves and peruse the titles on each spine. It would begin as a moment's distraction but would end in hours lost. A single window overlooks the domed roof of City Hall and the lower east end. His short, sharp movements are imbued with energy, an eagerness to hear our report.

'You have news of my son?'

'Before we begin, would you like to sit down?'

Barrows occupies a chair, his long legs folding like a crane's, his gaunt features tightening with concern. Uncomfortable in his presence, Josiah and I also sit.

'What have we learned?' asks Barrows.

I don't want to draw this out so I go straight to the heart of it. 'Nothing certain at this time, Mr Barrows, but a question has arisen.'

'You may ask me anything. I've absolutely nothing to hide.'

'While investigating another case, we discovered the remains of an unidentified man.' Barrows opens his mouth to speak but I press on. 'Of course, we at once thought of Jonathon, but this man cannot be named, you understand – not by his face nor his living likeness – that is beyond us now. There is but one detail that *may* aid us.'

'He has a broken arm. One that has healed.' Josiah points to a place below his own left elbow. 'Just here. Did your son ever break his arm?'

Grief overshadows Barrows' face as he turns to gaze from the window. 'I knew. Deep down, I knew he was gone.'

'That's a yes, then,' mutters Josiah.

'All the same, sir, the detail is not conclusive,' I say.

Barrows glances up, a hollowness in his eyes. 'What do you

mean, not conclusive? How much more conclusive could it be?'

'It merely suggests – '

'Suggests? What it suggests is my son is dead.'

'It merely implies the remains *may* be those of your son.'

'Remains…' Barrows rises to his full height and stalks the floor, his movements staccato. 'Pray tell. To what, exactly, do you refer when you say *remains*? How much of my son's body survives?'

And there it is. The question I've been dreading. I do not wish to sit here and explain to a grieving father the grim details of what is left behind, that fish have eaten the flesh clean to bone and ligament. I do not wish to tell Barrows that his son's face has gone and all that is left is a hideous mask, a slime-covered putrid skull. And that's when it hits me. I, too, believe it is his son.

Josiah steps in to fill the resulting silence. 'Regrettably, the remains are little more than bones, sir, but perhaps my colleague is right. Perhaps this is another who has also broken his arm at some previous time.'

I'm surprisingly impressed with Josiah's sudden turn of eloquence and offer him a mirthless smile. Good old Joe. He continues and it's just as well, for if he had not, Barrows would have pressured us for the details, I'm sure.

'The bones were discovered in the bowels of a wrecked galleon off Hatch Head, along with the bodies of several seamen. The ship went down over a month ago. We are investigating the circumstances.'

I cut in, hoping that's enough for Barrows to think on. 'Anything else we could say would be conjecture. In any case, Mr Barrows, that is the long and short of it. We shall, of course, make full report when we know more.'

Barrows collapses back into his chair, his thunder subsiding and it's like a daemon has vacated his body. The tall, black bird has gone, leaving behind only a broken husk; the sad, quiet figure of Death in a suit.

Riding from Peak Street, we head to Dockside to join the hunt for ship hand Anders, but our enquiries are tiresome and fruitless. Mardon and Penney are nowhere to be found and we drag our feet, ever more uninspired, from site to site. The afternoon draws low cloud in from the sea and the sun appears to have absconded. It grows prematurely dark and there is an unusual quietness about the place. We question residents and revisit Ander's shack, paw over the bric-a-brac of his backyard, look in vain for signs of his last movements and wander down to the sea's edge where smaller boats are coming in to harbour. Further towards the north end of the wharf, a galleon sways gently on the tide, steadied by its ropes.

Between us and the ship a stout figure bumbles along the quay: Inculus Legge.

'He's alive, then,' I mutter.

'Who's alive?' Josiah asks.

I nod towards the Harbour Master, glad he's not spotted us. 'Oh. Yes.'

Josiah's lost no sleep on Legge.

John Ferris greets us with a nod, while mooring his fishing boat. 'See yonder? A thicket in the sky. A storm coming, masters. I'd head home if I were you.' His leathery hands complete a cleat hitch and he straightens, stretching his back.

I nod. 'Thank you, John. Wise words, I'm sure.' And before long they prove to be true. The air changes as a wind arises and the coast turns cold. A dirty green fog suffuses the distant sea and slithers in, reaching with finger-like strands. Rain will surely follow the storm-head and I want to leave but before we can go anywhere, a crimson droplet, perfect in form, collides with the pale skin on the back of my hand. I stare, for the smallest time, wondering at its origin before my brow streams with blood. Pressing a handkerchief to my face, I turn back to the sea and scan the shoreline as the soft white cloth soaks to a deep red. Ahead, Josiah is already pointing.

'Do you see him, Mr Banyard? A shade man on the shore!' He makes the sacred sign, tracing a circle upon his brow before touching the shirt over his heart.

A tall, dim shape. Eyes like glowing white coals. Watching us!

Josiah says *shade man* but I know precisely what he means. Several other figures along the seafront turn and run, but I can't move. A fascination – the same fascination that strikes me at every such sighting – overwhelms me and I'm powerless to do anything other than stare back. Between the gawper and us is a fair distance, for which I'm grateful. And throughout the short encounter I'm struck by one detail: Although other people are present, mostly running from the scene in terror, it seems the gawper is watching only Josiah and me. Staring back, I amend the thought. It is me and me alone. It's more of a feeling than an observation and perhaps I'm wrong.

For moments, the gawper drifts towards us along the shoreline. Josiah turns to flee, his face pale, but I catch hold of his sleeve.

'Wait! I want to see what it does.'

We are the only ones left now. It's just us and it.

On it comes, legless yet closing on us, its broad, ragged base gliding over sand and rock and weed until the green fog hits the shore and envelopes it. A drop of rain lands on my forehead and I break my gaze, glancing skyward as the clouds open to shower the coast, dispersing the fog and, when the fog has gone, so has the gawper.

We stand for a moment, watching the empty shore.

I swallow a notion that it was trying in some way to communicate with me. Did it come for me, or for us? What did it want? Was there purpose in its visit and where, and how, did it go?

I wish I knew.

'Come!'

Josiah follows as I run to a giant set of steps built into the side of the Cogg. We descend and dash across a stretch of sand and then clamber over slippery rocks and onto more sand where we stop.

144

'It was here. It was right here!'

'Aye.'

'So, look! Notice anything strange?'

'Not really.' With a lingering fear, Josiah scans around as though the gawper is hiding close by, readying to jump out at us.

'The sand. Look at the sand.'

'Yes. Nothing there. It's gone.'

'But there's not a single footprint. Not a mark nor scuff!'

'Ah. Yes. I see what you mean.'

'So how did it get here? And how did it move?'

'Both *very* good questions, Mr Banyard.'

It's pouring heavily by the time Jinkers catches us by the alley, leaning out from beneath his porch. Lightning flashes violently in the sky and a deep roll of thunder follows, loud and close. The heavens appear to shift on a different axis to that of our world below, somehow out of sync with the ground. The moon creeps out between banks of churning cloud, low over the house and Mr Kaylock growls at it, as though bearing a private grudge. A gust of wind drives rain under the porch and Kaylock darts into the house.

'Another omen, Micky. A crowling with a broken foot! Hobbling in my backyard, it was. What do you say to that?'

'Not much. I'm sorry, Jinkers. It's been a long day. I bid you goodnight.' We hurry past, splashing a path to stable the horses. Jinkers' omens are nonsense but I don't like them, all the same. Where are Penney and Mardon? Arrested by Goffings or Legge? Trapped somewhere and in peril from Cullins or his henchman, Moor?

After dinner Josiah and I sit in silence. It's a tense silence, the sort that feeds on anxiety until it grows so prevailing that one is almost afraid to break it. Beyond the diamond-leaded windows the storm roils in an angry black sky and the flash and mocking cackle of lightning shocks the room, marking progress with its startling show. There's a sense that something is about to break, something heating, about to boil over to choke the world. Where are Penney, Mardon, Jonathon Barrows? And Anders?

I glare at the storm while tapping a rhythm on the polished arm of my chair.

'If I did that, you'd tell me I was annoying,' Josiah says, frowning at me.

'Indeed.' I don't bother to contradict, don't have the energy for it. And anyway, he's right. Things are annoying me and I, in turn, am annoying Josiah. There's a hierarchy, even in my house.

Restlessly I rise to visit the nearest window and study the sky. Lightning lights a figure standing a dozen yards from the other side of the glass, startling me. I look again, eyes straining in the darkness between strikes, but the figure is gone.

The tall figure – with white, gawping eyes – has vanished.

15

Visitors in the Storm

In which Banyard probes the dark

Clearly, I'm going mad. Or the gawper obsession is contagious, has spread from Jinkers to me, and I've come down with a sudden but no less tragic case. Perhaps it is a kind of madness, after all. That would explain a lot!

'Did you see that?' I ask, meaning the gawper in our back garden.

Josiah joins me at the window. 'See what?'

'Quickly! Snuff the lights.'

We extinguish candles and the lamp, plunging the room into a darkness more complete than the night outside.

'What was it?'

'A gawper. Right there outside the window, looking in.'

Josiah studies me with a look that suggests I'm crazy. 'Perhaps with the lightning and everything –'

'I'm not seeing things, Joe. It was there!' My hand shoots out to indicate the spot, as if to underline my lunacy and for a long time we stand in obscurity, silently watching the darkly glistening rain on bushes, the path and the stables.

My heart almost leaps from my mouth when an all-too-real face – pale, drenched and bloodied – lurches not five inches from the glass before me and in shock, a small squeal leaves my mouth, which for some reason has become desert-dry. Someone *is* outside!

'Mardon!' Josiah rushes to the back door. When it's open, Penney stands there, supporting Mardon as best she can, peering at us, soaked but apparently uninjured.

'He needs help,' she says. 'Now. We tried the front door but nobody answered.'

'Of course. The storm is loud. Come in!' I fetch towels and call Mother downstairs. She makes a good nurse and, while Mardon and Penney dry themselves and collapse into chairs, I bombard them with questions and Mother sets to work cleaning and examining a three-inch gash on Mardon's right temple, the only source of all the blood, from what we can tell.

'What happened? Where have you been?'

The widow steals in to watch quietly from the doorway.

'We tracked Anders to a shipyard north of Burrington Point,' says Penney.

'*We?*' I stare. 'Burrington Point? I thought you were interviewing Mr Fisher. You were supposed to be in Dockside. Working alone.'

'I did. I was.' She glares back, no nonsense. 'I'll tell you about Fisher later. Right now we have more pressing matters, don't you think?'

'So you found Anders.'

Mother has dabbed away most of the blood and the damage isn't half as bad as I feared, but Mardon is still dazed and groggy, his head lolling. Damp and bloodied towels litter the floor and the arms of his chair.

'Joe, fetch the brandy. There's a bottle in the cellar.'

He goes. Penney settles and Mother dresses Mardon's wound.

'Well, how did this happen? Where's Anders?'

'We were trying to find out when a barrel of rivets mysteriously toppled from a high stack and struck Mardon's head. He was out cold for a while. I thought he was dead.'

'Then thank goodness you were with him. Why *were* you with

him, by the way?'

'We bumped into each other in Dockside. He told me he had a lead and I'd finished with Fisher. Seemed like a good idea to tag along. He reluctantly agreed.'

'I'm sure he did,' I mutter this into my sleeve. 'And the lead was…'

'Mardon found a mariner who swore he'd seen Anders pass through the shipyard. The mariner pointed us to a boy. You pretty much know the rest.'

'A dead end.'

'Not entirely.' Mardon focuses for the first time since entering the house. Josiah arrives with the brandy and Mother has had the good sense to fetch the crystal. She pours measures for Mardon and me and looks around at the state of everyone else before filling more glasses. Downing the drink in one gulp, Mardon takes the bottle and attempts to refill his glass. 'Strictly medicinal, you understand,' he mumbles. I shift his glass to catch most of the stream and he downs that, too, and then sits back, the colour slowly returning to his face. 'Anders is out there somewhere. Before the barrels fell, we found the boy who reckons he saw Anders there less than a week ago. We were questioning the lad but he bolted when the stack collapsed.'

'Or was pushed,' Penney says.

Mardon raises his eyebrows acceptingly and shrugs. 'Either way, we have to go back and find that boy. He's our best chance of locating Anders.'

22nd Twinemoon

Penney sits in the visitor's chair, legs crossed, prim and all business. 'Indeed, Mr Fisher witnessed the wreck. He gave a full account. He even saw the ship turn starboard and drive into Hatch Head.'

'Interesting. The report and the papers all say the wreck was only discovered the following morning when bodies washed ashore. Why didn't Fisher raise the alarm? Lives may have been saved.'

'He tried. There are steep steps running up from his home, treacherous in the storm. He slipped, fell and was knocked unconscious. When he came round he was groggy, soaked and freezing. It was all he could do to drag himself indoors, where he fell into a feverish sleep.'

'I see. What about the false light theory?'

'He didn't notice any light. He said he wasn't looking for one but, from his house, he wouldn't have been able to see much of the coastline to the north. There's a rise in the land and buildings that block the view.'

'Another dead end, then.'

'Sorry.'

'It's too dangerous to work alone any longer. I won't allow it.' We are gathered around my desk in the case room, Josiah, Mardon, Penney and me. Mardon's head is bandaged.

'Then we'll go together,' Penney says, pristine in a grey and black ensemble: blouse, bodice, breeches and riding boots.

'Agreed. Do you think you'll recognise this boy if you see him?'

'Undoubtedly,' Penney says.

Mardon nods. 'Another second or two and we'd have had his name. It's a shame.'

'Well, it can't be helped. At least you're alive. How's your head? Can you travel?'

'I'm well enough. Let's be off.'

'One moment.' I lean in close to ask, 'Did any of you tell Elizabeth where you were going yesterday?'

They exchange puzzled glances, shake their heads and say, 'No.'

'All right.' On the way out I give Elizabeth instructions. 'Watch the shop and don't let anyone into the case room.' We slip our coats on.

'As you wish, Mr Banyard.'

'On second thoughts...' I fish my keys from my pocket and

return to the case room door to lock it. 'There.' Interestingly, Elizabeth seems oblivious. She sits at her desk reading a penny dreadful that she's brought in to occupy her, since I've excluded her from any part of our investigations and so limited her workload.

'All right. We'll be off now, Miss Fairweather.'

'Good day, then.' Not a glimmer.

Since we're travelling together and a measure of stealth is desirable, I hail a carriage and we climb in. We're all pensive on our journey to the shipyard – even Josiah – and barely a word passes between us until, glancing from a side window, Mardon lets out a cry.

'There he is, by thunder!' He lurches to point and bangs his cane on the roof. 'Stop the carriage. Stop, I say!'

We sprawl from the door as the driver slows the horses with a drag of the reins and a clatter of hooves. The boy, a sprite with a shock of blond hair and a rust-coloured waistcoat, spies us and in panic flees down the nearest alley, the soles of his naked feet flashing.

'Why's he running?' Penney asks.

'We've spooked him.' Mardon may be a better detective than me but he's a lousy runner. Josiah's not too bad, not for his size, though he has an awkward lumbering gait. All the same, I wouldn't want to be the one who tries to stop him once he's built momentum. Penney is too genteel to run anywhere and so it's only Josiah and me who tear after the lad. Down the alley, around the corner, another alley and another, two lefts, one right, two more lefts and he's vanished. Josiah and I stop at a junction of four alleys, the cobbles beneath our feet grimy with coal dust and oil.

'He's gone to ground, Mr Banyard.' Josiah's not even panting. I'm almost keeling over, my heart making a bid for freedom. 'Doubt we'll see him again this day. Do you think he's guilty? That he's involved somehow?'

'Not at all. Any lad would turn heel if a carriage of fellows set upon him. No, he's merely scared. He's a threader, right? No

151

shoes.'

'A threader, sure enough.'

'Stands to reason, then. He's probably spent half his life running from the Drakers.'

'I suppose.'

'We'd better find the others. Perhaps a systematic search will ferret him out.'

The search was a waste of time, merely achieving sore feet and weary legs but, meeting up at the shipyard after, Penney glimpses the boy fetching rivets to a worker on the far side of a half-built halker. Beyond this there's an open-sided warehouse with stacks of clinkers, steel plate and barrels, presumably the ones full of rivets. Penney has the good sense to say nothing but surreptitiously gestures towards the lad until we're all aware.

The ship sits in a shallow bay but is tall enough to provide the perfect concealment and, beneath its growing hull, we conspire.

Penney has a keenness about her that makes her even more attractive, if that's possible. She whispers. 'What should we do? We can't let him run again.'

Mardon grunts his approval. His feet are the sorest and he's only recently stopped wheezing from the trek. 'We'll need to employ a measure of stealth.'

'Split up and circle in,' says Josiah. 'Trap him like a wild pig.'

'What you mean to say is: *Trap him like you would a wild pig.*'

'Precisely.' He misses my point entirely.

'I've never trapped a wild pig,' states Mardon.

'All right, Joe. You work your way around and get on the far side of him,' I say. 'Mardon, take the walkway to the right. And keep away from the barrel stacks.' Chuckling at this, Josiah receives a scowl from Mardon. 'Penney and I will cover the left flank and the ship will block the lad's only remaining escape.' They nod. 'Now go.'

They go.

I circle around with Penney.

The boy is surrounded.

By the time he sees Penney and I, and recognises us from before, it's too late. Josiah steps out of the warehouse shadows and Mardon blocks the path behind.

'Don't try to run.' I say this loud and clear. 'We wish you no harm and you won't escape this time.'

He casts about anyway, seeking a route, but there is none. Unless he chooses to climb the half-built ship. Accepting this, his face falls as thoughts of escape drain away. We close in to form a tighter ring around him and the worker, who continues to rivet clinkers into place on an edge of the hull. He doesn't care. He simply curls his lip, amused by the lad's predicament.

'What's your name, boy?' I ask.

The boy looks around at us and decides to cooperate. 'Ebadiah. Ebadiah Joseph.'

'And what's your job, Ebadiah Joseph? Are you always to be found here, fetching and carrying for shipbuilders?'

'Not always. I shine shoes. Do a bit of this and that.'

'We're lucky to find you here, then.'

'I suppose. What do you want?' Eyes full of fear and determination.

'We're trying to find a man who may have passed through, a ship hand called Anders. I hear you've seen him.'

Ebadiah takes a long look at Penney and Mardon. 'Aye. I spoke with that pair yesterday, but that accident weren't nothin' to do with me. I swears!'

'We believe you, Ebadiah. We're not here about the accident. We only wish to find Anders. He's an important witness in a case we're working on.'

His entire face changes with this revelation. 'A case? Like a detective case? Are you lot detectives?' There's awe and admiration in his tone.

'We are. Will you help us?'

He nods, keenly.

'Then, you shall be rewarded. Please lead us to a suitable establishment of your choosing where we might buy you refreshment.'

'So, what's it to be, Ebadiah?'

'Cake. And black bean soup, of course.'

'Aren't you a little young for black bean soup?'

'Naugh. I always has black bean soup. Too young? Pah!'

'Very well. Black bean soup and cake it is.' I order the refreshments and give Ebadiah a moment to grow accustomed to his surroundings. He's not been in a silker soup shop before and is fascinated by the red and cream striped upholstery of the chairs, the highly-polished tables and the plush crimson drapes around the windows. The air is sweet and spiced with the scent of newly baked biscuits. Now he's relaxing, he has an open, boyish face and his eyes appear larger and less cunning.

'You still wish to help?' I ask.

'Oh, yeah. Of course. Can I join? Be a detective? I always wanted to be a detective!'

'Tell you what. Help us with this case and we'll see.'

'You swear?'

'I swear we'll see.'

Ebadiah spits on the palm of his hand and offers it. To Penney's revulsion, I spit on mine and we shake.

'It's a deal, then. What do you want to know? Anders, wasn't it?'

'Yes. Anders doesn't yet know he's an important witness in our case. We need to tell him. We wish Anders no harm and he's not in any trouble.'

'Not unless Cullins or Moor find him first, Shoe Shine,' adds Josiah. I throw him a disparaging look because I wasn't going to divulge anything more to the boy. Who knows who he's friends with or where his loyalties lie? He might even run the odd errand for Cullins or Moor.

'Ebadiah, you don't know either of these men, do you?' I mask my concern as best I can, though I get the feeling nothing is lost on this astute, sharp-eyed boy.

'Naugh. I don't know nothin'. Except, unless you're talkin'

154

about that *Nickolas* Moor. I do know him. A nasty blinder, is Nickolas Moor. Wouldn't tangle with him if I were you. I don't mind Shoe Shine, by the way. Everyone else calls me that.'

'All right. Be assured, we have no intention of tangling with Moor. Our case has very little to do with him. Indeed, the man is almost irrelevant. Now, back to Anders. What can you tell us about him? When did you see him and what passed between you?'

'It's like this. I saw him five days ago. He was passing through the shipyard, heading north. He sat and rested a while, all the time looking around as though someone might be watching. We talked. He had a scrap of bread he shared with me and I let him dip some in the stew I had on the boil – a campfire, you see. A pretty thin stew, it was, but he seemed to like it. He asked about the cliffs up past Windstrome Bay.'

'Oh, why?'

Our order arrives at the table and Ebadiah's eyes widen. 'Don't know. Didn't ask.' He picks up his slab of rich dark cake and chomps while silker customers pull faces. It is considered polite to use a fork. Once his mouth is as full as can be, he dumps eight spoonfuls of sugar into his soup and stirs it furiously.

'The cliffs beyond Windstrome Bay,' says Penney, excitedly. 'He must have meant Dorrington Rocks.'

'Is that pertinent?' asks Mardon.

'It is. Because Dorrington Rocks is an area of cliffs, full of caves.'

16

Caves

In which Ebadiah leads the way

Ebadiah plonks his cup down with zeal, slopping his drink over the tablecloth in the process. There's a line of black bean soup clinging to his top lip, which he wipes clean with his sleeve. '*I* know the caves. *I* can show you the way.'

I tell him. 'Definitely not. It's too dangerous.'

He argues. 'Them caves aren't *that* dangerous.'

'It's not the caves I'm worried about.' I lower my voice because we're drawing unwanted attention. 'There are people trying to stop us. Take the "accident" with the barrels, for instance. And there have been other occurrences.'

Ebadiah stares into his soup, genuinely crestfallen. I watch Penney soften, her heart melting right before me and it's not that I'm untouched but, ultimately, she isn't the one responsible here.

'Can't he come with us?' she asks. 'He does seem *very* keen.'

Josiah shrugs. 'It could be useful to have someone along who knows the caves.'

Ebadiah brightens. 'I'll be no trouble. I promise.'

Outnumbered, I turn to Mardon for support. Fruitlessly.

'It doesn't bother me, one way or the other.' He seems more focused on his soup and his sore feet. He lights his pipe.

And with a sigh, I give in. 'All right. You can come, but on condition you do exactly as I say. *I* am in charge. Got that?'

'I got that all right! If my ol' ma could see me now – a detective!'

I laugh. 'You're not a detective yet. You'll have to prove yourself first.'

We catch another carriage – all of us – and head north to Windstrome Bay, hugging the coast until the outskirts of the city run out and the judder of the wheels on the metalled surface of the roads slows and softens to an easier vibration – one that sings of a dirt track, sandy with grass – and then the carriage stops altogether.

We climb out.

We stand.

We look around.

The track runs on, following the coast, but we've arrived. At least, we've come as close to the caves as the driver can take us. Without a word, he thrusts his riding crop towards a narrow path to our right, one worn to bare sand and edged with tall dune grass. That's the way to the caves. I've never been before and neither has Josiah, so I'm actually quite glad of our scrappy guide, who sets off with quick steps and head held high, brimming with importance. He's revelling in his new role, glowing with it.

Our driver has a pair of lamps, one of which I borrow. 'Wait for us here.'

He nods and looks around at our barren surroundings, a nervous twitch in the corner of his eye. There's no sheltering tavern nor a croft for miles.

The narrow path bends to the left and drops, gently at first and then steeply, diving through dunes that recede on the seaward side and eventually slip into rocks and cliffs and then thin air. A decline of steps cut into the cliff edge leads us to the first of the caves with still a fair drop to the sea below. This one, Ebadiah ignores. He also marches straight past the second and third, but stops in the shadows of the fourth, waiting for our line to gather.

'This is it.'

'What about the others?' asks Mardon.

'Oh, they don't go nowhere.'

'But this one does?' I wonder if we'll truly find Anders somewhere inside. Somehow, I doubt it. Ebadiah nods and we follow him in. A few minutes along our undulating route, he stops and turns, the cave ceiling barely a foot from his head.

'We're nearly at the junction. The way splits into five passages and some o' them split into more passages and chambers and they goes on for miles. If you don't know what you're doin' you can get proper lost. Folk have died down here. Starved to death trying to escape.'

'Enough of the horror stories, Shoe Shine. Lead on.' I bring the lamp up to show the way. It's dark now and we stoop to go further in. For a full hour we tour the cave system, ducking where necessary, crawling occasionally and it's endless. Guilt strikes. Penney only has fine clothes and she's probably tearing them to shreds or wearing them through, grovelling on all-fours through the low passages in the near dark.

Ebadiah stops in a widening cavern and, hands on hips, peers at the impressive stalactites overhead. 'You know what? I don't think he's here, Mr Banyard.'

I must confess, I'm *convinced* he is not. This whole thing has been a colossal waste of time and effort, the five of us dragging pointlessly through tunnels and caverns.

Josiah huffs. He's bored to death and the low passages are a liability for his skull and a nightmare for his back. 'If he *was* here, wouldn't there be signs?'

'If he *were* here,' I correct him. Again.

'Yes,' agrees Mardon. 'He'd have to eat somewhere, sleep, most likely cook or boil water at least, but there's nothing here but bat dung and cave spiders.'

He's right about the bat dung. There's a cloying stench in the air.

'Perhaps we should think about leaving,' I say, sweeping the light around the formations slick with mineral deposits that line the chamber walls and give the impression they are melting. 'The lamp will eventually run out of oil. We'd better turn back before it dies.'

Penney's pale face flashes across the beam. She looks anxious, has done since we entered. She's barely said a word.

To his credit, Ebadiah does appear to know his way. In the darkness I have no concept of where we are or where we've been, but as long as we can get out, I don't much care.

At long last the soft sheen of daylight blooms in the tunnel ahead and we leave the cave to gather once more on the sandy track outside. There's a line of dune grass running alongside the track that rises a few yards to the edge of a cliff so that it appears a very good place for a person to step off the edge of the world, if they had a mind to. It's like this all the way along until the path spills out onto the rocks below. I imagine someone trying to live here amid the sand, the caves, the cliffs and the rocks, and know I wouldn't want to. Not even for one night.

It's late afternoon now and the sun is weak and low, sinking with the heavy mileage of the day.

'Well, you can't say we didn't try,' says Ebadiah, disappointment marring his face as he turns to trudge up the path. He has an easy way about him and the sand between his toes somehow suits him. He's at home here as much as anywhere. Josiah follows him and I'm next, with Penney and Mardon behind me.

That's when we smell it.

All of us.

We stop, except for Ebadiah, who continues.

What we detect is a faint trace of smoke. It's not enough to see and it's coming from the second cave, one of those Ebadiah led us past when we first arrived.

'Someone has set a fire,' says Penney, peering into the passage. Mardon and Josiah look to me.

'Josiah, the boy!' I urge, because Ebadiah has twigged we're onto him and is dashing away. Josiah bolts after the boy but it's hopeless. The boy runs like a lantern dog: light, lean and as fast as they come. We're stood in the entrance to the cave with the smoke and, if Anders is inside, he's not going anywhere. I watch the two run up the path, Ebadiah stretching out an easy lead, but then he stumbles and falls. In three giant bounds, Josiah is on him, lifting him around the waist and hauling him, kicking and fighting, back to us.

'These caves go nowhere, you say.'

Josiah deposits the boy before me, still clamped in his vice-like hands.

'All right, all right. Let me go!'

'Tell us the truth and I'll think about it.'

He meets my gaze but quietens.

'Suit yourself. You're coming with us.'

'Augh,' he complains, eyes blazing.

Inside the cave the floor slopes back under the cliff and an initial narrowing turns to broaden into a sizeable cavern. Here the invisible taint of smoke is stronger. To our right, a tight passage twists from that cavern for a while before leading to a wedge-shaped chamber – high at one end and low at the other – that hooks back around, leaving me with a sense that we must have come full circle. Again, the smoke is stronger and now wisps the air with traces of grey. A cool breeze draws it in from the far end where a dimple of light betrays the presence of another exit.

There, a shadow moves.

Mardon puts a finger to his lips as we creep towards the glimmer. He waits until I draw level and together we turn the corner, blinking in the sudden light, to face whatever is on the other side: a grubby, scuffed-looking man in his twenties crouches by a fire in the cave's final cavern, a modest one that opens on to the sea, nothing but a hole in the cliff. The sound of waves crashing on rocks reaches us from far below. The others join us.

I take a wild guess. 'Ship hand Anders, I presume.'

He stands, neither confirming nor denying. 'Who are you?

What do you want with Anders?'

Anders – if that's truly who this is – is a handsome fellow, or at least, I imagine he would be if he washed and dressed in clean clothes. As it is, he carries the look of a beggar, albeit a beggar with confidence and a comfortable acceptance of the fact.

With a sudden bodily twist, Ebadiah slips from Josiah's grasp and nips across to join the man on the other side of the fire. The man grabs Ebadiah and takes a step perilously close to the edge of the cliff.

'Come any closer and the boy dies.' His pupils dart from the rocks below and back to us. 'I swear it!'

Ebadiah's face contorts with fear.

I believe Anders and I have no wish to see the lad perish, whatever his shortcomings.

'There's no need for that. We simply wish to talk to you about a pending court case. You're an important witness to the premeditated wrecking of the *Dollinger.*'

He narrows his eyes, keeping hold of the boy for surety. 'You mean to silence me.'

'No. Quite the opposite, in fact. We wish to amplify your voice on the matter. In short, we need your testimony – your testimony against one Jacob Bartimaeus Cullins.'

'Testify against Cullins? Now I *know* you're lying!'

'It's the truth!' Penney steps forward to emphasise. 'This is private investigator Michael Banyard. He has your best interests at heart. He's taken a case from a widow who Cullins defrauded. We think Cullins had the *Dollinger* wrecked, thereby murdering the crew. You may now be the sole survivor.'

'But surely Geofferson – '

'Has disappeared since we first questioned him,' I explain. 'And Cullins may be behind it.'

'Say what you will. I don't believe you. Cullins wants me dead. His man Moor tried to kill me once already. You're just the latest in a line of would-be assassins out for my blood.' He drags Ebadiah an inch closer to the edge and the boy yelps.

'All right!' I throw out my palms. 'You don't believe us and we understand why. We'll leave, but think about what we've said and, if you change your mind, come to Burrington Point Lighthouse tomorrow at noon. I'll be waiting for you, alone and unarmed.'

'I'll think about it. If you leave right now. All of you. Right now.' Anders nods towards the exit.

I bow my head solemnly. 'You have my word. We're leaving and shall disturb you no more.'

Mardon, Penney and Josiah turn away and, with a final glance at Anders, I follow them out. We find our way out and climb the steps and the sandy path back up towards the waiting carriage. The lamp has managed to stay alight and it can stay so, because the sun is setting and the coachman will need it soon anyway. He'll have spare oil, I hope. Before we reach the top of the path where it broadens and flattens out onto the clifftop, Mardon halts me with an arm across my chest.

'Wait. Something's bothering me.'

We stop.

'Oh. What?'

Penney almost walks into me. 'What's wrong? Will he kill the boy?'

'No. It's not that. Quite the opposite. I fear we've been duped.'

'Duped?' she asks. 'How?'

Mardon thinks. 'Does he really strike you as the sort who'd throw a young lad to his death?'

Penney looks at each of us in turn. 'Well, now you mention it...'

And I'm right behind Mardon. About three seconds behind each of his steps of logic. It's infuriating.

'Come. I believe young Ebadiah will be crossing our path before long.' Following Mardon's lead, we clamber off the path and up onto the rising dunes where, behind a bank, we hunker down to hide, spying through the tall tufts of dune grass at the track below. The very fact that we're all hiding and waiting is a silent admission that we're in agreement. The boy has tricked us.

I know it. Mardon and Penney know it. Even Josiah knows it.

The confirmation comes tramping up the path not ten minutes later, their words reaching us long before their faces.

'Leave it out.' Anders' voice. 'I told you. It's all right. You did your best. Anyway, it was my fault for lighting a fire. Should've waited till nightfall. No one goes poking around the caves after dark.'

Ebadiah. 'Yeah, well. I'm sorry. I tried. I didn't mean to actually lead them to you, I swears! It's just... well, I always wanted to be a detective, like. I thought – '

'I know. I know. Now let's hear no more of it.'

'You gonna meet the silker at the lighthouse?'

Presumably, I'm the silker in question.

'Maybe. Maybe not. Haven't decided. Do you trust 'em?'

'Don't know.'

'Me neither.'

'All right. You'd better go back in case someone's about up here.'

'Tomorrow night, then.'

'Aye.'

'And you won't forget the bread...'

'Course I won't. You's worse than my ol' ma!'

We can see them now, grinning at each other like brothers before Anders turns back for his cave. As he drops beyond view, Ebadiah draws level with us and I spring out to block his way while Josiah has the presence of mind to get in behind him. Hapless Ebadiah is trapped again. He takes a good look at our expressions, which range from outrage to mild surprise, before shrugging.

'Seeing as you lot's still here, you might as well give me a ride back to the yard.'

17

The Black Ledger

In which a story unfolds

23rd Twinemoon

It's a blustery day, out on the headland. Burrington Point is a highly exposed peninsular and a dreadful wind tears at my coat and hair as I cross the open ground leading to the lighthouse. Beyond it and below, the sea thrashes and froths, raking at the rockface in a merciless assault. My tricorn is gripped tightly in my hand to save it from flying to the horizon.

It's not raining. Rain would be worse. In fact, I enjoy the fresh lick of the wind on my skin and, up here, there's no stink of rotting crab and old nets but pleasant sea salt on the air. What I don't enjoy is the ensuing hour of waiting in the cold while Anders, presumably, warms himself by the fire in his cave. In short, he doesn't show. The blighter. Not while I linger in plain sight at the foot of the lighthouse, nor as I walk back to the road where my carriage awaits.

Oh, no. Only once I've climbed in and tapped the carriage ceiling with my stick and the horses have set off, does he venture out from the trees at the side of the road to call.

'Michael Banyard!'

Glancing out, I give the ceiling a double tap and the

164

coachman halts the horses awkwardly, jolting me in the process. They clop in protest. Anders hugs his tattered coat and watches me. It seems the coachman is not to be trusted.

Fine.

I disembark and walk to the wind-torn treeline where a loud conversation takes place over the roar of the gale. It goes like this.

'You've had me wait all this time. I do hope you'll make it worth my while by testifying in court.'

'So, you're legit, then? I had to be sure it wasn't a trap.'

We can barely hear each other's shouts.

'There's no trap, I assure you, but I understand. Can't be too careful when people are out to kill you.'

'Aye. 'Tis the truth.'

'Would you mind terribly if we were to find somewhere to talk out of this wind?'

The lighthouse keeper lets us shelter for two pennies and leaves us to talk as we head inside. Anders takes one last look behind before closing and latching the door, apparently satisfied that I am alone as promised – he seems to have forgiven me the coachman's presence – and the wind is at last confined to the outside.

'That's better.' Ahead, steps lead up and around the tower. We climb as there is nowhere else to go. Perhaps this is an apt meeting place. The high lamp chamber will provide an excellent view of the wreck site and the Eyes of Myrh, the two isles a league from Dockside. At the top we walk around the enormous lamp and gaze from the myriad windows at the raging billows below, the Eyes and the open ocean, now devoid of ships. The storm has driven them to harbour.

'You truly are not sent from Cullins or Moor? You do swear it?'

'I swear it. I would say it a thousand times if I thought that might convince you. Take a good hard look around. I have brought nobody with me, not even my business partner. I have risked my own safety to come here.' I open my arms, letting my coat hang loose. 'Here. Search me for weapons. You will find none, nor ropes, nor manacles, nor poison or sleeping draughts. I am not armed in any way.'

'All right.' His eyes burn into mine. 'I trust you.' He has a determined look about him.

'It's about time.'

'It still doesn't make me safe.'

'No. Indeed. That's an issue we must address.'

'Agreed.'

'You'll need safe haven until you testify in court. The case has yet to be registered, so there'll be a wait. Just as well, though. We'll need to build our argument, go over your account. Which I've yet to hear, by the way.' He begins to speak. 'No. Save it until my associates are listening or you'll have to say everything twice.'

His gaze settles on the rocks at Hatch Head. I don't know if the *Dollinger's* mast is protruding from the sea or not – it wouldn't be visible from this distance in any case – but that's where he's looking.

'You want me to accompany you back into Camdon. I'm afraid I can't oblige.'

'Oh?'

'It's too dangerous. I'll go to testify but that's it, so I'll give you my account here and now. Take it or leave it.'

'Very well.' I take out my notebook and pencil. 'Wait. Where will you stay? Surely not in the caves?'

'It's best if you don't know.'

'We can find you a safe house. We could –'

Glancing at the floor he shakes his head. 'Best leave the hiding to me, Master Banyard.'

'We could keep you safe if only you'd let us.'

'You'd have me holed up in a townhouse surrounded by Cullins' spies. He has many. More than you know.'

'We could hide you in another town. Take your pick.'

'I'm touched by your concern but, if it's all the same to you, I'll find my own sanctuary.'

'And if I need to contact you? I *will* need to inform you of the trial date, if nothing more.'

He thinks for a moment, looking back to the wreck. 'The lad will get a message to me. When you need to contact me, find the boy.'

'If you insist.' It's my turn to stare at the wreck site. 'We found a caged man, a skeleton, in a secret chamber in the bowels of the *Dollinger*. Do you know who he was or why he was there?'

'I know nothing of this man, yet it doesn't surprise me. On that galleon we all heard strange noises – sometimes voices from nowhere, odd and unaccountable cries. Such things are commonplace on Moor's ships. There was talk of ghosts.'

'Moor's ships?'

'Nickolas Moor runs the ships for Cullins, though the two are tighter than new-born twins. Nothing happens on those ships that Cullins doesn't sanction. If a man was caged in a secret chamber, it's because Cullins ordered it.'

'Do you know a man named Jonathon Barrows?' I make notes.

He shakes his head, no glimmer of recognition. 'No.' He begins to spill the details of his last voyage aboard the *Dollinger*. 'We set sail with the usual crew of luckless dogs, scoundrels to a man, except for Geofferson and me. A rough crew, you understand. With our cargo safely stowed, we voyaged to Urthia. There were fights and the expected cruelties our tyrannical Captain Solomon was known for: lashings, ropings and keel-haulings. Nothing unusual.

'But while docked at Morracib, a rumour surfaced. A dangerous one.' Anders pauses as though afraid to say more, even here, alone and as far from prying eyes and ears as we could be.

'What rumour?'

'One that was to seal the fate of the entire galleon. It was said a letter had been stolen from the second mate, a letter addressed to Cullins himself. The unfortunate ship hand, a lad named William, concealed the fact that it was him who took the letter, but old Solomon punished the crew in cruel ways hoping they'd give up the thief. The first day, the captain merely forbade us to disembark. He gathered the crew and marched up and down before us, demanding the letter's return and the voluntary surrender of the thief. When no one came forward – and who would? For we all knew the fate that awaited that man – things grew worse. The next day he had the crew systematically flogged. The same the following day and the next, only the floggings got harder each time. Of course, all the while the words of that stolen letter were circulating the ship. By day three, every jack 'n' cook knew of it.'

'So, it wasn't merely a rumour. It was true.'

'Oh, yeah. It was true, sure enough.'

'And the letter?'

'Was penned by a fool who thought he could blackmail Cullins. A fool who claimed he had proof Cullins was smuggling goods via secret compartments in his ships.'

'What kind of proof?'

'Whenever Moor uses the ships for smuggling, he enters the details in a black ledger, a closely guarded ledger that he keeps in a secret place.'

'It doesn't make sense. If it's illegal activity then why keep records at all? Surely that's just asking for trouble.'

'Ah. I said Cullins and Moor were tight. Not that they trust one another.'

'So Cullins has Moor account for the smuggled goods to be certain he's not being cheated.'

'Precisely. Everything is recorded so that, in the event of a discrepancy, Cullins can check Moor's dealings and prove he's being cheated. Well, that was the general idea, anyway. The black ledger was stolen and hidden before the voyage, but now the entire crew knew about it and the blackmail attempt. Solomon was in a deep quandary. He delayed the return voyage of the *Dollinger* for a week while he tortured the crew one after the other. Then, one morning, it all stopped. He had the ship loaded with barrels of fine wine, gunpowder and black soup beans and ordered us to set sail for home, but what we didn't know was he had sent word ahead on a faster ship that left before us. He had already reported back to Cullins. You've probably worked out the rest of it by now.'

'Cullins heard what was happening and took no chances. To silence them, he decided to murder the entire crew: captain, officers and all. Tell me about the false light set to drive you onto the rocks.'

'I saw the light and knew at once it was a ruse. Unfortunately, the bosun wouldn't listen. He shoved me aside and turned us to Hatch Head, thinking he was heading out to sea. That was when the ship broke upon the rocks.'

'And that was that.'

'Not quite. Moor had a surprise in store for those strong enough to fight themselves ashore. Those poor, half-drowned souls. He was waiting with his men, club in hand. I saw it happen. I clung to a floating barrel and waves bore me south to the far end of Lytche's Cove where I grasped the moorings of a fishing boat and clung tight. They never saw me or I'd have been murdered like the rest.'

We gather in the case room: Mardon, Penney, Josiah and me. I've also called the widow and Mother – her moral support – to attend, as the agenda has a marked bearing on the case. Although I try to keep the details of my work from Mother's ears, she's heard every morsel of this case from Widow Blewett. They sit opposite the door, close, glimmering with hope and anticipation. It must have been the way I smiled when I invited them.

I take my time relaying Anders' story, being sure to include every detail and render it accurately. The horrors of the *Dollinger*'s final voyage seem even uglier when voiced before gentle and refined women. Penney hides her face in her gloved hands at several points and by the time I'm done, a haunted look has fallen over her.

'Do you believe his tale? Is this the truth?' she asks.

169

'I believe it. I see no reason why Anders would lie, and his words had an honesty about them.'

'Then we've done it,' says Josiah. 'With Anders' testimony, the case is solved! It proves Cullins had his own ship wrecked, and what court would then reject the notion of him lynching the rest of his assets to claim the insurance?'

'It doesn't prove Cullins set the false light but it's pretty damning all the same,' adds Mardon. 'What judge could be presented with two and two and not make four?'

The moment has rather taken me by surprise. 'I believe you may be correct.'

The widow, who has remained silent until now, displays an expectant half-smile. 'Well done, Master Banyard. I knew you were the right man for the job. I knew you could do it.' And in that moment, I love that old woman, her fire and her crooked smile.

'So, you were right, by thunder!' Mardon directs this to me, banging the butt of his cane on the floor in celebration.

I hadn't thought about that but I do now. 'Yes. Yes, I was right.' Anders' account was more or less in line with my prior supposition, give or take a few details. I didn't know about the ledger, of course, but perhaps I'm not such a dreadful detective after all. I allow myself a glance at Penney as reward and from her depths she draws a smile, her face warming to meet me. I stand and the others follow suit. 'Black bean soup all round, I think, for it seems the time has come to take the industrious Mr Cullins to court! I can't thank you all enough for your diligent work.'

'You can keep your soup,' Mardon says, fetching a silver liquor flask from his inside pocket and raising it to the gathering. 'Congratulations!' He takes a long swig.

Penney plants a kiss on either side of my face and I steal a deeper look while she's close. A flicker of – is it contentment or mutual admiration? I can't fathom – passes between us before Josiah fills my view, lifting me from the ground in an almighty bear-hug that squeezes the breath from my body. The meeting has lost all sense of decorum and it's not until later, while the others talk and continue to congratulate one another over drinks, that Mardon approaches me, his face darkly sober.

'You do realise it's not over? In some ways it's only just begun.'

I take a moment. 'Yes. I know. We've a lot of work to do – a lot of preparation – and our case would be far stronger if we could locate the black ledger. Can you stay?'

The following few weeks rush by. The first thing I do is register the case against Cullins at the city courthouse. This has two direct results. Firstly, Cullins is served with a notice of intent to prosecute, so he now knows we're on to him and that we likely have evidence to support an accusation. Secondly, I feel a sudden and overwhelming pressure to order my argument and ready my case. Mardon has gone home to deal with his Loncaster surgery with a promise to return if he's needed and, meanwhile, Josiah, Penney and I have made little headway tracking down Moor's black ledger. Still, at some level I'm now determined to prove I can do this without my cousin's help. I need to find the black ledger myself or forever believe he's the better detective.

The date for the hearing does not appear until a third week has passed. Three things happen that day, the fourteenth of Elventide, three encounters that are worthy of note.

The first is the arrival of a letter to the Mysteries Solved office. Before I can stop her, Elizabeth opens it and reads aloud to Josiah and me.

'To Masters Banyard and Mingle, proprietors of Mysteries Solved. You are to attend the City of Camdon Courthouse on the seventeenth of Trimoon to present your case against industrialist and city entrepreneur Jacob Bartimaeus Cullins of Highbridge, Camdon, and Nickolas Moor of Dockside, Camdon. Failure to attend will result in the absolution and acquittal of any court action against the accused. In such an event, no further prosecution may be pursued.' She adds, 'It's signed by the Chief Justice and bears the city seal.'

'The seventeenth of Trimoon? That's three months away!' The news rattles me. How is the widow supposed to survive on nothing until then? How are *we* supposed to, for that matter? The Barrows case has dried up and I don't dare return to Mr Barrows for further payment, not when I've already exhausted all leads on his son's disappearance. Having questioned his entire family and friends and investigated everything, we are left with the unsatisfactory conclusion that the man in the cage probably was Jonathon.

'Perhaps we could request an earlier date,' says Josiah.

For once I'm in complete agreement with him. 'Yes! We must!' I have Elizabeth immediately take down a letter to the Chief Justice and deliver it myself to the courthouse.

The second encounter of note happens on my way back to the office. It's a fortunate coincidence that I spot young Ebadiah, looking dubious, on a corner of Market Street in Old Camdon. I spy from a shop corner. My quarry has yet to see me. Good. I'm hoping to give him a fright. He's watching a group of workers loading a cart with bread, fresh from the bakery. No doubt, he's planning a way to bag some for himself. I risk several steps closer before slipping up behind him and grabbing his earlobe.

'Awwah!'

'Quit complaining, Shoe Shine.' I drag him into the shadows at the edge of the street.

'Oh, it's the detective.' His eyes dart, seeking my associates and, seeing I'm alone, he appears to relax a little.

'A word, if I may.' I release his ear, instead holding his sleeve to deter him from running. 'Are you still in touch with our mutual friend?'

'You mean – '

'Don't say his name. You know who I mean.'

He nods. 'Yes. We're in touch.'

'Is he safe?'

'As safe as he may be.'

'Good. I need you to get a message to him as soon as possible. Tell him the court case is set for the seventeenth of Trimoon, though I'm hoping to have it brought forward.'

'The seventeenth of Trimoon. Right away, boss. Anything else?'

I study him momentarily. 'Yes. Do you know where my office is?'

'I do.'

'When you've delivered the message, meet me there if you still wish to be a detective.'

'But I thought… After what I did at the caves – '

'What you did at the caves was impressive. You fooled four grown adults, for a time, at least. You could be useful to me.'

He nods again.

'Now go, before someone sees us talking.'

He shoots off with purpose and I continue on my way but double back. I can't help myself. I want to know where Anders is hiding. For one thing, what if Ebadiah disappears or – heaven forbid – has an *accident*? How will I get a message to Anders then?

I shadow the boy through Old Camdon, full of admiration. He's cautious, careful not to head off straight for Anders in case he's followed, instead taking a route that hooks around. It's all I can do to keep track of him and I nearly lose him several times. First, we move north and then east, before finally turning south for Rook's Bridge and out, through Crowlands where the town dissipates around us as we enter countryside scattered with hamlets and villages. We pass fields of grass and stubble, where the occasional ancient burial mounds rise to dome the surface. Reminders of a long-forgotten past.

Miles from the city, he eventually slows his pace on the edge of Curlston Marsh, an inhospitable stretch of boggy ground beyond which, the land grows ever more arid until hitting the Borderlands and then Mors Zonam. Curlston Marsh is known as the last wet ground before oblivion.

There's an outcrop of stone ahead and this is where Ebadiah

stops.

He whistles. Three short blasts. A signal.

Sensing something is about to happen, I duck down, throwing my body low to the ground, staining my shirt with mud while hoping the tall grassy tufts around an isolated boulder will hide me.

Ebadiah appears not to notice. To his side, a rock moves as though of its own accord. It jiggles and shifts until falling over, and what was once a rocky knoll is revealed as a hollow cell. Anders' head fills the space left by the rock, followed by his shoulders and the rest of him. He and the boy greet each other and walk off towards the coast, too far in front for me to hear the conversation but I can take a fair stab at it. Ebadiah is delivering my message.

They walk for a while until they reach a clifftop overlooking the sandy beach and shallows of Halfer's Bay. Here Anders takes out a telescope and focuses down. From my position, I can't tell what he's looking at, but it's on the beach below. They talk and watch for a while and it's not until after they've moved off, back to the rock chamber on the edge of the marsh, that I venture to the cliff and see for myself. Below, a woman leads a child across the sand. The girl, little more than a toddler, has to reach high while the mother has to stoop. She does so willingly and the strong bond of love between them is visible, even from this distance. I don't need a telescope to see their beauty and the woman's extended shape. She's with child and only now do I comprehend who they are and the stakes for which Anders is playing.

18

The Third Encounter

In which Banyard has an unwelcome guest

The third encounter is waiting for me a short while later when I walk into the office. Of the three, the last is by far the worst. I see him through the windows, sitting in the visitor's chair, waiting for me like a hangman awaits the condemned. There's a second during which I consider turning away, for he has yet to see me and I feel distinctly unprepared for a fight. Jacob Cullins is a man of considerable stature both in the authority he wields in this city and in his physicality. At a guess, he's three times my age and probably twice my weight. I can't afford for this to get ugly. I squint at his face through the glass to assess the situation.

Mr Cullins is not a happy citizen. He glowers across the room, lost in his thoughts. They're wretched ones, I'm quite sure.

I enter, despite my impulse to run. This is a confrontation I cannot avoid.

Curiously unsettled, Elizabeth rises to gesture towards our visitor. 'Ah, Mr Banyard. Mr Cullins is here to see you.'

I drop my hat on the stand. 'Thank you, Elizabeth. Is Mr Mingle about, perchance?'

'I'm afraid he went out before our guest arrived.'

Wonderful.

'Very well.' Turning to him, I offer my hand. 'You must be Mr Cullins.'

Looking me up and down, he rises but declines the handshake. 'What was that you were wearing? A tricorn? How fashionable.'

I withdraw my hand. 'If you must know, it was my father's.'

'Your father was a snipe, just like you, Banyard. Always snivelling on about threaders' rights.'

'My father was a good man who cared about people. He was kind and generous.'

Cullins seems to have not heard me. 'He was weak. Pah! Threaders' rights? Threaders don't have rights. They shouldn't have rights. That's the way it's meant to be. We're silkers, by thunder, and we should act like silkers. These low-brained threaders need keeping in place!' He concludes his tirade with the silker creed. 'The threaders thread the silk. The silkers wear the silk.' There follows a stunned silence and there's hate in his glare. It bears down upon me, oppressively. 'So, *you* are Michael Banyard. I might have guessed as much.'

'Why, whatever do you mean, sir?'

He huffs and grunts. 'You're the jumped-up scoundrel who's taking me to court.' He's on the balls of his feet and a redness rises to the skin beneath his bulging eyes.

'I *am* taking you to court, sir, though I'm no scoundrel. I think you'll find I'm a very reasonable and well-adjusted fellow – '

'I don't care what you think you are! You will abandon this case immediately or suffer the consequences. Do you hear?'

I think, *Has he recognised me from my disguised visit?* I can't be sure. 'My apologies but that would be counterproductive.'

'Rescind now, or I'll see you regret it, I swear!'

'Elizabeth, please note the details of this conversation and record anything further that passes from our honourable guest's lips. I'm sure the court will be fascinated to hear every threat and fear-mongering word. Oh, and do be sure to date the document. We must present a thorough and orderly account along with the rest of our considerable evidence.'

'Very well, Mr Banyard.' Elizabeth rushes to find a new sheet of paper and dips a quill to scribble frantically while the air is still loaded with words.

'Evidence? Why you...' Cullins lowers his brow like an aurochs about to charge.

'Yes? Did you wish to add something more?' All this time I've been watching his hands, for the cocked flintlock on his belt hasn't escaped my notice. Now, the sound of Elizabeth's quill scratching across the page behind me stops, as Cullins reaches for his gun.

'I wouldn't do that if I were you,' she says. Cullins becomes statue-like as though frozen in time. I turn to see Elizabeth brandishing a small snub-nosed pistol. I have no idea where she's had that hidden, but it's trained upon Cullins' broad chest.

He grunts again. 'Never mind.' He leaves his flintlock, instead grimacing and heading for the door while Elizabeth tracks him with her gun. 'I'm sending someone over to take a statement from the widow. Be sure to have her here in one hour's time.'

When he's gone, Elizabeth locks the door. 'He was nice.'

I collapse into the visitor's chair, exhale a long breath and mutter. 'Yes, charming. Where's Josiah when you need him?'

A revelation strikes me like a rock between the eyes: Elizabeth is a trooper. My fears of her betrayal with Cullins and Moor dispel and the realisation dawns: I've done her a great disservice. As she tucks her pistol discreetly back into the secluded holster on her thigh it's time to confess. 'Lizzy, I've judged you poorly. Can you ever forgive me?'

'I'm not sure what you're talking about.' She meets my gaze with a blank, slightly frustrated look and, now that Cullins has gone, colour gradually returns to her face.

'Josiah and I saw you conversing with Nickolas Moor across the street. I thought you may be in league with them.'

'I talked with Nickolas Moor? Really? When?'

'Three weeks ago. It was definitely him.'

'Oh dear. I'm afraid I don't know what he looks like. I don't know him at all. If I did speak with him, I was not aware it *was* him. I do talk with a lot of men, because a lot of men – '

'Yes, of course! You *are* rather pretty.' For this I receive a glare. I make a hasty retreat. 'By which I mean, you are rather wonderful.' *Pretty? What was I thinking? What kind of a compliment is that to offer the woman who's just saved your life? It's not appropriate in the slightest. I should be thanking her profusely and upping her pay.* 'Thank you, by the way, for what you just did. You rather saved me. I really must wear my pistols. Tell me, would you have truly shot him?'

Stupid question. The look says it all.

Ebadiah arrives soon after, clutching his cap to his chest. He slows, taking in the reception room and Elizabeth behind the desk, and I usher him through to the case room where Josiah sits chewing on an aurochs sandwich.

'You got an easy life, ain't ya?' Ebadiah says, looking around.

I sweep Josiah's feet from the desk and snatch the penny dreadful (the one about the man-eating monster from the Borderlands) from his hands. 'Straighten up, Joe. We have to set a good example to our young detective in training.'

'He's joining us, then.'

'We're going to give him a trial period. What do you say?' I aim this at Ebadiah.

'I'm listening but I needs the terms and conditionals.'

Josiah laughs. 'Terms and conditionals? Exactly where do you think you are, Shoe Shine?'

'Don't matter. There's always terms and conditionals, even on the street.'

'And that's exactly where I want you,' I say. 'To begin with, at least. No one must notice anything different about you. You are to keep the job a secret. Can you do that?'

'You wants me to spy.'

'Exactly.'

'I got ya. How much?'

'How about we pay you for information received, piecemeal? You bring us useful knowledge from the street and we'll pay accordingly. Much more than that and you won't be able to keep up the pretence of your other jobs. Does that sound reasonable?'

'I suppose. It's a start,' says Ebadiah.

'Precisely! It's a start. We all have to start somewhere, don't we, Joe?'

'Indeed, we do, Mr Banyard. Indeed, we do.'

Pressing the tips of my fingers together, I think about the best way to engage Ebadiah's services. 'The first task is for you to help us track down a certain ledger. It may be perilous work, mind. Under no circumstance must you take any unnecessary risks.'

'I get it.' Ebadiah nods.

'Good. A certain black ledger has been stolen from Nickolas Moor. I want you to find out who has it and where it's hidden. Can you do that?'

'I'll give it a go, though Moor ain't no pushover.'

'He's a dangerous man. You are to stay well clear of him. Listen, I'll tell you what we know.' I go on to recount the story of Anders' voyage on the doomed galleon and the theft of the black ledger.

When I've finished, Ebadiah is speechless for a moment and then he says, 'You really do trust me, then. You're trusting me with all this information.'

'We're trusting you with our lives, Ebadiah. This information is top secret. When it gets out, men die, so it's imperative you keep it to yourself.'

Josiah leans forward and tilts his head at Ebadiah. 'Make him swear.'

Ebadiah looks at us, one after the other. 'I swears on my life. I won't tell a soul.'

'Very well. I suggest you begin by looking into every man on this list.' I present a comprehensive list of the *Dollinger's* hapless crew. 'No one's talking to us silkers since Cullins learned of the court case, but they may be a little freer with their tongues around you.'

Ebadiah visits us regularly after that, always with a progress report on his attempts to track down the ledger, going through the names on the list, each in turn, and delving into the history of every dead mariner as thoroughly as he can. He never mentions Anders, but I can tell he's consulted him from time to time, hoping to learn something of the fateful voyage, the *Dollinger* crew or the location of the black ledger.

Of the twenty-four crew, not including the officers, he's found five who were pretty much labelled cowards. The officers and these five, he suggests, are unlikely to have ever attempted theft from Moor. Removing the two good men, Anders and Geofferson, and excluding others for a variety of reasons, we are left with only six suspects remaining. It's these six dubious fellows – either drowned or clubbed – that he's been investigating. Today he reports.

'Of those six crewmen, three were proper rogues, by all accounts.'

'Their names?' I ask. Lizzy prepares to take notes (I've taken to calling her Lizzy since the incident with her pistol).

'Balroy, Flinders and Knight. I think it was one of them what did it. One of them or all three.'

'Were they known to work together?' I ask.

'Now and again. Knight was their ringleader.'

'This is fine progress, Shoe Shine. Very fine. We'll need their last known addresses. Perhaps the ledger is hidden in a cellar or a loft.'

Ebadiah drags a crumpled note from his pocket, straightens and presents it. Taking it, I see three names and addresses pencilled in Ebadiah's erratic hand. The spelling is mostly questionable but it's readable and that's good enough.

Ebadiah takes his payment with a tip of his cap and leaves.

I dictate a letter.

Dear Mardon,
Following some interesting developments, we are a step closer
to our goal. We need you. Please come at once.
Your cousin,
Michael Banyard

While Lizzy takes the letter to the post office, Josiah and I drink black bean soup.

Josiah gazes into his cup. 'It's all very well us having three addresses, but there will be people living there, families and the like. They could have hounds. How are we going to search for the ledger?'

'Hmmm. Only the Drakers have the power to kick people out of their own homes to search and seize. I don't suppose old Bretling would stretch that far for us.'

'Not a hope.'

'Perhaps Mardon will think of something.'

For some moments, Josiah is lost in thought, but then he animates. He has that look again, the one he gets when that dreaded spark of inspiration hits his brain. 'Wait, Mr Banyard.' And here it comes. 'I do believe I have a most excellent idea!'

I'm not holding my breath. The last excellent idea of his could have killed the Harbour Master. I shake my head. 'All right. Let's have it.'

'Well, it's obvious, really. If we need to have the powers of the Drakers, we've got to *become* Drakers.'

'As I thought. Preposterous.'

'Hear me out, Mr Banyard. What if we disguise ourselves as Drakers – all we'd need is a couple of uniforms – and raid those three houses, one after the other. Quick, like.'

Once again, Josiah has me considering one of his ridiculous plans. 'How would we source the uniforms?'

'You leave that to me and Shoe Shine. We'll sort it.'

'If we were to do this, we'd need fool-proof disguises. I mean *fool-proof.*'

'Indeed, but you can do that. Just look what you did with

Cullins. He never suspected a thing, not even when he saw you here, face to face.'

I'm not actually sure that's true but he didn't mention anything.

'I don't know, Joe. Any number of things could go wrong. The real Drakers could show up while we're in the middle of a raid. Someone could report us and then where would we be?'

'We'd be long gone by the time any real Drakers could arrive. We'd have vanished on the wind, disguises gone, the uniforms ditched.'

I'm desperately trying to think of all the other things that could go wrong. There must be many but I'm coming up empty, and that's when I realise. He's right. 'We'll do it.'

His head spins to me. 'What?'

'I said, we'll do it.'

His mouth gapes open. 'That's what I thought you said.'

19

Uniforms, Drakers and Thugs

In which Jinkers dances and uniforms are procured

Josiah can't believe his luck. He's up and out of the office like a hound on the scent, no doubt tracking Ebadiah down, hoping to put phase one of his *excellent* idea into action.

He returns with a worryingly satisfied grin on his face and I don't even ask. I only wait. It's just as well I sent for Mardon if we're to perform these raids. The more of us, the better. I'm having grievous doubts already.

Very little happens for a day or two but then, late one afternoon, Ebadiah shows up hauling a sack on his shoulder. Without a word, he marches in and tips the contents over Lizzy's desk. Draker uniforms fill the space and several black hardhats and batons roll to the floor. Drakers don't carry guns, not the honest ones, anyway. The weapon of choice, the one with which it is deemed suitable to enforce order upon our twisted society, is the club, affectionately known as the baton. As if a more refined name lessens the damage... What nonsense. It's a club and everyone knows it.

'Three Draker uniforms, as ordered,' Ebadiah announces.

I rush to retrieve the hats and collect up the clothes. 'Are you insane? Hide them, now!' I glance out of the shop windows to see if any passers-by have noticed. The others jump to help and

183

soon the uniforms are safely back in the sack.

Josiah ruffles Ebadiah's hair. 'Well done, Shoe Shine.' He's like a proud father.

Ebadiah is pink in the face. 'Yeah, well. Sorry about the – '

'Not to worry,' I smooth things over. 'No harm done but we must be more careful in future. No more slip-ups. No one must know we even have these, especially not Lizzy. You know what a stickler for the law she is.' Lizzy is out right now, thankfully. A horrible thought occurs to me. 'They can't be traced back to you, can they?'

He shakes his head. 'Naugh. Not a chance. It were too dark for – '

'Stop right there. I don't want to know. Joe, please put the sack in the case room.'

He takes the sack with a look that says, *Why can't you do it?* He seems restless. 'So, when's the first raid?'

Fishing in my jacket pocket I take out a letter, unfold and pass it. 'Tonight, and not a moment too soon.'

He reads. The letter is from the Justice and tells of the new court date. We have but one day to prepare for battle, and the day of the trial also happens to fall upon the same day that the cremated bones of Great King Doon are to be transferred to Yorkson's Bank. That could scupper my plans.

We make a start without Mardon as there isn't time to wait for him. The first raid begins with promise. It's later that afternoon and already growing dark when we arrive to stake out Knight's house – a run-down hovel in Dockside – only to find it empty.

'That's good, isn't it?' asks Josiah.

'Yes. Excellent. Let's hope they're all like this.'

I've sent Penney home as I don't want her caught up in any dubious activity – her father would kill me – and Ebadiah is watching for Drakers at the busy end of the street. His job is to sprint the distance between, to warn us if any head this way.

With the occupants elsewhere, we have the house to ourselves, but it does mean breaking in. Just as well I'm a dab hand with locks. We're dressed as Drakers and heavily disguised anyway, so if someone spots us, they'll hopefully think we're on legitimate business. Josiah's uniform is too small for him and this is a concern. He's bulging all over the place, threatening to split the seams.

Once inside, he closes the door and we both peer from the windows at the empty street.

So far, so good.

We search, Josiah taking the upper floor while I systematically go through everything downstairs. I riffle through drawers, chests and bric-a-brac but find nothing of interest. In the second room, there's a tall bookcase with a broken shelf. I pay the whole thing special attention, checking each book in turn to be sure it is not the black ledger. I even pull out the larger books and open them, in case the thief had the mind to hide the ledger inside one of them. He hasn't, not if this was his house, and he also has appalling taste in literature. *Tom Rotlings and the Fight for Savington*, what an awfully dreary book!

The search goes on. We check everywhere, pulling up floorboards and emptying a coal bin. By the time Josiah clomps back down the dusty stairs, there's only the backyard left unchecked. I suppose I'm hoping for a secret underground chamber or at least an outbuilding with a false floor. No such luck. Knight was surely a man of limited imagination. The yard is small, made of compacted dirt and populated by the remains of a solitary stone-ringed fireplace.

'We should check the ground in case he buried it,' says Josiah.

'Good idea.' We search for recently disturbed soil. I also pace the low stone wall, looking for any hiding places.

Nothing.

The ledger is not here.

I check my pocket watch. It's getting late so we leave, empty-handed, tired and hungry. We sneak into the office through the back lane and change back into our own clothes. I think, wouldn't Jinkers have a field day if only he knew what we get up to. As though summoned by my thoughts, he catches us later as we arrive home.

'You've been slithering here and there, I see.'

'I honestly do not know what you're talking about,' I say.

'Oh, I think you do.'

Is he psychic all of a sudden? 'What do you mean?'

Josiah trudges past, in no mood for Jinkers' nonsense.

'Good evening, Josiah,' says Jinkers.

'Is it?' asks Josiah over his shoulder. He seems genuinely peeved that we didn't find the ledger.

Jinkers returns his attention to me. 'I've seen you, coming and going. You're up to something, aren't you? Something secret.'

I almost breathe a sigh of relief. All he wants is to know what we're doing. He can't deal with the fact that others know things he doesn't. 'We're private detectives, Jinkers. *Most* of our work is secret.'

'Hmmm. Well, it can't be good – that's all I'm saying – or else why would it all need to be secrets?' As he speaks, a small dark shape darts in the air above us. He tracks it before losing it against the darkling sky. It prompts him to touch his shoulders in turn with the first two fingers of his left hand. This is the godly sign. He then steps from foot to foot, a repeated motion that swells until it's a dance as he turns about on the spot.

'What *are* you doing?'

He continues to swirl and step. 'It's the seven steps, Banyard. You must dance the seven steps at Elventide or you'll have the gawpers down on you! Didn't you know?'

'I didn't, as it happens.' I think, *He's beyond saving.* 'Goodnight, Jinkers.'

He's indignant. 'Goodnight, indeed!'

The next morning I buckle on my rapier and belt up my flintlocks, one hanging either side of my hips. They're heavy and cumbersome, but if I'm to defend myself against the likes of Cullins and Moor they're necessary. I sit alone in the case room, armed and dangerous, not a threat in sight. Feeling ridiculous. My hat observes me from the end of the desk where I tossed it. It calls to me. 'Violence is never the way, Micky.'

'What would you have me do? These people, they're unworkable.'

'Do you think I didn't see that for myself?'

'Did you never wear guns, stand up for yourself?'

'Guns were never my way. What will you do? Become a murderer to save yourself? There'll be nothing left worth saving.'

'It's not murder if it's self-defence.'

'It's still killing, son.'

I ditch the gun belt, letting it clatter onto the desk, but keep the rapier. 'Happy now?' I'm sure the hat would nod if it could, but it can't. It just sits there as Josiah enters with cups of black bean soup. I sip, eye the pistols and think.

Josiah also glances pensively at them. 'Not wearing your guns, Mr Banyard?'

I spend several hours pawing over my case notes. I've had a vague plan of attack for a week or so, but that won't win us the case. I need facts and figures, details, all laid bare in chronological order. I could use another week but by the time Penney arrives, around midday, there's enough prepared to give her the general idea.

'Of course,' she says when we're done combing through it. 'It would all swing more weight if we actually had the ledger.'

'No luck there, I'm afraid.'

She doesn't know we're breaking the law and raiding properties as Drakers. I'm pretty sure she wouldn't approve. She doesn't know about Josiah's previous life as a threader, though I've occasionally caught her regarding him quizzically, and she must surely have noticed my constant corrections. I wonder. Whether she suspects something or not, she's never said a word. She's also unaware that, before the *Dollinger* wreck, I spent my last guinea buying false papers for another threader in dire need of a new life. With the silker papers tucked in her pocket and an expensive wardrobe of silks, Annabel Stafford set off for Rochington to meet my contact there. She's one of a growing list, and I will worry about her until a letter arrives telling me all's well.

The next in my sights is that poor girl from the butchers, Jemima. I call there later that day to get my head out of the widow's case for a few minutes and to see how she fares. She's not in the shop when I arrive. Maddox is also out but the butcher points to the passage behind the counter.

'You'll find her out back, burning the sweepings.'

'Thank you.'

The corridor leads to a courtyard with an open fire burning at its centre. With her back to me, Jemima tends the fire, adding more sweepings, which appear to be blood-soaked sawdust and bits of mouldering pig and aurochs' sinew and bone.

'I thought the rag 'n' bone man took this stuff.'

She jumps at my voice. 'Oh! Master Banyard. He does, but sometimes it stinks so bad Master Maddox has us burn it before he gets here. The bone man only comes once a week.'

Around the flames lays a scatter of charred bone fragments among the ash.

We both look around. We're alone. It's an opportunity I've been waiting for. I lower my voice. 'Did you buy that new dress?'

'I did. Thank you.'

'No problems, I hope.'

'No problems, except it hasn't stopped Master Maddox...'

'Listen, I have a friend in Loncaster. I'm going to see if he can take you on, get you out of this place. I plan to have new papers made for you, set you up in a new position.'

Jemima's face contorts with fear. 'I won't leave Master Maddox. It's a hanging offence.' She studies my face, eyes wide.

'I'm not testing you, Jemima. This is no trick.'

'You mean it? You really mean you'll get me out?'

'Yes.'

'Why? Why would you risk everything for a threader?'

'Because the system is all wrong. Because you are worth every bit as much as I or Maddox. Because it's not fair or just.'

Her expression of dread softens into hope and she makes the sacred sign. 'Then do it!' she hisses through her teeth. 'Do it as soon as you can.'

For the briefest of moments, I glimpse the sheer desperation she hides inside, like a fragile bird through a curtain of bars. 'I will,' I promise. 'You'll need a new name, a new history, but we can deal with the details later. I'll have your papers drawn up. Do you have any brands?'

She shakes her head as hope topples back into the present, tumbles into sorrow. 'Master Maddox prefers to inflict his punishments in a more... personal way. The scars he leaves will be seen by none other than him.'

I hurry back to the office, where Mardon arrives with the usual style, his Double Heart polished and purring. He offers Penney a ride and, to my annoyance, she accepts. That's the last I see of them for the next hour but, when they return, I manage to get Mardon alone.

'We need your help, raiding houses.' I explain everything he's missed since he left. 'It's urgent.'

'You really are asking for trouble, Micky,' he says. 'Why can't you ever take the easy way?'

'I must have been absent from class the day they taught that.'

'Huh,' he grunts. 'By thunder, you'll get us all locked up, or worse.'

'You'll help, then?'

'I suppose.' He takes a swig from his flask and lights his pipe.

'Good. Be careful you don't self-combust.' I nod towards his pipe and flask and check my watch. 'We leave in an hour. There's a uniform for you in the case room, along with a toupee and false moustache. Don't let the girls see you.'

He looks at me sideways. 'Is it too late to change my mind?'

I'm more nervous this time. The longer we do this, the deeper the fear of getting caught burrows into my mind. Josiah stands with us at the front door of what used to be Balroy's terrace house, hammering with his fist. The make-up I've applied makes us all appear ten or twenty years older than we are.

'Open up,' I repeat. 'It's the Drakers.'

Shortly, the door opens a crack and an old woman's face fills the space.

'What is it?'

Swallowing the temptation to ask *What is what?* I reply. 'I'm sorry to disturb you, madam, but we've received reports of unlawful behaviour in the area and we're conducting random searches, just to be sure, you understand. You and the other occupants will have to vacate the property for the duration of the search. Shouldn't take too long.'

She retreats, bellowing into the house in a thick Dockside accent. 'Harold, those rogues the Drakers are 'ere again. We 'ave to get out.'

We stand back to allow the entire family to leave and they file grudgingly past to gather outside; it's surprising just how many there are. With three of us searching, the job is considerably quicker, which is good, because among the family are several brutes who look like they'd snap our necks at the first chance. I see them through the window, watching, waiting, pacing like captive animals. They hate the Drakers. That much is clear.

We each take different rooms and scour the place, ending once more in the backyard, a rough patch of ground where they've made a poor attempt to grow vegetables. The soil is black and grimy. Probably poisoned by toxins from Dockside industry – oil and the like. At the end of the walled yard, a tall iron gate is chained shut.

Again, the ledger is not here but, when we turn back to the house, a Draker is.

A real Draker.

Standing in the doorway.

With thugs one to three backing him up.

'So, this is a Draker raid, is it?' he asks.

I take the lead as Mardon and Josiah exchange glances. 'Yes, indeed. This is a Draker raid. We're from Division Six. Secret business. You probably won't have heard about it at Dockside HQ.' I smile confidently, almost convinced myself.

'Well, you're right, there. We've heard of no such raid. Division Six, you say?'

'Yes, a new operation. So, if you'd be so kind as to vacate the property, we'll finish our business and be on our way.'

'They ain't no Drakers,' says the bald brute on the right.

Now they empty into the yard to oppose us. We're outnumbered and although Josiah is probably the strongest man here, the three behind the Draker are all weighty. I don't fancy our chances in a fist fight so I draw my Draker baton and level it at the officer. 'Call these men off and leave, or your name will find its way into my report. What is your name, incidentally?'

'You'll not have my name,' says the Draker, drawing his baton. 'Get 'em, boys!'

Blows reign from both sides as the yard fills with thrashing limbs, batons, cries and shouts. The Draker's fist finds my ribs with an impact that steals my breath. Josiah does the fighting of two men and lays one of his combatants out cold with an unstoppable uppercut to the chin. He lifts another clean off the ground to throw him through a window, back into the house, where the man lands with a crunch and moves no more as shattered glass and splintered wood rain. The others gather in the doorway, watching us to reassess their odds. Outmatched in men and weaponry, they retreat.

We're bedraggled, our disguises falling apart. Mardon's moustache is dangling from one side of his lip and Josiah's Draker coat has a large tear in the seam of one arm and another in the shoulder. Our make-up is mostly smudged or gone.

'Quickly, Joe. The gate!' I point to the iron that blocks our escape. It's solid yet a good stamp from one of Josiah's boots sends it flying with a crash and we flee, empty-handed, bruised, but alive.

20

The Smiling Judge

In which Josiah finds trouble

Daylight is ebbing away and, with it, our chances of finding the ledger. I'm edgy. More so than any other time I can recall. 'Where's Mardon?'

'Buying spirits and tobacco. Said he needed a drink. Back soon. Still no sign of Ebadiah.'

'He probably ran when the Draker showed up.'

'He was supposed to warn us.'

'Who knows? We'd best get ready. Repair our disguises. Do you want the moustache or the beard this time?'

Ebadiah finds us in the street.

'Some watchman you are!' says Josiah.

'I tried to warn you when the Draker came but the family wouldn't let me through. By the time I ran around to the back of the terrace, you'd gone.'

'Never mind, Shoe Shine,' I say. 'At least you tried.'

Mardon returns, puffing on a fresh pinch of tobacco. It's our last chance to find the ledger. There's one more house on our list of likely suspects and our court hearing will open, ready or not, at the stroke of nine tomorrow morning. I can focus on little else, my mind consumed with arguments, facts and figures, and preparation, but I have this one last task that must be done first.

Flinders' house is the largest of the three, though the most dilapidated. Tall and narrow, it leans, three storeys high, between ramshackle properties in the roughest end of Dockside.

It appears empty as we approach.

'Perhaps they're all at work,' says Josiah, when my knocking raises no answer. He nods to Ebadiah – now watching further down the street – and we skirt around to the back.

The house is wooden-framed, the gaps between timbers cobbed and whitewashed. I attempt to pick the lock of the back door.

'There's a pane missing, up there.' Mardon points to a window on the second floor, ten feet above our heads. There's no ladder.

'All very well, but unless you've recently learned to fly...'

I'm not getting anywhere with the lock. I look to Josiah but he's left my side to snoop around at the back of the yard. He returns, a rusty old pickaxe hanging from one hand, and walks right past.

'Wait a minute, Joe. What are you –'

Ignoring me, he swings the pick, thwacking it with great force into the cob wall to the side of the door.

I retreat. 'Joe, stop! You'll –'

Thwack! Again.

Thwack, thwack! The strikes dig into the wall and each one sounds like a cannon. With the final blow, the one remaining seam on Josiah's uniform rends.

Thwack!

He drags the pick back, tearing away part of the wall with it, to leave a head-sized hole. 'Sorry, Mr Banyard. Thought you wanted to get inside.'

'Yes, but... Never mind. You've done it, now.'

He dumps the pick, reaches into the hole and, a moment later, there's a click and the door swings open. 'After you, Mr Banyard.'

'Really, Joe, you give a whole new meaning to the term *breaking and entering.*' I step into the kitchen, now convinced there is no one in the house. Josiah's din would have raised a corpse. The others follow. 'All right, you know the drill.'

We search.

The interior is gloomy and we haven't brought lamps, so that's the first thing we look for. Mardon finds a couple in a cupboard and lights them, pausing, then, to refill and light his pipe, which irritates me to the extreme.

It seems there are no more lamps to hand so I make do with a candle in a brass holder, padding around by its yellow flickering glow. With each step the floorboards creak. The entire place is cold, dusty and worn out. Shelves are crooked and the furniture wonky and in a bad state of repair. The few surviving drapes are threadbare, moth-eaten and faded.

Mardon has vanished deeper into the house. I've lost track of him so I nod towards the stairs and Josiah obliges. He ascends, the steps groaning with each tread until, halfway up, one splinters beneath his weight as his foot goes right through the rotten wood. While he curses and continues upwards, I finish in the kitchen and move on to a room mostly occupied by a table and a scatter of mismatched chairs. I'm not overly concerned about searching the obvious places. No one would ever hide a secret ledger in the open. It's unlikely to be in the cupboards, nor on shelves, nor in a chest. No, if the ledger is here at all, it is surely in a special place: a covert compartment, behind a hidden door or beneath the false bottom of a drawer. I check everything anyway, even opening the few old books to be certain nothing is concealed as before.

Out of the three houses we've raided, this one's the most interesting. It has weird primeval-looking paintings on the walls, all hanging crookedly, and a plethora of strange artefacts collected from foreign lands: Flinders' voyages, perhaps. Several primitive sculptures stand guard in the corners and either side of the fireplace. Wooden masks portraying hideously distorted faces, painted in gaudy colours, line the dining room walls. I check behind everything and knock on the walls, listening for a hollow response that never comes.

There's no sign of Mardon, but Josiah's feet clomp clearly on the boards overhead. His footsteps distance as he explores the far side of the house. A moment later, a shout from above startles me and, dashing from the dining room, I run for the stairs to leap up, four at a time, as my candle flutters out.

'Mardon? Joe?'

No reply, except somewhere, startled voices echo. I recognise one of the voices as Josiah's. The other is unknown to me. I reach the top of the staircase and, following the sounds, head for a door, but before I can enter the room, two loud blasts shock the air. For a second I fear Josiah has been shot. There's no time to wonder by whom because a loud crashing noise follows, quickly followed by another from the ground floor.

In the gloom, I rush through the door to find a decrepit old man in a nightshirt and nightcap, frantically reloading a pistol. Beyond him, dust rises from a gaping hole in the floorboards as he shouts. 'I thought I told you lot the first time. We ain't got nothin' of yours!'

I rush to close the door. So much for the house being empty. This old boy must be quite deaf to have slept through Josiah's explosive break-in. Deaf or drunk. Perhaps both.

I tear down the stairs as the man shoots lead at me through the door. Below, firelight bounds from the walls and, reaching the lower landing, I pause in an open doorway. Inside, Josiah lays unmoving as fire from his broken lamp licks up the tinder-dry drapes. Oil spills across the floor, blazing as it spreads.

'Joe, wake up!' I run to him and try to drag him from the hole. It's no good. He's too heavy.

Mardon arrives in the doorway. 'What are you doing, Micky?'

'Don't stand there gawping. Help me!'

The fire spreads quickly, the room filling with smoke. It pools overhead and streams out of the door seeking higher realms. The old man flees past the open door, not stopping to inflict further injury.

Pulling together, we drag Josiah free of the splinters and it's my plan to keep going until we're all outside of the doomed building, but glancing back to the broken boards where he landed, I'm compelled to return as, all around, the house blazes.

A minute later, we gather across the street, gasping the blessedly cool clear air of the night, watching the inferno swell. Beneath my arm I clasp a package wrapped in an oilskin.

29th Elventide

On the courthouse steps, I catch a street boy by the sleeve and press a letter into his hand.

'I'd be much obliged if you would run this to the Draker City Headquarters in Tower End. It's most urgent and must be delivered into the hand of Lord Bretling Draker, no other. Do you understand?'

He nods and accepts two coins before taking to his heels. We enter the courthouse and proceedings swiftly begin.

Where is Anders? Perhaps Ebadiah has been delayed and prevented from delivering the message. There's no other option but to string out my presentation of the case for as long as it takes. I have a feeling we'll lose if he doesn't show, with or without the ledger.

On our bench, Mardon sits to my left, Josiah to my right and beyond him, the widow. Across the room, our opponents also sit facing the three judges and the stand. The jurors occupy benches that ascend at our sides.

The empty space at the end of our bench watches me with anticipation as Josiah leans close to whisper. 'Where on Earthoria *is* he?'

'On his way, let us hope.' Hearings are usually short affairs lasting, at the most, two hours. I've no reason to think this one will be any different.

The trial opens with the clerk reading the charge. 'Announcing the first case of the day. Jacob Bartimaeus Cullins of Highbridge, aided and abetted by one Nickolas Moor of

Dockside, stands accused of embezzlement to the costs of six thousand guineas and insurance fraud of an unspecified amount.'

Shock ripples through the courtroom. It's to be expected but is a bad sign, all the same. Taking a man of Cullins' social standing to court is almost a direct challenge to authority, and that's the reaction before they know the true depths of our accusations. I allow myself a secretive smile. This case is ground-breaking. It may enter the annals of history.

For now, it's enough to know they're about to learn the acting prosecutor, that's me, is representing a threader.

Judge Marshall, bespectacled, round-nosed and pot-bellied, peers out from his throne-like seat. 'And who is accusing this upstanding gentleman, this worthy pillar of society, of wrongdoing?'

No bias there, then. He's quite famed for his speedy and crushing sentences, which doesn't bode well when he's clearly in favour of Cullins.

My turn to speak. I stand and clear my throat to address the magistrate. 'Michael Banyard, Your Honour, representing my client, Koslyne Blewett.' I motion to the widow.

Judge Marshall has notes in front of him on the bar. I imagine our case and some scanty details of it are among them as he peers from them to the widow and back again. 'Mr Banyard, perhaps I'm wrong, but it does in fact appear that your client is… a threader!'

Howls of outrage and mocking laughter encircle us and it feels as though we are sheep, hemmed in by wolves.

The judge's smile expresses amused abandonment. He's clearly pleased with the reaction. We are doomed. He has already decided our case is a joke. What follows for him will be a welcome frivolity to liven up an otherwise dreary day.

And nothing more.

Despite the smile, his eyes are as cold and unyielding as iron.

Swallowing hard, I take one last glance at my notes before launching into my argument.

'Your Honour, Your Graces and members of the jury, it is my solemn intent to present to you today undeniable evidence proving Mr Cullins, previously of Golden Shores Imports, has committed gross embezzlement and fraud to the detriment of my client. Not only that, but that he has instigated the murder of numerous merchant sailors in his employ, in the calculated wrecking of the *Dollinger* galleon – a wrecking that occurred on the twelfth night of Honourmoon, in the waters off Hatch Head.' The ensuing gasps force me to pause. 'That he – '

'Just one moment, Mr Banyard. You cannot prosecute for these ridiculous accusations all at once. Kindly restrict your argument to aspects pertinent to the case in hand.'

'Quite, Your Honour. We have called the case for embezzlement and fraud, yet I will explain in due course how evidence of these other crimes supports our case. If justice is to be served, this trial will likely spawn several more. To fully comprehend this, the jury must first understand that the wrecking of the *Dollinger* was only the first of seven apparent disasters that brought Golden Shores Imports to ruin. It is my intent to prove these misfortunes were in fact created by Cullins' own hand and that, in purposefully bankrupting his own company, he has stolen the widow's investment.' I look to the door but Anders is not there.

The judge weighs me, leaden-eyed, and glances with subtle concern to Cullins who, along with Moor, has not ceased glaring at me since I entered the room.

One of the judge's aides leans in to whisper in his ear.

The judge responds just loud enough for those close by to hear. 'Indeed. A splendid idea!' He addresses the court. 'Very well, Mr Banyard, we shall indulge your preposterous accusations but, be warned: you shall be fined heavily for any judged by this court to be false. Such slurs against the good gentleman's name will not go unpunished.'

I incline my head and dig a finger in to loosen my collar. 'May I continue, Your Honour?'

'I was hoping you would.' His voice is sickly sweet, insidious.

'Not only shall I prove these aforementioned accusations, but that Mr Cullins is also guilty of smuggling, an offence he has perpetrated for some years. In all these crimes, he has been aided by the man at his side, a ruthless killer and swindler, one Nickolas Moor.' A general rumble of unrest rises around our bench and I raise my voice to continue. 'Moor is the kingpin of Cullins' operations. He was the foreman of Golden Shores Imports and took part, personally, in the clubbing to death of the wreck survivors as they fought their way ashore.'

The noise has risen beyond my own voice now and the judge has to call order or risk a riot.

'Silence!' He waits as the atmosphere quells. His smile has gone. 'And you say you can prove these allegations?'

'I have a witness who will swear to these truths and there is this.' I gesture to Josiah to present the ledger I took from beneath Flinders' floor. 'Permission to approach the bar, Your Honour.'

'Granted.'

Moor growls something beneath his breath as Josiah crosses to lay the ledger before the judge.

'Behold, the black ledger. Therein lies account of every item Moor ever smuggled through Golden Shores Imports, logged by his own hand.'

Again, the room erupts with noise. Several people leave from the rows behind me – heading for the papers, with any luck. Surely Moor and Cullins can't get out of this, however much they've paid the judge, or bribed the jury. Only one shadow casts doubt on the thought: the absence of Anders.

21

Small Victory

In which a witness arrives

Judge Marshall levels at me. 'Smuggled, you say? Unusual for a smuggler to record his misdemeanours. A little *too* convenient, don't you think? And how, exactly, did you come by this *black ledger*?'

I swear Moor would be foaming at the mouth if his jaw wasn't so tightly clenched. Beneath the surface, he's writhing in fury, boiling like lava.

'I'm aware it's unusual, but my witness states the ledger was kept to ensure a level of trust between the two conspirators. You see, without the ledger Cullins had no way of knowing what had been smuggled and was open to treachery, but this way he could occasionally check on proceedings and challenge discrepancies. You'll see every barrel of wine, every crate of spirits, is accounted for and signed off by Moor and a witness – usually a ship's officer, also in on it. All fair and above board, so to speak, except that it was all smuggled.'

This raises a modest laugh from the rows.

'And you have a witness who will testify to these things?' asks Marshall. 'I dare say, I've never met a rarer creature!'

'I do indeed have such a witness, summoned to this very court.'

The judge looks around. 'Well, if he's here, bring him out and let's get this sham dealt with!'

'Sham, Your Honour?'

'Yes, by thunder. Sham! This entire trial is a waste of the court's time. A threader accusing a silker? What in the King's name were you thinking?'

'Alas, my client is indeed a threader but the accusations are all true, I assure you.'

'Enough time-wasting. Bring out your witness or I shall rule the trail annulled this very minute.'

A glance at the door gleans no help and the snide smirk on Moor's face is discouraging. 'Before we hear from our primary witness, I would like the court to hear the account of my client, an innocent threader widow, most maligned by the actions of Mr Cullins. I call Koslyne Blewett to the stand.'

The widow glances at me before rising and crossing to the stand where she grips the podium.

The judge sighs. 'Very well. State your name for the court.'

'Koslyne Blewett, widow.'

'Pray continue.' He's deeply irritated.

I begin. 'Widow Blewett, please tell the court what happened when you sought help with your hard-earned savings, savings that were the culmination of your life's work and that of your dear departed husband's. Perhaps you could start by confirming for us the exact figure of the savings you managed to accrue.'

'The amount I took to Master Cullins was six thousand guineas.'

A murmur or awe passes around the room.

'That's an exorbitant amount of money for a threader to hold.' The judge says what everyone is thinking. 'How ever did you and your husband raise such a sum?'

'We worked hard all our lives, Your Honour, beneath a silker who was generous and good friends with my late husband. Our silker master treated us very well. I believe he was fond of us.'

The judge frowns and sounds disappointed. 'I see. Please continue.'

'And so, you gave this money to Master Cullins. Why was that?' I ask.

'As you know, a threader – by law – may not invest in any other's business unless it's done through a silker. Master Cullins was the silker I chose.'

'What happened?'

'Not long after the money was invested in Master Cullins' business, Golden Shores Imports, the company was declared bankrupt and all debts void.'

'Do you recall the date of the investment?' I consult my notes.

'I do. 'Twas on the seventeenth of Hexmoon. The deal was set to pay out a return on a three-weekly basis. I have the signed document here.' She waves the paper before passing it to the bench, where it is examined.

'Ah, yes. A return you never saw.'

'Indeed.'

'So, what took place over the following month, between that day and the declaration of bankruptcy, that might account for the demise of Golden Shores Imports, as far as you understand it?'

'There were seven incidences. The first, as you say, was the wrecking of the *Dollinger* on the twelfth night of Honourmoon. 'Tis all in the insurance claim.'

Waving the claim in my hand, I begin to ask, 'Your Honour, may I appro–'

'Yes, yes. Do get on with it.'

I deliver the claims report, which he studies.

'You will see the seven events that brought down Golden Shores Imports clearly marked. After the wreck of the *Dollinger*, there was a break-in at Golden Shores warehouse during which many expensive goods were purportedly stolen.'

I consult my notes. 'This is recorded as taking place on the fifteenth of Honourmoon, Your Honour.'

The widow continues. 'That was followed by the mugging of the Golden Shores company clerk and the theft of the company cash box, the death of the treasurer, a warehouse fire, the pirating of the *Ingleford* and, finally, the loss of another of the fleet's ships to fire.'

'These all occurred during the next six days. Yes, quite a list of calamities,' I add.

'Master Banyard,' says the widow, 'you asked me what took place that may have caused the bankruptcy. Isn't it obvious? Surely no man has ever suffered such a catastrophic run of misfortune before. And so it is, in this instance, also. This man has not suffered unduly at the hand of fate but has brought these events about by his own hand. Master Cullins has bankrupted Golden Shores Imports for personal gain.'

'But, madam, this is preposterous!' The judge is livid now. 'What nonsense! This man has lost three ships, suffered a cruel run of thefts and misfortunes... What would ever drive a man to do that to his own fortunes? I'm sorry, but I must halt this case immediately. We have real crimes to judge. Case diss–'

The words spurt from me like a fountain. 'Your Honour, if I may address your question...'

He pauses, eyes boring into me. 'My question?'

'Yes, Your Honour. You asked what would drive a man to ruin his own fortunes, though, I must point out that Mr Cullins has several fortunes of which Golden Shores Imports was but one.'

'You have evidence of such a reason?'

'I do.'

He offers Cullins a fawningly apologetic look.

I continue. 'During the last voyage of the *Dollinger*, the crew learned of the black ledger and its theft from Mr Moor. The captain sent word on a fast ship to warn Mr Cullins ahead of the *Dollinger's* return. When the galleon neared Dockside in darkness during a storm, a false light was set to drive it onto the rocks. Any survivors who made it ashore were bludgeoned to death by Mr Moor and his men, all – that is – but two; ship hands Anders and Geofferson.'

'My Banyard, we have three thefts, a housing dispute, a

beating and a very real murder to get through before the end of the day. Please. Hurry. Up.'

'My apologies, Your Honour, but these details are necessary to support our argument.'

'Bunkum!' says the judge. 'Your argument…'

At the back of the room, the doors open and in walk Penney and Bretling Draker. Marshall appears to lose his thread while Bretling finds a seat in the rows behind me and Penney, red-eyed and tear-stained, runs to me.

'Ebadiah's been badly beaten,' she whispers as Mardon and Josiah lean in. 'The surgeon says he'll not see morning.'

'Who did it? Where's…' I realise this conversation cannot happen now as the judge clears his throat. Penney sits at my side. My head reels with the news and across the room Moor grins. This is *his* doing. I know it. 'Anders?'

'No word,' says Penney. 'No one's seen a glimmer of him and Ebadiah's unconscious, can tell us nothing. Your mother tends him.'

Through the maelstrom in my mind I fix upon one fact. Bretling received my message and has responded.

'Mr Banyard, I really must insist you move to conclude or drop this case.'

'Thank you, Your Honour. I've finished with my witness.'

Receiving a nod from the judge, Cullins' lawyer, Porter, rises to cross-examine. 'Widow Blewett, is it true that gawpers were sighted around the time of these events?'

I rise. 'Objection. Your Honour, what has this to do with anything?'

'Be seated, Mr Banyard. Pray continue, Mr Porter.'

'Thank you, Your Honour. Widow Blewett, please answer the question.'

'It is true. There are some who've witnessed gawpers down by the docks.'

'And it is your belief that these gawpers are real?' asks Porter.

I know exactly where this is going but am powerless to prevent it. I try to catch the widow's gaze and subtly shake my head. To no avail.

'Why, yes, Mr Porter. Gawpers are as real as you and me. I know, I've seen them.'

At this, Porter turns to the judge with a casual, if melancholy, expression. 'It seems to me this dear elderly woman should be forgiven these ridiculous accusations and allowed to leave the house unaccosted, Your Honour. She appears to be mentally impaired, a disability that, I'm sure, is no fault of her own, yet she is mentally impaired, nonetheless. Clearly, she sees beings that are not really there. Should we not, in good grace and kindness, discharge the case and release her?'

'Yes, I see your point,' says Marshall. 'Gawpers indeed! Quite clearly deluded.'

In a desperate move to prolong the trial I stand. 'Your Honour, I call Lord Draker to the stand!'

During the ensuing murmurs, Bretling rises and watches the judge in a wordless challenge. This is Marshall's jurisdiction but everyone knows Bretling could have him extricated from the Order of Judges with a single word in the right ear. When no objections are forthcoming, Bretling takes his place before the court. The room quietens and notably, nobody troubles him by asking for conformation of his identity. Everybody knows who Lord Draker is. The judge looks hard at me and checks his pocket watch before muttering to one of his aids in a voice loud enough to reach me.

'Postpone the rest of today's cases until further notice.'

It's a small victory for which I have Bretling to thank. He will be hurried by no one and, by bearing witness, he's showing his support of my case. Old Marshall has no other option than to hear me out, now.

'Lord Draker, it was said among the crew that the *Dollinger* was a cursed ship. This came about because of strange, disembodied voices and unaccountable sounds in the night, all witnessed by the crew.'

'Who are not here to corroborate,' interrupts Porter.

'Very true,' adds the Judge. 'Move on, Mr Banyard.'

'Your Honour, evidence has come to light that explains perfectly well where these voices and noises originated, evidence pertinent to the case.'

'Oh, very well. Continue if you must.'

I ask, 'Lord Draker, do you recall the events of the twentieth of Twinemoon when my associate, Mr Mingle, and I visited your office in Tower End?'

'I recall them very well.'

'Please tell the court what took place that day.'

'You informed me of a grim finding, the discovery of cadavers trapped within the wreckage of the *Dollinger*.'

The judge interrupts. 'Cadavers in the wreck?' He directs this at me. 'How would you know of these bodies? It's my understanding that the wreck is submerged.'

'It is,' I confirm. 'Mr Mingle and I employed diving equipment to investigate.'

'I see,' says the judge. 'Do continue, Lord Draker.'

'I ordered a team to dive the wreck. My divers recovered the bodies of five merchant sailors from the lower decks. The skeletal remains of a sixth man were also found, caged in a secret chamber, deep in the *Dollinger's* bowels – a chamber only revealed by damage done to the hull when it split upon the rocks.'

'What conclusion do you draw from this discovery?' I ask.

'It's clear to me this caged man was confined and hidden from the remaining crew for some reason.'

'Such as?'

'Mr Banyard, there *is* no legitimate and legal reason that I can think of. It's my opinion that this was, therefore, illegal activity and likely murder. I'm afraid without further evidence I can conclude nothing further.'

'Thank you, Lord Draker. You've been most helpful.'

The judge asks, 'Does the defence wish to cross-examine the witness?'

Porter stands. 'Yes, Your Honour. Lord Draker, you say a skeleton was recovered by your men. Were you able to identify this poor soul?'

'Alas, we were not.'

'And were you able to ascertain the approximate date upon which this man perished?'

'Our findings were inconclusive because the remains had been submerged for a time.'

'Oh, I see. So, a man we can't name died at a time we don't know and his bones were pulled from the sea. Is it even possible to say with certainty that this man was ever alive on the doomed ship? It seems to me the implication of murder is far-fetched, at best.'

'When you put it like that, yes, it sounds so. *But* my men carried the cage from the ship and I saw it with my own eyes. The man was still clinging to the bars as if in his final moments of life, his bones fully articulated, though stripped of flesh. That man died in that cage and that cage was only removed through the break in the hull. Until the wreck occurred, it was trapped – as was the man – within the secret chamber. There is no other interpretation.'

Grimacing at defeat, Porter sits. 'Thank you, Lord Draker.' Cullins turns to mutter in Porter's ear. Nothing encouraging, I'm sure.

Relieved from the stand, Bretling reoccupies his seat in the rows behind.

With little choice I present what other evidence we have, working down the list of catastrophes to debunk each in turn. There's not much I can say about the warehouse break-in other than to suggest it was instigated by Cullins and executed by Moor and his cronies.

I can only say the same for the mugging during which the Golden Shores company cash box was stolen. 'It's fair to assume that this, too, was by arrangement.'

I call two witnesses for the attack on the company's treasurer, Doncley Maples. Both neighbours were at home when Maples died.

'The coroner who attended the scene recorded Mr Maples'

cause of death as heart failure but I propose an addition to this finding.'

'What do you mean, Mr Banyard? You do not have the power to rewrite the coroner's report.'

'I suggest to you, that Mr Maples' heart failure was triggered by an invasion of his residence by men who wished him harm, men who would have murdered him if his heart hadn't first given out.' I go on to question the two witnesses about the event.

'Yes, Mr Banyard. We heard shouts and someone was banging around in that house. We saw two men run away shortly before Mr Maples was found dead.'

The defence declines an invitation to cross-examine.

'Thank you. You may step down.'

The witnesses leave the stand.

I press on. 'In conclusion, it seems clear that the treasurer was visited and murdered, most likely to silence him and remove his objections to Mr Cullins' and Mr Moor's lawless actions.' Pointing out the dismaying fact that the Drakers' findings upon the discovery were either forgotten, lost or simply unreported, I move on beneath the brooding glower of Sergeant Goffings, calling Mardon to the stand and introducing him as a surgeon and a man of science. 'It is paramount that for this court to fully comprehend the circumstances surrounding the *Dollinger* wreck, we consider the false light, of which my primary witness will later testify. As a scientist, Mr Mardon Banyard, can you tell us the likelihood of the *Dollinger* crew actually seeing Burrington Point Lighthouse from their location off Hatch Head?'

'Oh, I'd say it's highly likely they would have seen it. If it was lit,' Mardon says.

'Even in the storm and a league away?'

'Indeed. That's what lighthouses are for.' This raises a laugh.

'Your Honour, if I may, we have prepared a map to demonstrate the *Dollinger's* possible positions.'

'Proceed, if you must.'

Josiah takes the map to a corner where the entire room can

view it, and I borrow Mardon's cane to point with. 'You'll notice the location of the *Dollinger* wreck, being approximately here, off Hatch Head.' I point. 'For the crew to be fooled by a false light, two circumstances must have been created by the wreckers. Firstly, the true lighthouse was extinguished or its light covered. If this was not achieved, then the crew would have seen Burrington Point much earlier as they navigated their way towards the harbour, along the north side of the Eyes. Secondly, a false light was created, probably from the rooftop of the Golden Shores' warehouse, here.'

Cullins' supporters rumble their discontent. 'You can't prove that,' says Porter.

I continue. 'No. Because the evidence was destroyed by the warehouse fire some days later. And I can't prove it was Cullins' men who set the false light, but ask yourselves this: where else could such a light be raised that would lead the *Dollinger* to turn starboard onto the rocks at Burrington Point? The crew thought they were turning back into open sea. It surely came from Dockside and instead of open waters, they found the treacherous rocks of Hatch Head. In your scientific opinion, Mardon, what do you conclude from all this?'

'Whatever the facts, it is surely clear that if a false light turned the *Dollinger* to its doom, it was done with callous premeditation.'

'Callous premeditation, indeed.' Pause for emphasis. 'Before my next question, I must offer some details of the warehouse fire suffered by Golden Shores. The insurance claims report lists a healthy inventory of expensive goods present at the time of the fire, purportedly all lost to the flames, you understand.' I itemise each, drawing special attention to the two thousand bottles of whisky and rum and ask if the glass bottles in the warehouse might have vaporised in the fire.

Mardon clears his throat. 'I've conducted experiments to provide an accurate answer to this question and my findings are thus. The glass would have melted and pooled on the warehouse floor but, as you know, no glass was found there. My only conclusion is that no bottles of whisky and rum were present at the time of the fire.'

I add rhetorically, 'And why would this be so unless the accused had arranged for the bottles to be removed prior to the fire? In fact, does this not strongly suggest that *all* the goods were also removed and, therefore, not lost to the fire at all?'

I'm considering what to say about the pirating of the *Ingleford* and the burning of the *Parrot* – probably not much, as both events happened so far away that we've little evidence of what happened – when the doors open again and for a moment I think Anders has finally arrived and we are saved, but it's not him. Instead, ship hand Geofferson enters and sits scruffily at the end of our row. There's silence while Moor, Cullins, Goffings, Legge and my entire row turn to gawk at him. I wait, watching the man, because I'm half-convinced he's about to vanish before I wake and find the last few moments have all been a dream, but he doesn't vanish and I don't wake. It's no dream.

Words rush from my throat. 'I call ship hand Geofferson, witness to the wrecking of the *Dollinger*, to the stand.'

Geofferson takes Mardon's place, bowing politely to the officials. He confirms his name and station.

'Ship hand Geofferson, please repeat to the court your experience of the twelfth night of Honourmoon.'

Marshall grunts.

'That night there were a terrible storm at sea. The *Dollinger* were wrecked on rocks near Hatch Head and I were on board when the black took her.'

'Did you or any member of the crew see a lighthouse during those harrowing last moments of the voyage?'

'Yes, indeed, Master Banyard. There were a light on the land, though our vision were impaired by the storm. Anders and the bosun disputed the light. The bosun says it's Burrington Point Lighthouse but Anders says it's a false light. No matter. The bosun had us turn the ship and soon after we struck rocks.'

'You managed to survive the ordeal. One other also

survived.'

'Aye. Anders survived and I heard his account!' Geofferson points wildly at Moor and Cullins. 'He witnessed these savages butcher the crew as they fought their way ashore, already weakened and breathless. Moor and his black-hearts bludgeoned them to death!'

The jury and bystanders erupt with a combustible mix of outrage and awe.

Moments pass, drowned in noise until, through the quietening, Geofferson points again. 'And now, Moor has struck down Anders in cold blood to silence him! Murderer!'

22

The Bank and the Bones

In which the judge calls order and the trial concludes

'Order! Order! You will be silent!' The room quietens. 'Now, Mr Geofferson, these are *very* serious accusations. I trust you have supporting evidence.'

I cut in. 'My witness is saying that Mr Moor has murdered Anders to prevent him from testifying here today. Anders is my primary witness, Your Honour. The witness I've been waiting for! If he is dead, it is but more evidence that the accused are ruthless criminals.'

'Mr Banyard, the law deals in fact, not hearsay or groundless accusation.' Marshall smiles that same cynical smile, the one that heralds doom. 'Ah! I understand. I see perfectly well what is going on here. The court should know we have reached a pivotal point in this hearing.' He peers around at the gathering over the golden rims of his spectacles. 'We have heard all the evidence brought to bear against the accused and, you will note, a simple absence of a person is not proof of murder. Where is the body? Can you even prove this fellow Anders is dead? No?'

Geofferson scowls but has no answer.

The judge addresses the defence council. 'Mr Porter, we've endured the considerable ramblings of the prosecution. Would you care to say anything more on behalf of your clients?'

Porter stands. 'No, Your Honour. It seems to me there is very little here to defend. No real evidence of any substance. Mere speculation, at best.' He sits.

Marshall nods. 'I must say, I agree. Very well. Since this man Anders has decided not to appear, we shall waste no more of the court's time. Members of the jury, you may consult one another briefly before presenting your findings.'

Unbelievable! 'But, Your Honour – '

'Hold your tongue, Mr Banyard. You're done here!'

'But, I've not – '

'Be quiet, or I shall have you ejected!'

I simmer and seethe, robbed of my chance to sum up, while tense moments slip by and the jury mutter among themselves. Eventually they, too, fall silent and the allotted spokesman stands to face the judge.

'Your Honour, we have concluded.'

'Very well,' says Marshall. 'On the count of embezzlement, how do you find the accused, Silker Cullins?'

With fear in his eyes, the spokesman reports. 'Not guilty.'

The ranks behind me roar their disapproval as Cullins' supporters crow.

'And on the count of aiding and abetting embezzlement, how do you find the accused, Mr Moor?'

'Not guilty.'

The roars reawaken but subside as Marshall prepares to pass judgement.

'Thank you. It seems to me the jury have reached the just conclusion. There is, indeed, a distinct lack of evidence against the accused. It is this court's ruling that Mr Cullins go free, unencumbered by any slur to his good name, and that Mr Banyard be fined a thousand guineas for his time-wasting and slander. However, there is circumstantial evidence of crimes committed by Nickolas Moor, not in the least a ledger of allegedly smuggled goods bearing his mark. He will, therefore, be detained in the silker prison until further investigation into his activities may be made. Case dismissed.' He bangs the gavel on the block.

I'm on my feet, as are many others. 'This is an outrage!' I shout. 'A gross miscarriage of justice! Judge Marshall, I demand a retrial at the earliest opportunity!'

Marshall either doesn't hear over the clamour or chooses to ignore me. At my side, Mardon, Penney, Josiah and the widow look forlorn.

'Don't be too hard on yourself, Micky,' says Mardon. 'You gave it your best shot.'

'I'm down a thousand guineas which, with all the wages I owe, puts me in serious debt. Cullins and Moor have ruined me.' I add that crime to their growing list. My blood boils and I have to get out of the courthouse. I stalk into the street not caring if any of my team follows and, seething, ride home.

Ebadiah is flat on his back, unmoving, as I enter the sitting room. Mother has fed the fire into good heat and made a comfortable enough bed from our old bench.

There is no perceptible rise and fall of his chest.

'How is he?' I ask, desperate to hear he lives.

'I fear life is leaving him. He's been witless this whole time.'

I'm shocked by the bruising and the bloody dressings around his head, but mostly he's hidden beneath blankets. One eye is heavily dressed. 'He *is* breathing?'

'Yes, weakly.'

A clutch of heated stones, wrapped in cloths, surround his feet.

'He's terribly cold. I'm doing what I can to help him.' She rests a hand gently on his brow. 'Michael, Surgeon Harrow says we're wasting our time.'

Mardon blusters in, closely followed by Penney.

'Let me see the lad.' Setting his surgeon's case down, Mardon examines Ebadiah, feels for a pulse and leans an ear to his chest. He assesses Ebadiah's wounds, the worst of which Mother has dressed. While Mardon works and all eyes are on Ebadiah, I fish around in the case, lift a phial of dark powder and slip it secretly into my pocket. When he's finished his examination, the bleak sorrow of Mardon's face says everything. The boy is as good as dead.

'Well, he's in the best of hands, Aunt Sarah,' says Mardon. 'You're doing all the right things. Perhaps another blanket. Has he woken at all?'

Penney brings a blanket over and Mother tucks it around Ebadiah and shakes her head. 'He's stirred once or twice, as though dreaming.'

'Were there witnesses?' I ask.

'None,' Penney explains. 'Elizabeth found him like this in the street outside the office and sent for me. We think he may have crawled there before passing out.'

I head for the door, calling over my shoulder. 'Stay with him. And spare no expense on his recovery.' Cullins' acquittal and Ebadiah's attack have only cemented my plans.

'Michael, where are you going?' asks Mother, but I'm already leaving the house as Josiah rides in. He reins in Willow.

'No. Don't dismount.' I quickly untether Blink, mount up and turn him about. I check my pocket watch. Half-past two. 'Hurry! We've no time to lose. At three, King Doon's bones will arrive at Yorkson's Bank.'

'Is that today?'

'Yes.' I dig heels. 'And we're going to rob it.'

Flinging open the office door, I enter, ignoring the *Gone for lunch* sign. Lizzy will be back soon and she must know nothing of our plan.

Josiah follows me in. 'You did say, we're going to rob the bank?'

I drop my tricorn on Lizzy's desk. Anders' no-show has cost me precious time. 'Yes. Cullins has the widow's money in that bank and, by thunder, we're going to take it back.'

'What *is* this? Plan B?'

'Did you really think we ever stood a chance in court? Marshall and the others are crooked. Not an honest man among them. This has been plan A from the start.'

215

'You might of told me.'

'*Have*. You might *have* told me.'

'How are we to do it?'

'Exactly as you said we should. By taking advantage of the distraction, the arrival of King Doon's bones. And by turning that into a bigger distraction. Now, where is it?' I hunt around in the room and snatch up the top newspaper from a small pile that Lizzy's arranged at one end of her desk. 'Ah, here.' I tear off the front page containing a large imograph of Great King Doon's funerary urn. 'Take this.' I stuff the page into Josiah's hand. 'Hasten to Jacob Sproat's. You will find in the shop window an urn very similar to that one. Buy it.' For weeks, I've been hunting a replica but this is the closest I've found and time is up. I take a hammer from one of the drawers in the case room where we keep a few basic tools, and hand it to Josiah. 'Here, hide this about your person. You'll need it.'

Once I've briefed Josiah in the role he must play and made sure his disguise is suitably convincing, he leaves, not bothering to shut the door. I pocket my own disguise for later, taking a beard and thick-rimmed glasses, and select a coachman's hat of black silk from the shelf in the secret room.

My father's hat is looking at me. Considering me.

'What now?' I ask and listen for my father's words.

'Is this an act of revenge, Michael?'

'Perhaps. What if it is?'

'Revenge fixes nothing and will only leave you embittered. Seek to forgive.'

I pause to think. 'It's not about forgiveness. It's about justice.'

'Be careful, son. Mind you don't join the ranks of those you despise.'

I collect my rapier and gun belt, checking both pistols are loaded and, with trepidation, grab my tricorn.

With the topper tucked under my arm, I dash to the butcher's shop where, to my relief, Maddox is again absent. Jemima Gunn is there, though, which is as equally important to my scheme.

'Jemima! How are you?' Allowing no time for her reply, I draw her to one side and she looks at me strangely.

'Are you all right, Master Banyard? You seem... feverish.'

Across the shop, the oblivious butcher continues to cleave meat and bone. I am glad to be the only customer.

'I'm fine,' I say below breath. 'Merely in a hurry, my dear, and in need of assistance.'

'Then how may I help?'

I hunt for a container about my person – a bag or box – but, in my hurry, I've left the cloth bag I planned to bring back at the office and I decide my purse is too small. My pocket watch reads twelve minutes to three. Time's running out. Stooping awkwardly, I remove my right boot, drag off my sock and present it. 'This will have to do.'

'Your sock? What for?' she asks, understandably, and wrinkles her nose.

'Oh! I didn't say. I need some of those burned bones from the firepit out back. Would you be so kind as to fill my sock with them?'

'You want a sock full of bones?'

'Yes, and a little ash, please, but you must breathe not a word of it to anyone.'

'Have you lost your mind?'

'Not yet, but the day is young.'

She looks at me doubtfully, but takes the sock and disappears through the back of the shop while I pull on my boot. A few moments later she returns to hand over the sock full of bones.

'Here you are.'

'Thank you. What do I owe you?'

'Nothing, Master Banyard. Will that be all?'

'Jemima, I could kiss you.'

Weapons are not allowed inside the bank, for obvious reasons, so I've stashed mine, along with my tricorn, behind a large iron bin in a narrow alley not far from here. Josiah has been instructed to do the same. Only one pistol do I keep, stuffed into my belt and well hidden beneath my long coat.

Crowds extend from the bank's entrance into the street. I arrive, breathless, in time to witness the grand procession's climax as, at a solemn pace and amid a trumpet fanfare, a royal carriage approaches Yorkson's. Six magnificent black horses, plumed with crimson feathers and heavy ornamental brass work, draw the urn along the last few yards of its journey. The urn itself is carried in the podgy hands of an official from the Loncaster Museum, a small man with a large moustache who is dwarfed by ceremonial pomp.

I squeeze through the crush of bodies to reach the bank doors, where a red carpet has been rolled out and rope barriers erected to prevent attendees from blocking the way. The interior is less crowded, to my relief. I slip past the rope barrier as the driver brings the horses to a halt and the museum official stands to make a speech. While he waffles on about matters of history, state and grandeur, I watch nervously for Josiah's face among the crowd and view my pocket watch again to be sure it's synchronised with the Highbridge tower clock. The clock tower stands on the same street as Yorkson's Bank with but three buildings between. When that bell strikes, it is loud and reverberating.

Bank guards line the roped walkway and one is stationed either side of the entrance. Inside, however, there are mostly tellers and a thin scatter of folk, some of whom are even here to do their banking.

Yorkson's is one of the finest banks and has some of the highest security measures available. The entrance hall opens to a windowless atrium where double doors lead on to the banking room, also windowless. This was purpose-built to prevent break-ins through windows or outer walls and to make tunnelling a more challenging option for robbers. There is, however, a weakness in this design: no natural light can penetrate this far into the bank and so the occupants are solely reliant on gas, piped along the walls to feed a dozen or so lamps.

This is an oversight we intend to exploit.

I keep a security box here, one of many that constitute part of Yorkson's sterling service to the community. Obviously, my security box is, at the moment, as barren as Mors Zonam. The boxes are, basically, locked iron drawers that line the walls of a long strong-room, kept locked until a key-holding customer requests entry to make a deposit or withdrawal. This first barrier, then, is no issue. I simply need to present my key and ask for admittance. On occasion, a teller has accompanied me into the strong-room, but I've noticed that on busier days – and surely today must count among them – the tellers are less stringent and happily leave customers unattended there. After all, what harm could they do? They only have the key to their own box.

Doon's bones are not headed for a simple security box, of course. They will pass through a similar vault and on into an inner vault which lies beyond a further iron door with a huge and impressively complex lock. There is, therefore, a fair chance that right now the box room will be unattended.

I go over the plan one last time in my mind. Precisely on the first bell strike of three, Josiah will loiter at the back of the crowd, unnoticed. He'll swing his concealed hammer and flatten the main gas pipe in the banking room, where Doon's funerary urn will be temporarily on display. He must aim well and strike hard because it has to happen in sync with the covering din of that first bell. There is no room for error. There are four seconds between each bell strike. That should be enough time for the remaining gas in the pipes to burn off and the lamps to die. The result? The room will be plunged into darkness.

During those eight seconds between the first and third bells he must get from the gas pipe to the urn (navigating the darkness and the foreseeably bewildered crowd), hide the real urn behind its plinth and prepare to smash our fake urn, with its burned bones, on the floor. The smash must be timed to coincide with the third and last of the bells, because at that precise moment I shall blast the lock of Cullins' security box clean open, and I need all the noise I can raise to cover the sound of the small explosion.

Four minutes to three.

Where are you Josiah, I think in desperation. Perhaps we won't rob the bank today after all. If Joe doesn't make it, the whole thing's off.

I feel a nudge at my elbow and turn.

Jinkers. Just what I need.

'Good day, Micky. I didn't have you down as an old traditionalist.'

'Jinkers – I mean, Mr Jinkers – what a pleasant surprise! I didn't expect to see you here, either. Excuse me. I have urgent business to attend to.' Hoping to lose him, I duck away between the other visitors and hook round to peer at the entrance from the other side of the room. I can feel his eyes following me, as there are simply not enough people here to hide behind. That will change when the urn is brought in to be placed on its plinth.

Time to change. In the gentlemen's room, I glue on the beard with its excessively bushy sideburns, don the thick-rimmed glasses and topper, and re-enter the banking room looking a little like my great-uncle Bernard.

Josiah. At last! Looking odd in his disguise: moustaches, an aged-make-up job and a brown bowler.

His face bobs towards me through the gathering. He's perspiring but he's made it, clutching to his chest a brown paper bag the size of a small loaf.

'Sorry, Mr Banyard. They've temporally banned horses from the street to keep it clear. Had to run to get here.'

'The word is temporarily. The urn?' I whisper, when he's close enough.

He taps the bag and grins, enjoying this far too much.

It feels, all of a sudden, like a ridiculous plan that is doomed and yet, no one has stopped either of us from entering, nor searched us and, if anyone has noted Josiah's bag, it's not unimaginable to think they might take it for a precious heirloom on transit to the vaults, or coin bound for a deposit box. In any case, no one is paying us a blind bit of notice. Doon's urn holds all the attention and, under such circumstances, we may just succeed.

'Here!' I hiss, dropping the sock of bones surreptitiously into his long coat pocket. 'Remember, on the first stroke of three, precisely. Time to go.' Leaving Josiah, I approach a teller at her desk. 'I'd like to make a withdrawal, please.'

'Certainly, sir. Your key?' She smiles. She's pretty, pretty enough to have distracted me on a different day.

'Here.' I pass the key, which she studies briefly to ascertain its authenticity before returning it.

'This way, sir.' She leads me to the vault door and unlocks it. Opening it, she steps aside as a great roar of celebration reaches us from the street. The speech is over and Doon's bones are on their way into the atrium.

'Will you need assistance, sir?' she asks, in a hurry to get back to the main attraction.

'No. Thank you.' I bow my head.

She leaves and I take a final look over my shoulder to see Doon's urn carried in and placed on its plinth, raising a further round of applause. I enter the box room, closing the door quietly behind me. I find my security box, number 258, and unlock it, leaving it open with the key in the lock, before taking a folded slip of paper from my pocket. On the paper is written a number in Ebadiah's irregular hand: 842.

I know the number well – memorised it more than a week ago – but it still seems fitting to view it now in all its glory. Without it, my plan would be futile; yet, at what cost has it come to me?

Well done, Ebadiah, I think, swallowing guilt. *Who knows what mischief you undertook to acquire the number of Cullins' security box, but you did it. May you live to be a hundred!*

My watch ticks loudly, counting down. Thirty seconds to three o'clock, twenty-nine, twenty-eight…

This is for you, Koslyne Blewett, for your late husband, Jonty, and for Ebadiah, you brave, brave boy.

Sixteen.

Fifteen.

Fourteen…

Cullins' box is lower than mine, being one of the larger ones that run in two rows along the base of the wall. Taking the phial of Mardon's special mix from my inner pocket, I remove the stopper and tip gunpowder into the lock of Cullins' box until it overflows.

If all is going to plan, Josiah has by now discreetly emptied the contents of my sock into his urn and is preparing to strike out the lights.

I recork the phial and pocket it.

Only I don't.

What I *actually* do is miss my pocket and let the phial slip to the floor where it smashes on the tiles, the powder exploding with enough noise to alert the guards and make me leap.

Nine seconds.

Eight.

Seven…

I'm stunned by my ineptitude and expect the guards at any second, but then I hear another bang, almost like an echo of the first. Josiah has reacted and come to my rescue, striking the gas pipe in the banking room. He's brought the plan forward to distract from my mistake, although in doing so has risked discovery.

Brilliant! There's still a chance. I imagine Josiah slipping the hammer back into his coat pocket and hiding among the crowd as heads turn.

A rumble of concern rises from the gathering crowd as the lights go out beyond the door and, a second later, a ceramic smashing sound that can be only one thing.

I'm also plunged into darkness. I fumble for the packet of Sulphurs in my pocket and strike a match. I take three paces back and draw my loaded flintlock, cock the hammer and take aim with one eye on my watch in the flickering light. It's a tricky operation, holding the match and the watch in one hand while aiming with the other, and the flame creeps ever closer to my finger and thumb. Four seconds to the first bell strike. I'm committed, now, guards or not.

Three.

Two.

One.

Holding my breath, I squeeze the trigger.

23

The Shadow

In which Banyard and Mingle flee

The clock strikes three, the din resonating through Yorkson's as hot lead hits the keyhole and Mardon's special mix explodes. It's not a great blast, but is bright and fierce enough to blow a hole in the security box where the lock used to be. I drop the match as the flame burns my fingers, and strike several more, piling them on a floor tile to make an improvised work light. Cullins' box is full of Doleks, large gold coins from Urthia. Marvelling at the sight, I hurriedly remove and pour the Doleks into my deposit box. When it's full to the brim, there's still a good deal of gold left.

That won't do!

I close and lock my drawer, pocketing the key. Whipping off a boot, I remove my remaining sock and stuff it hurriedly with handfuls of coins from the box while Joe rallies alarm and confusion with his hastily rehearsed lines. They, too, penetrate the vault.

'It's the king's bones! Someone's tried to steal old Doon's bones!'

Another's voice. 'Look! The ashes of King Doon!'

I smirk. It's working.

'There he goes,' cries Josiah. 'After him! Catch that man!'

There's a commotion outside the door and a loud banging and clattering as somebody hits it from the other side, though the expected appearance never comes. The door remains closed.

I imagine, by now, the guards and officials have found storm lamps or candles from somewhere and the banking room is no longer in darkness.

There are too many Doleks. My sock full, I take off my topper and curl the sock inside before replacing my hat and cramming handfuls into my pockets and my purse. I take every last coin, even slipping some into the tops of my boots, before stamping out the little fire and opening the door an inch to spy on the mayhem beyond. It doesn't want to open because the stunned body of a guard is slumped against the other side.

Looking pleased with himself, Josiah watches for me, his role complete. I imagine him gleefully tripping the guard in the gloom to prevent him from entering.

The atrium writhes with motion. Guards rush about with no discernible sense of purpose. Several wander with storm lamps, filling the space with half-light. Onlookers stand, bemused, while the museum man, also knocked down in the confusion, is helped up from the floor by attendants. On the red carpet at the centre of this chaos, a group of tellers, guards and officials gather around the plinth and the broken shards of an urn, pieces of burned bone and scattered ash.

I squeeze through the open door, close it and hurry to Josiah.

'Go!' I say. 'Walk. Don't run.'

The whole town has turned out to see Great King Doon, including Penelope Danton. We meet, jostled nose-to-nose in the throng as I'm trying to leave and, for a moment, she stares perplexedly into my eyes. Her exquisite features crease. Her lips part to speak.

I affect a northern accent, 'Excuse me, my dear,' and brush past.

We thread the preoccupied crowds, who are still trying to determine what has happened, and leave the bank as rain begins to fall. On the street, I see three Drakers heading our way, batons drawn, and tug Josiah's sleeve to steer him around the next corner. We walk briskly, pushing past pedestrians and guards and more Drakers, all running to Yorkson's amid the din of shouts and Draker whistles.

A Draker calls from the atrium. 'It's the king's ashes!' They catch on quickly around here.

The weight on my head is significant. Concealing a quantity of socked-gold, my hat feels ungainly and likely to slide off at any moment, giving us away, but we continue, silently watchful.

Two corners later, we enter an altogether emptier street and our eyes meet.

'Run!' I hiss, keen to distance ourselves from the bank.

I've a feeling we've been followed from the start. A feeling that persists. At first, I put it down to paranoia – who wouldn't think they were being followed, having just robbed a bank?

Our weapon stash is in an alley down here. We find it and quickly belt on our guns and rapiers. We hurriedly remove our disguises and I swap the top hat for my tricorn, dropping the topper into the bin. There's still a good distance to cover before we reach the safety of home.

We speed up and turn another corner towards the stalls where our horses await but, at the other end of the street, a line of Drakers search. The robbery has been discovered. Word is out and the Drakers' confusion has turned into an organised hunt.

'Back!' says Josiah.

We hastily retreat to duck into another alley, hoping it leads somewhere. It does. It leads to Jinkers. Speeding around the corner, I run into him with enough force to send us both sprawling. Doleks fly from my pockets and spill from the sock which, along with my tricorn, falls to the ground. Gold rolls and flashes in the alley's shadows.

Jinkers sits up, frowning at me from the slick dark cobbles.

'Micky? But…' He spies the gold, eyes widening.

'Jinkers, what are you doing here?' I smell the pungent reek of urine and notice his shirt tails hanging loose. 'Oh.'

Josiah hurries to gather the spilled Doleks, retrieving my bulky sock and hat. I get up, as does Jinkers, who quickly tucks in his shirt.

'Now, I know what this looks like,' I begin.

'There's been a robbery at the bank.' Jinkers' greedy eyes flit from me to Josiah, who is still gathering gold. 'A good amount of gold was taken, they say.' His voice is heavy with insinuation.

'Indeed,' I say with urgency. 'The Drakers are out, chasing down the culprits as we speak.'

Josiah is just about finished collecting.

''Twould be an awful shame if all that lovely gold was to disappear unaccounted, like.' Jinkers nods towards the gold in Josiah's hands.

'It would. I don't suppose you would be interested in helping with the unaccounting. Say, for example, if you were to unaccount for these…' I grab handfuls from my laden pockets and release them into his hastily cupped hands.

'I see what you're saying, Mr Banyard.' Jinkers looks greedily to his growing coin pile and then back to me. 'Consider this unaccounted and we shall say no more on the matter.'

'Very well, consider this a long-term investment and, next time I ask for a loan, I'll expect you to oblige. Farewell, Mr Jinkers.' I drop one more coin in. 'For Mr Kaylock.' I receive my hat from Josiah, replace it along with the loaded sock and venture deeper into the alley.

The rain stops and, leaving Jinkers behind, we work our way further from Yorkson's but, each time we try bearing south for Crowlands, Drakers block our path, forcing us into another route. We head east, hoping to skirt the main throng of Drakers who appear to be forming a ring around Highbridge.

That's when I notice the large bulge in the side pocket of Josiah's long coat. A horrible possibility calls me to a halt. I point.

'What's that?'

He looks at me. 'What's what?'

'*That*. In your pocket.' The bulge is about the size of a small loaf of bread or, to put it another way, it's urn-sized.

'Oh, that. Yes, well. I had to hide it quickly and then one thing led to another and we had to get out, quick.'

'Tell me you didn't just steal the nation's most cherished historical artefact. I need to hear those words right now, Joe.'

But I don't hear those words. I can't hear anything over the screaming in my head. The screaming that cries, *The whole world will be after you now!*

He parts the top of his pocket to show me the urn.

'You did smash the fake one?' I'm doubting everything, my sanity included.

'Yes, of course.'

'But stealing the urn… That wasn't part of the… I said hide the…' I can't think straight. 'How could you…' I can barely speak.

'I'm sorry. I didn't think it was *that* important.'

'Not important? The ashes of Great King Doon, not important!' I feel the blood rising to my cheeks. 'It's a national treasure!'

'I know you said to hide the real urn but I was standing there, in the dark, with the urn in my hands and I had a better idea – an excellent idea.'

'You and your excellent ideas…' I should have let him hang.

'Just hear me out.'

'I'm listening.'

'The whole country's going to be looking for this urn, right? The robbery will be famous.'

I nod enthusiastically. 'That is, more or less, why I want to kill you right now.'

There's nothing for it. We must keep moving and deal with this disaster later.

Dodging the law, we stumble upon a street with several clusters of people, talking, walking and generally behaving themselves. We walk, trying our utmost to appear calm and innocent. Halfway down, a side road branches to the left and, on the corner, a couple lean in to kiss. A certain familiarity draws me to look again. Gerard Monkfield and Jennie Lowery touch lips. They clasp hands and walk on, neither noticing my presence. That's interesting – Jonathon Barrows' business partner and bereft girlfriend...

I push it from my mind. We have more pressing matters. The follower, for one. There's nothing concrete, no real evidence, but I swear I glimpse an occasional shadow, always in our wake. It lingers at the edges of buildings and vanishes when I turn. Perhaps I'm seeing things.

Planning to bend south at the first opportunity, we hurry ever closer to Dockside until, on the edge of this forsaken suburb, we see shadows, long and violent. Venturing near, the scene grows clearer.

Silhouetted and framed beneath an arched bridge, Moor towers over a shrinking figure, whose cries for 'Mercy!' pass disregarded. Beyond the arch, a lone Draker runs closer, blowing his whistle, yet Moor continues to beat his victim with the heavy knob of his cane, desperate to finish the job and, swung forcefully like a cudgel, it is lethal. We rush to intervene – as does the heroic Draker – yet arrive too late. The man is dead and Moor is in the wind, his footsteps echoing into the distance. The Draker stoops to turn the broken man, blood flowing from concave wounds on his barely recognisable face, temples and cranium.

There is nothing more anyone can do for ship hand Geofferson.

I lean on the arch wall for support. 'Murderer!'

'I thought they were locking him up,' says Josiah.

'He must have broken free and run.'

We steel ourselves to give chase.

'Stop that man!' shouts the Draker, piping on his whistle with frantic blasts.

Moor is agile and quick, weaving through streets and alleys he knows well. The sea is in the air and soon we chase him into the lower ranks of the town. He knows we follow. His backwards glances confirm it.

As our pursuit lengthens, it seems fate is on his side: a mist rolls in from the sea to swamp the glossy streets and darken the day and the longer we follow, the quieter the Drakers' calls and whistles become, dampened by distance and fog.

'They've lost him. Useless wastrels,' says Josiah.

'On the positive side, they've lost us, too. I'm sorry we can't say the same for our shadow.'

'Our shadow?'

We search the haze behind us and I call out. 'Who are you? Show yourself!'

But no one steps out as the mist continues its crawl.

'Where are we?'

'Dockside, somewhere. I don't recognise the street. Wait. There!' He points further down the road where a sign protrudes from the miasma ten feet from the veiled ground.

The Ship Keepers.

'Have we come that far?' I don't know why I'm surprised. I'm exhausted and feel like I've been running for miles. 'Where's he gone?' The fog-shrouded shape of Moor has vanished from the street ahead. 'We can't lose him now!' I glance behind for the follower, but there's no one in sight.

Josiah spies movement. 'Behind the barrels, down by the water.' He leads on.

As the Cogg emerges before us, he turns left, heading towards the dockyards, and I hurry to catch up. Moor is a blank form running the length of the sea wall that stretches out to Lytche's Cove.

The place looks different in the failing light and the fog. The details are vague and hazy, the piles of netting, the boats, the barrels, crates and ropes, seem barely there. So, too, the rocks, sand and weed of the foreshore – or is the tide in? It's impossible to tell. Instead, the landscape is formed of vast stretches of characterless planes. The sea is an expanse of grey, disappearing into eternity. Even the smell has changed. The stink of stale nets and dead crab is subdued by a damper, saltier air.

On we run.

To our right, galleons loom from the harbourside, creaking and shifting on the tide with soft, ghostly movements. The noise of the Drakers is so distant now that I strain to hear them. Every small sound – our footsteps, our breath – drowns them and, somehow, I know that however this ends, it will not involve the lawmen.

The first few ships we reach are quiet, seemingly unoccupied. Josiah halts suddenly, his searching movements fox-like.

'Where are you?' he hisses.

Is Moor hiding or has he escaped us? We probe the drifting mist and study the ships for signs of life. He's vanished again and perhaps we've lost him for good.

After the commotion of the bank and the chase, this near-silence is uncanny and now the only sound is the soft lapping of the sea against the clinkers of galleons and the harbour wall.

We watch.

We wait.

After what feels like an hour but is only moments, I can stand it no more.

'He *has* to be here somewhere.'

Slowly. We advance. Scrutinising every speck of temporal shadow. The murk hangs over everything, disguising, concealing, obscuring, deceiving. We attempt to make sense of the little we can see. There are barrels, crates and small upturned boats littering the harbour's edges and a row of iron columns, some with mooring ropes that hang, looping up to their respective vessels in the water, each column paler than its forerunner, until the fog swallows all. We near a scatter of dockyard shacks that rise from the mist and, as we creep from one to the next, Moor leaps from a gap between them, flying at us, raging and swinging his cane.

His assault is flailing and desperate. He knows he's outnumbered and outmuscled. Josiah steps in to take the brunt of the assault, receiving a clout around the shoulder that was meant for his head. The impact has little effect on Josiah and on the second strike, he catches the cane in his fist and wrenches it from Moor's grasp.

Moor's eyes widen in alarm and he draws his rapier, knowing that gunshots would bring the Drakers and lessen his chance of escape. He knows Cullins has given him up and will back him no more. He's on his own and the realisation glows from his face.

We have no more wish to alert the Drakers than he. We draw our rapiers and prepare to meet him. Still, he knows he's made a bad choice in confronting us. It's in his eyes, nestling with an inner madness.

'Two against one?' He sneers. 'How gentlemanly.'

I answer him. 'I've no objection to a fair fight. Would you prefer my sword or my companion's?'

My guard down, he lashes out.

I recover in time to parry. 'Oh, but it seems you are no gentleman.' We stand, point to point.

Josiah is itching to skewer the man. 'Let me take him, Mr Banyard. Can't think of anything I'd rather do.' He ditches his coat to move more freely, rolls his shoulders.

'Now, Joe, we should take him alive. He's a wanted man, don't forget. It will be far more satisfying to see him hauled before the judge and this time there'll be no escape. His master has abandoned him and we *must* observe the law.'

'The law is a joke,' sniggers Moor.

'We agree on something, at least,' I mutter.

Moor smirks, stretching the scars on his cheek and chin. His glare bores into Josiah. 'Come on, then, boy! I'm not afraid of you. I've beaten larger whelps.'

'Then, give it your best!' Josiah lunges in with surprising speed, aiming for Moor's heart and it seems these boys are going to fight, whatever. The problem is, Moor's vastly superior experience in this arena is likely to outweigh Joe's stature, muscle and reach.

'Stand down, Joe! I'll fight him.' My words go unheeded

beneath the clash of steel.

Josiah's doing well. His anger and muscle are working to his advantage, but for how long? They circle, lunge, part, until Moor's undeniable skill with a blade shines through. He stops retreating to stand his ground and lets Josiah run into his sword on each approach. Josiah takes a slice to the upper arm but doesn't even glance at the wound so it can't be bad. Perhaps it's only his sleeve that's cut. I can see no blood, though visibility is poor. The mist is thickening to a denser fog, forever flowing in from the limitless ocean.

Now Josiah is retreating, edging nearer to the sea wall edge. It's all part of Moor's plan, he's steering him there, thrusting left and right, shifting his angle of attack to force him towards the water.

'Joe!' I cry and move in to assist, but there's no time to help because Josiah's had enough of the fancy blade work and what happens next is over in a flash. He makes a mighty sweep with his sword that clashes against Moor's with such ferocity that it sends Moor's blade flying into the sea. Stunned, Moor glances after the rapier but pulls a dagger and lunges into the gap before Josiah can recover from his swing. The dagger lodges in Josiah's shoulder as he grapples with Moor, finding his wrist and overpowering the attack, muscling Moor's dagger hand slowly back and so drawing the point free from flesh.

Now, there is blood. It spreads upon the creamy cloth of Josiah's shirt like spilled wine. His sword rendered useless at such close quarters, he follows up with a left hook that catches Moor on the jaw.

I run in as Moor sprawls, and bring the point of my blade to his throat, his dagger outreached by my rapier. Josiah recovers to level his rapier, too.

'Enough,' I say. 'Surrender, or suffer the…'

Moor draws a pistol, scrambles backwards to his feet and backs away. The fog swallows him. Dropping my sword, I draw and fire as his shot tears a hole in my tricorn, the lead thumping into gold.

'That was close! Are you all right, Joe?'

'It's just a scratch. After him!' He reclaims his coat.

We search but, injured or not, Moor has gone. I've missed my chance to capture him and I hate myself.

I've used Ebadiah and led him to slaughter.

I've allowed Josiah to be injured.

I've let Moor escape.

I am the worst detective in the world.

24

The *Bartimaeus*

In which Banyard makes a critical error

Moor knows he has to flee the area, and fast. Our shots must have echoed halfway across Camdon City, even with this wretched fog.

Josiah turns about. 'I think he went this way.' He points to a street that runs directly inland, just beyond the shacks. It's the last road before the dockyard warehouses, so we're close to the Golden Shores yard.

He heads off.

'Wait,' I call. He stops. 'Do you think Cullins has other ships?'

'I don't know.'

I watch the line of galleons gently rocking on the water, monsters slumbering in cloud. 'He's bound to have other ships, I reckon. Don't you think? Surely, he has.'

'If you say so. Mr Banyard, he's getting away!'

I pace along the sea wall, reading the ship's names and stop beneath a hulking galleon that would surely have outdone the *Dollinger* in every way. The intricately carved name plate on the bow reads *Bartimaeus*. I smile to myself. 'Jacob *Bartimaeus* Cullins. Let Moor go. I've a notion he'll be back.'

We make ourselves as comfortable as possible, tucked away in the last of the old shacks, which is so dilapidated that the lock has disintegrated. Everything is damp but we find places to sit anyway, Josiah taking a sturdy lobster pot while I perch on an upturned bucket that reeks of festering fish guts. Through gaps in the shack's wall, we watch the galleons slowly rise on the tide as late afternoon blends into evening and the sky darkens further.

I badger Josiah until he allows me to examine his wounds. He has a cut that other men would call deep, though on Josiah's massive frame it looks small. He has many scars and it's obviously a relatively minor injury compared to his past sufferings. The stab wound from Moor's dagger is worse.

'The bleeding has slowed but it should still be stitched.'

'It's nothing. Stop fussing.' He bats me away, watching for Moor through a crack.

'He'll return,' I mutter. It's become my mantra.

'So you've said.'

'Am I boring you, Joe?'

'Yes.' Josiah is angry and tight like a spring, coiled for action.

I do hope Moor doesn't disappoint. 'It is surely high tide, now. If the *Bartimaeus* is going to sail, it must be soon.' Doubt plagues me. 'Can a ship sail into the wind? Would they leave harbour in this fog?'

Josiah shrugs. 'Do you think Moor knows its schedule?'

'Probably. He's been Cullins' right-hand man up until this morning.'

The gold and Doon's urn and ashes are now safely buried beneath a floorboard in the shack, ready to be reclaimed once we've dealt with Moor, and I feel lighter for it. I've also recovered my socks, though the one that carried the bones and ash is hideously gritty around my toes.

A noise outside draws our attention. On the *Bartimaeus*, crew are moving, rigging the vessel, preparing to sail. I wonder again about the limiting wind conditions.

'This is it, Joe. He has to board within the hour or risk

missing his chance.' I check the other ships as far as I can see, but discern no other movements. In fact, they all look abandoned. I want to go out and run along the sea wall to be sure but, if Moor *is* staking out the docks, he would see me and know we lie in wait. Better to stay put and observe. Our success hinges on this one hunch: the *Bartimaeus* is Cullins' ship, named after himself, and Moor thinks he'll escape Camdon if he can board her.

For now, we can only spy.

'How does a ship sail?' asks Josiah, by way of killing the boredom. People think what we do is exciting but the reality, at least for much of the time, is waiting and watching. Boring stuff, really.

'What do you mean? It floats on the water and the sails catch the wind. The sails propel the ship.'

'But why does it float? Why does it not sink?'

'Wood floats, doesn't it?'

'Does it? I don't think all wood floats. If so, then why do some ships sink?'

He's got me there. 'I'm not sure. Never thought about it that much. I think it's something to do with the displacement of water. Ask Mardon. He'll know.'

After a moment of thought, he changes the subject. 'What do you think caused the cataclysm? Was it men, the Old People?'

This takes me by surprise. 'There are many theories, Joe. Some say there was a great war with explosions so large they reshaped the land. Some say the planet was struck by a field of meteorites that turned the sky black. Others say the Old People polluted the atmosphere so badly that it became too hot, crops failed and the waters rose – that the Old People fought among themselves for survival. They say it was called Earth before it happened.'

Did the planet fight back in an attempt to eradicate its nemesis, I wonder?

'Earth…' he mutters. Mind blown.

'Well, we've proved one thing, Joe. It is possible to rob a bank without anyone getting hurt.'

'There!' A quick, shifting dab of light. It's him. It *has* to be. We watch in apprehension as the dab moves closer, coming in from the yards beyond, skirting buildings, walls, flitting through shadows like an alley rat. His shape grows ever sharper until…

'That's him. There's no doubt.' I hardly dare believe I was right.

'What now?' asks Josiah.

'Let him board. Once he's on the ship he'll be easily cornered.'

'Don't you think that's risky, them being Cullins' men an' all?'

'It is, but if we face him now, he'll scarper again and we'll have gained nothing. Presumably, they'll have to wait for a more favourable wind before sailing.'

'Right.'

Moor dashes across the walkway to the sea wall, and for a moment it looks as though he's going to board via the gangway but, before reaching it, he stops as though in doubt. He leaps up to grab the balustrade of the gunwale, hanging flat to the clinkers and from there heaves himself up and over, onto the deck and out of view.

Josiah looks at me, dismayed. 'Can we go, now?'

I check the positions of the few crew members visible to us. The ship is so large and tall that from here, the upper decks are hidden. 'Yes.'

We rush out and scurry across the walkway to board in much the same way as Moor. Watching him, I wondered how he made the leap up to the gunwale but I now see a row of gun ports, the closed shutters of which offer excellent footholds. Using these we climb and haul ourselves up to poke our heads over the rail and peer around. No one is watching. The fog is our friend and the mariners are busy. We clamber onto the deck and slip behind one of the upturned lifeboats to hide.

Moor has vanished.

The *Bartimaeus* is enormous, its upper deck long enough to utterly disappear into the fog. It's also populated by an entire village of crew and is well underway to make sail. The ship rolls gently beneath our feet. Mariners set the fore, main and mizzen sails at a tight angle and lash their ropes. To my bewilderment, the wind fills the sails.

I learn something in this pivotal moment: it is quite possible to sail a ship into the wind. Of course, one cannot sail *precisely* into an oncoming wind but, with enough of an angle and some skill, a good captain can still harness the wind's power. It is happening now as we cower, our fate unravelling.

Voices volley.

The gangway is withdrawn.

The mooring ropes are loosed.

The crew work on, the *Bartimaeus* leaves dock and, in an instant, the gap between ship and land widens.

We are trapped on board.

'Moor knew!' I hiss, furious with myself for letting this happen. 'He watched them rig the entire ship, knowing full well that the time approached. He left it until the very last minute.' Stowing away was *not* part of my plan. Nor was being stuck on a ship full of Cullins' men.

'He's clever,' mutters Josiah.

'Yes, and he knows considerably more about sailing than us.'

'I'm going to kill him,' he growls.

Things get worse. Up on the quarter deck, the captain is joined by a familiar figure: Moor steals from the shadows and offers his hand. The captain shakes it, greeting him warmly.

'Oh, no.'

'Now we're in trouble,' says Josiah.

'I don't suppose the captain knows he's a wanted man.'

'I don't suppose we'd be that lucky. Anyway, if the captain works for Cullins and Moor, he's probably a criminal as well.'

'Hmmm. We need a better hiding place and we're going to

need some pretty good disguises if we're to survive this. Unless we swim for it.'

'I can't swim.'

'Of course.' I lay down in the shelter of the lifeboat and cover my face with my mortally wounded hat.

'What are you doing?'

'Getting some rest. At nightfall, a skeleton crew will be left to navigate and watch. We shouldn't risk moving until then.'

Darkness shrouds us and we welcome it. A mariner lights lamps around the gunwale, marking our small floating zone of dryness in an all-encompassing black ocean. Quite suddenly, I feel awfully insignificant in the greater universal scheme.

Josiah snores so I elbow him in the ribs and he grunts awake.

'What? What is it?' he says, rising to smack his head on the lifeboat above us. 'Ah!'

'Shush! Wake up and get ready. We need to move.'

The fog has thinned to a mist that I hope will cloak us as we tread the most moon-shadowed parts of the ship, avoiding the areas of cloudy lamplight. Flitting adeptly from lifeboat to mast and from mast to forecastle, we pause, warily checking around. Up on the forecastle a single mariner watches, though his attention is mostly on the inscrutable waters beyond the bow and we quickly flatten ourselves against the forecastle's sternward edge, beneath his line of sight. High overhead, another man watches from the crow's nest. There'd be no escaping his gaze if he were to glance directly downward, but his job is also to watch for rocks and other ships, so why would he? In any case, all we can do is hope he doesn't spot us. By far our likeliest threat comes from the three officers gathered high on the poop deck opposite, although they are some distance away with the quarter deck in between.

Our next and most dangerous move is to reach the trap leading to the steps down into the gun deck where we might explore with less fear of being noticed. Once at the trap, we must lift it and descend, all in view of the officers. We watch them, waiting for an opportunity, and when one of them points out to sea, we dart out as they all turn seaward. Josiah is quick to heave up the trap, its hinges squeaking. We hurry down as he lowers it behind us and it seems we've gone unnoticed.

Down below, we stand in a deeper darkness for some moments, waiting for our eyes to adjust. There are no lamps alight on this level; the deck holds only lines of cannon and ammunition. No disguises to pilfer here.

'We must find the sleeping quarters.' Further down the gun deck there's another hatch and, edging our way in the gloom, we descend. This is the lower deck, the crew's quarters, and there are ample clothes for the taking. We don't need much and it will pay not to steal anything nice. *That* would only lead to a hunt. No, we grab the shabbiest pieces we can find, hoping their owners will not miss them and, creeping around hammocks and the laboured breath of men, their scant baggage and paraphernalia, we take our humble prizes and slip away.

Back on the gun deck, we change into our motley rags. They're ill-fitting at best but Josiah has done well to detect several of the larger men by their bulky, low-slung beds and he looks convincing in a yellowed, patched shirt and dun hose. Of course, the tables have turned in his favour. By my very bearing, I am conspicuous among these threader mariners. I'm clean-shaven, my hair has been cut and I lack their common stoop and musculature. There's a rawness I'd have to work on for years to perfect. Unfortunately for me, the officers are far fewer in number and infiltrating their ranks is not a conceivable option, so there's nothing else for it. We're stuck with this lot. Josiah is going to fit right in with little effort. That's obvious from the start.

I catch a whiff of my stolen clothes. They stink of sweat and who knows what else. 'At least my smell will be convincing,' I mutter.

'What do we do with our silker clothes?' he asks, looking around as though for a laundry basket.

The question stumps me for a moment until I realise we can

easily open a gun port and ditch the clothes overboard. We're in the process of doing so when I think again.

'Wait!'

Josiah pauses, his arm drawn back to hurl the first bundle overboard. 'Why?'

'Because we don't have anywhere to sleep, not unless there are spare hammocks below. Did you see any?'

'No, but I don't think they'll be any.'

'Hmmm. If nothing else, we can wad our clothes into makeshift pillows. We'd better hide them instead.'

Behind Josiah is a cannon, its bore wide enough for his fist. He balls up his clothes piece by piece and rams them in.

'Brilliant!' I shove my clothes down the neighbouring cannon.

Josiah sits to rest, a hand on his wounded shoulder. 'Let's hope we don't meet pirates. Now what?'

'Well, it's the first night of a new voyage. There's bound to be fresh crew aboard. We have a good chance of fitting in.'

'But we know nothing of seafaring.'

'True.' I wonder. 'How hard can it be?'

Josiah shakes his head. 'You silkers are all the same. It's hard. Very hard.'

'Then we'll just have to hide away, shirk duties. The main thing is to avoid Moor.'

'Or take him down before he knows we're aboard.'

'Agreed. He's a silker so they'll have housed him with the officers. Let's look around. We might find a good hiding place where we can sleep.' Despite dozing uncomfortably beneath the lifeboat earlier, I feel exhausted enough to slumber, even in the shadow of Moor's unsettling presence.

It doesn't take us long to realise every area of the ship is partitioned by class and use. The lower deck and the orlop are given over to cargo, in this instance, quarter casks and firkins – of rum, judging by the vapours.

'Let's hope no one strikes a Sulphur down here,' I whisper on our way back up the steps.

Sternward of the crews' quarters, we find a series of ration stores, locked, of course.

I peer inside through the barred window of a door. 'This would be perfect if only we had a key.'

'Guess one of the officers holds that.'

'Perhaps there's a spare we can pinch.'

'Let's go see.'

Back up the steps into the gun deck we climb, to creep over to the upper deck hatch. An animal squeal startles me and I realise there are livestock on board: several pigs and hens, all penned in traps sunken into the upper deck. I nearly clock my head on the corner of one of these enclosures but we make it to the hatch unscathed and there, ascend quietly out onto the deck.

The night watch pass their rum allowance around, talking animatedly. We hurry down to the stern and, beneath the quarter deck, peer through a window into a lamplit chamber. I polish the murky glass. It's an exquisite room with cushioned seating, cabinets and a writing desk. A door is set into the panels of the wall opposite.

'That'll be the lower officer ranks' quarters,' I surmise.

'Will the key be in there?'

'Possibly. I'd like to look in those drawers.'

A brass clock on the desk takes my attention. It looks like a pocket watch, though one too large for a pocket. I've seen the same thing somewhere before, though it takes me a few moments to recall where. The clock is unusual in other ways. In the gleam of the lamp I see four hands on its dial and around this, an outer dial with intricate markings.

'There was a clock like that at Hunt and Slaker's,' I whisper.

'The watchmakers?'

'Yes. It was on Jonathon Barrows' desk. I wondered what it was. It's not a regular chronometer.'

'Of course not,' says Josiah, with just a hint of *don't-you-know-that?* 'That's an Abrahams Maritime Chronometer.'

'A what?'

'An Abrahams Maritime Chronometer. All the ships have

'em these days. They help with the navigation and that. Oh, yeah, the Abrahams Maritime Chronometer is the best advancement in maritime technology since the mercury barometer.'

My last remaining tower of pride crumbles to dust. It was a bastion named Knowledge, a vestige that stood firmly between Josiah and me. I'm not sure how or why he knows so much about the latest advancements of nautical technology – and now is not the time to ask – but, in any case, the Abrahams Maritime Chronometer is a link I previously missed, *the* link between Moor and Jonathon Barrows, perhaps. It begins to make more sense to me and I'm convinced Moor had something to do with Jonathon's disappearance.

But back to the now.

The *Bartimaeus*.

The dark.

The officers' quarters.

The chamber is unoccupied. I test the door and the latch clicks open.

I have half a foot in the room when a shout goes up. An officer peers down at me from the deck above.

'Where do you think you're going?'

25

The Latch

In which a discovery is made

'Run!' we chorus.

We run, racing to the hatch. There's only one way to go from there, and that's down, accompanied by the outraged shouts of the officer and his fellows, who are giving chase.

We have one chance because leaping overboard is certain death. No, our only hope lays in the sleeping crew below – the soon-to-be-waking crew. If we can reach them before we're apprehended, we might hide among their number and never be identified. I'm not entirely sure but I reckon I saw more than a hundred sleeping in hammocks. Surely that's a large enough crowd in which to lose ourselves.

We make it to the crew's quarters a good fifteen seconds ahead of the officers.

'Wake them!' I hiss at Josiah before tearing between hammocks, screaming in my best threader accent: 'All hands on deck!' To my astonishment, it works. The sailors awake and, bleary-eyed, dash from their beds, throwing on clothes, stumbling, falling, rising, rushing. By the end of that fifteen seconds so many are on their feet that we're pushed to the clinkers, but it doesn't take much effort to weave our way deeper into the crowd. The pursuing officers arrive, invading the steps to face a swarm of mariners, all of them scrambling for action.

'Quiet!' The watchmaster bellows, a petty officer: three stripes on his shoulder. 'Which two of you blighters were creeping around the officers' quarters?'

No one answers, of course.

'Come on, now. Step forward or you'll all be on half-rations.' The petty officer is tall with mean eyes and waxy skin like soap. He paces back and forth, berates and threatens but, before too long, it's over. The penalty is set, the officers slope off back to the upper decks and Josiah and I skulk as the crew climb back into their hammocks. Tomorrow we will all suffer half-rations, thanks to our deplorable behaviour.

For now, Josiah and I slink up to the gun deck to retrieve our silker clothes and sneak back down the steps into the orlop where we sleep uncomfortably, hidden among the vaporous casks, lulled by the hideous roll of the ship, our heads on our bundled clothes.

We're woken at sunrise by a commotion on the decks overhead. The officers are back, barking orders and, with much stamping around, the crew are mustering.

'What should we do?' asks Josiah.

'We either hide down here and learn nothing or join them on deck.'

'We'd better go, then.' Josiah rises to his feet but glancing at me, stops near the steps. 'Wait. There's something not quite right.' He studies me in the dusty haze of the orlop as lamplight glows down around us from the hatch. You still look like a silker. You're too pale, too... straight.'

I know. It's not the first time the upright nature of my spine has been thrown into question. I do my best to affect a stoop. 'I'm not sure there's much I can do about my skin tone.' I rub at my chin. At least there's a healthy stubble developing. The floor is grimy down here. I collect a little dirt on my fingers and smear it onto my face.

'Now you look like a silker with dirt on his face. Here.' He revels in this, kneeling to swab his massive hands all over the floor, getting a good thick greasy coating of filth. 'Hold still.' Easy for *him* to say. My face is enveloped in his rough hands as he rubs and smears the muck on, being sure not to miss my neck, behind my ears or any crevice that his fat fingers can reach. My hands and wrists get the same sandpapery treatment and with a final flourish, he wrestles my hair into disarray. With an exaggerated slouch, he points out that I've already lost my stoop.

I adjust my posture. Again.

He grins. 'Better.'

We climb.

On the main deck the crew assemble before the officers as the captain addresses them. The petty officer with cruel eyes stalks along the ranks scrutinising each man, his pale face turning on each of them in turn, longing for a victim.

'It has come to our attention that there may be stowaways aboard.' The captain pauses, watching the men line up, while Josiah and I halt instantly on the hatch steps before backing up to remain hidden. Keeping to the shadows I risk one step up, to spy on a portion of the deck where the petty officer counts men, marking tallies on a board. At the captain's side, Moor watches over everything as though he's in charge.

'This calls for extra vigilance from all of us,' the captain continues. 'I want any stowaways apprehended on the spot and brought directly to me, whatever the hour. Do you understand?' The crew nod and mutter affirmations. 'Good. You will not attempt communication with any such fugitives. Understood?'

'Understood, captain,' murmur the crew and officers.

'Goood.' He draws out the word. 'What is the count, Mr Philips?'

Philips, the petty officer, says with an air of disappointment, 'One hundred and seven, captain. All present and accounted for.'

'Very well. You men will remain while the officers search the lower decks.' With Moor close behind, the captain leads the way to the nearest hatch which, happily, is at the opposite end of the main deck and, while they and the officers descend, Josiah and I hurry up the remaining steps and slip out to join the crew. They're too preoccupied discussing the prospect of stowaways to notice us and, once we're among them, we *are* them. It feels safer to be hiding in the crowd, although the smell of stale sweat is overpowering.

The officers return before long.

'Nothing,' concludes Philips. 'They must have taken their chances with the black.'

I glimpse Moor's frustration as Josiah and I slink our way through the men and descend to the orlop.

It's moderately lighter now, as more daylight is filtering down through the hatches above and, taking a storm lamp from a higher level, I stop to examine the end wall of the orlop, a planked wall identical to one we've seen before. Josiah's gaze meets mine with understanding.

'There's a hidden chamber.'

'Just like the *Dollinger*.' And so, it follows, is there also a cage?

'Quickly. Look for a lever, a latch, anything.'

We search the planked surface of the wall but, at length, find nothing.

'Perhaps we were wrong.'

Josiah knocks on the planking with his knuckles. 'It sounds hollow, don't you think?'

'Perhaps the latch is somewhere else.'

'Where else could it be?'

He raps again, further across and, as if in answer, a muffled noise issues from the other side.

'Did you hear that?'

We listen intently. There is the creak of the ship, the distant rush of the waves and... That noise, again. A muted, wordless voice.

'Someone's in there!'

With renewed vigour, we scrutinise the area, seeking the

secret latch. We tug at lamp hooks overhead, check joists and props, run our hands over dark timbers in shadowed corners and, finding nothing, we sit there, thinking, our backs against the clinkers.

'When's breakfast?' Josiah asks. 'I'm starved.'

'I don't know. Soon, I hope.'

'What do mariners eat for breakfast?'

'Weevils with a little biscuit, I think.'

Suitably discouraged, we gaze around hoping for some inspiration.

After ten minutes or so Josiah throws his head to the side, staring at an area of floor between his feet and, reaching out, hooks a finger into a small gap in the decking. With a tug, he levers up a piece of wood the length of a hand and a click sounds somewhere in the wall, releasing the hidden door.

'There's your latch, Mr Banyard.' The words parade from his mouth like a small victory march, albeit a hungry one in the belly of a dangerous floating island of wood.

'You found it!' Getting to my feet, I go to investigate, Josiah on my heels. I ease the door further open to peer inside at a man I've never before met, who is familiar and looking back at me with wide, desperate eyes, his face pressed against the bars of a cage. He is gagged, his lanky form kneeling with hands bound behind his back. It's his gaunt features that are the most reminiscent thing about him, though, for Jonathon Barrows is a younger copy of his father.

26

The *Lantern*

In which a dead man speaks

'Jonathon Barrows,' I say, a thousand thoughts hounding my head. I loosen and remove his gag. He's in bad shape: exhausted, malnourished and filthy.

'Yes.' His brow creases. 'How did you – '

Josiah follows me into the hidden room. 'So, the skeleton we found – '

'Was another hapless victim. I'm Michael Banyard, and my friend here is Josiah Mingle. Your father employed us to find you. He believes you to be dead. Turn around.'

'Death's grasp is but an inch from my throat.' Shivering, he turns, allowing me to untie his bonds through the bars. 'Get me out. I beg you.'

Josiah and I search again, this time for a key or something with which to break open the cage.

'How is my father?'

'He was well enough when we left him.'

Jonathon's features crumple with pain, relief and rage.

The chamber is small, the cage occupying most of it. A gap on all sides prevents Jonathon from reaching the clinkers, so he can only touch the cage and the floor. Hunting around in this gap we hear feet approaching. We dash for the door as, to our horror, someone on the outside pushes it shut. Moor, I'm guessing.

The latch engages.

We're trapped.

In total darkness.

The hurry drains from us. There is suddenly no rush. In fact, we have all the time in existence. We have, quite possibly, the rest of our lives.

Think! 'There has to be something here that will help us.'

Jonathon's sobs sound like hope bleeding away.

'I don't suppose anyone has any matches?' I ask.

'No matches,' says Josiah. 'We're going to miss breakfast,' he adds, trying to make light of the situation, I think.

The hunt takes on a new design as we feel our way around the cage, our fingers probing the boards of the deck and the curving walls. I hear Josiah straining to bend the bars of the cage. There's a groan of iron followed by a sorry voice in the darkness.

'It's no good. The cage is just too strong.'

My fingertip brushes something sharp and hard. I collect the object, knowing it by touch. 'I've found a nail.' I soon find another. 'Two nails. Perhaps we can pick the lock.'

'I've found... Well, I think it's a dead rat,' says Josiah.

'I suppose we could eat it if we get incredibly desperate.' A rotten odour reaches me.

'It's too far gone for that.'

'So, we have two rusty nails and a dead rat.' We meet in the darkness on the other side of the cage, our search complete. 'I'm not entirely sure we're going to get out of this.'

'I was just thinking that very same thing, Mr Banyard.'

'All the same, we must try.'

'What do you suggest?' asks Jonathon.

'I'll try the lock on the cage. If we can get you out, we'll be part-way there.' I feel my way around the cold cage to a hinged door of iron bars. 'They must have fed you something to keep you alive this long.'

'A little water and a ship's biscuit once a day, if I'm lucky, a bowl of watery stew.'

'There's a chance, then. When they open the door.' Josiah's optimistic.

'That was before Moor boarded the ship. Before they trapped us in here. We'll be lucky if they open that door again this side of Trimoon.'

The lock is a thick, riveted slab of metal with a hole in the centre, half an inch wide.

The Bad News
That means the key is probably quite large and my paltry nails – the length of a little finger – are likely too short.

The Good News
Sorry to disappoint. There isn't any.

I try the nails anyway. 'We could be here some time, so you might as well tell us what happened. I take it Moor visited your shop and asked you to repair an Abrahams Maritime Chronometer. What I can only surmise is what passed between you that made you a liability to him?'

Jonathon pauses before speaking, I presume, to compose himself and collect his thoughts. 'He did come to the shop. He left the maritime clock with me, demanding I mend it before the week was up. Examining the clock in his presence, I immediately noticed the stamp pressed into the underside of its base – a small mark in the brass, you understand, one he may not have noticed himself. In all innocence, I mentioned the mark because it named the ship for which the clock had been commissioned: the *Lantern*.'

'What's so special about the *Lantern*?' asks Josiah.

The name jogs a memory. 'I think I read about the *Lantern* in a paper last summer. A merchant galley, pirated on a voyage to Amorphia. It never returned.'

'Indeed. Pirated by one of Cullins' ships, perhaps by Moor himself. Who knows? Whatever the case, Moor didn't like me knowing the clock was from that ship. The next day they took me on my way to work. They jumped me in the street, a sack over the head and a cosh to the skull. I didn't stand a chance. I came around, bound and gagged in this hideous cage, hidden in a smuggler's hold. Do you have any food? I'm near-starved.'

'None, I'm afraid.' I jostle the tip of a rusty nail inside the lock mechanism and, probing as deeply as I can, feel something give a little.

'I wonder why they've kept you alive,' says Josiah.

'I've wondered the same thing every day since. Perhaps they plan to sell me to Amorphian slavers.'

'And why did they take you but not your partner, Gerard Monkfield?' I ask.

'I rather presumed he was in a similar cage somewhere, in a similar room,' says Jonathon.

'I can assure you he's not.' I try again, the nail tip slipping as I press with my finger and thumb jammed hard at the keyhole. Again, the slip. If only I had a longer nail.

I measure the two nails by touch to be sure I'm using the longest and then it strikes me. Both nails are curved. They've been used and drawn from the wood. Straightening them would make them longer. Not by much, granted, but longer, all the same. I get to work, pressing the longer of the two against the boards, trying to flatten and straighten it.

I recall Gerard Monkfield and Jennie Lowery kissing in the street. 'Tell me, did Gerard witness the exchange between you and Moor?'

'Oh, yes. He was there, keeping his thoughts to himself, as always.'

'He said nothing?'

'Not a word.'

'Interesting.' Should I tell him his bereft girlfriend is on the arm of his business partner? For now, I decide to keep quiet. We've enough to think about.

It's worked. The nail feels straight. Straighter, at least. I try again, teasing the nail into the keyhole and locating the point inside that promised to move. On my third attempt the inner lever gives. I test the door. Still locked. There's another lever to go, possibly two.

I work on in silence until there's a satisfying click. At last the cage door is released. The squeal of the hinges informs Jonathon.

'You did it!' He rushes in the darkness to leave his iron prison, only to remain confined in the smuggler's room.

'Now for the door. Can you break it down, Josiah?'

'I can try.' There's an audible thud as he bruises his shoulder. 'No.'

'There has to be a weakness. We must find it. Let's see. This side is hinged. The other must hold the latch.' Feeling in the darkness, it's hard to discern the door at all, so well crafted are the joins.

Right now, I'd give anything to be on the other side of the clinkers, swimming freely. I'm sure the sharks out there are friendlier than those on this despicable ship. Perhaps we should have jumped when we had the chance.

The wood I'm touching trembles under Josiah's probing weight as he tests its strength. After minutes of trying, he hits a sweet spot that warps the plank door enough to allow in a faint sliver of light. Josiah's face flashes before me and the light is gone.

'There. That's the place.'

'We could do with something to use as a wedge, Mr Banyard.'

'Yes, but what? There's nothing here but us and the cage.'

'The cage!' whispers Josiah. 'Help me shove it back.'

The three of us push the cage along the floor towards the back of the room. It slides and scrapes a few inches at a time but it doesn't take long. It hits resistance and we can force it no further. I haven't bothered asking what his plan is because I think I know. He's going to brace his shoulders against the cage and push at the door with his feet. A second flash of light enters the room to confirm my thoughts. I join him at his side to help, the problem being that Josiah is the only one of us tall enough to bridge the gap. All the same, we try, laying on our backs and pressing at the door with the soles of our feet. Ultimately, we tire and the door remains firmly closed. In one of those fleeting glimpses of light I catch the reason why. Josiah is stretched too far, his legs almost straight. We could do with the cage being a foot or so longer (or the chamber a foot or two shorter). I'm sure then he would have the leverage to splinter the door, but alas...

Time slouches by, trickling seconds like sand grains in an hourglass. We're going nowhere. Nor do we have the energy to continue our fruitless escape attempts. I marvel at how quickly we've given in. One hour? Two hours? Who knows? The truth is, there is simply nothing we can do. We are trapped and that is that.

Some Facts
We are cold.
We are hungry.
We are hopeless.
We are going to die.

'Did you hear that?' asks Josiah.

'What?' I ask. We listen.

A series of noises fall down to us from the upper decks. They are jumbled and confused, but among them are distant panicked voices, men running and officers' shouts.

'What is it?' asks Jonathon. 'What's going on?' He sounds groggy, as though the disturbance has roused him from a stupor.

'I don't know,' I confess.

Our conjecture is short-lived because a voice close enough to be clearly distinguished shouts, 'Fire!'

'Incredibly, I do believe our situation has worsened,' says Jonathon.

'Hmmm.' I stand and feel my way to the hidden door,

wondering how long we have before the smoke reaches us. There's no hint of it yet, but then the wall before me is well built and devoid of gaps.

The sound of quick footsteps penetrates the barrier. Someone has descended into the orlop. I hammer my fists against the wall and shout. 'Hey! We're in here! Get us out!'

Josiah repositions himself against the cage and starts stamping at the door. Dabs of light flicker with each thump. I sense Jonathon join us in the darkness.

An iron point appears in the gap. A chisel, perhaps. I can't be sure. The limited orlop light is like a lighthouse to us. It streams in. The iron works deeper, widening the space between the corner of the door and the wall until an eye gazes in at us.

'There's a latch in the floor back there. A hidden latch!' I shout to the eye.

'Wait,' it calls back to us. 'It's too dark.'

I've heard the voice before.

The iron ceases to move. Quick footsteps distance and a moment later return to us, a flickering lamp swinging past the gap. I press my eye close to peer through. Beyond, the figure wielding the lamp studies the floor in its light.

'Further back!' I call. 'To the right!'

The figure follows my directions and finally finds the latch. The door bursts open and we fall through, staggering to find our feet. For the first time, we see our saviour in full.

I can barely believe it. The follower. Of course.

Four climbed aboard the *Bartimaeus* that night at the docks: Moor, Josiah, me and, very much alive…

'Anders?'

'I'm sorry I couldn't make the trial. I'll explain later but, right now, we need to get off the ship. I've an inkling it may be about to sink.'

'*You* set the fire?' I hurry to rescue my tricorn.

'I needed a distraction,' shrugs Anders, heading for the hatch. 'Was out of ideas.'

We rush up, leaping steps, scrabbling, scrambling, helping

Jonathon, who can hardly walk. The entire crew must be on deck because the lower levels are deserted. There's no sign of fire until we reach the gun deck where smoke wafts down through the hatches and when we spill out onto the main deck, a scene of chaos meets our eyes.

The crew, including most officers, fight the fire. A barrel of tar is overturned and alight, its viscous contents thinning with heat and spreading the blaze wherever it runs. At least one lifeboat is aflame, along with the main mast and its lower sails. It already looks like a fire that will consume the entire ship. Desperate mariners haul buckets of water from the sea to the deck only to dash their contents into an inferno.

I stop. 'Anders, I do believe you may have killed us all.'

Flames reflecting in his eyes, he doesn't take the news well. He grabs his head in disbelief. 'I only meant to – '

'It doesn't matter. We were going to die anyway,' I add. 'We have to take a lifeboat. There!' I point and run for the boat laying upturned near the port gunwale halfway down the deck.

'Look out!' calls Josiah.

Up ahead, Moor and half a dozen of his officers step from the smoke to stand between us and the boat, among them, the captain, the chief officer and Philips.

'What did I tell you? These are our stowaways.' Moor draws a newly acquired rapier and waves the tip towards us. 'We knew all about you two.' He gestures to Josiah and me. 'But you've come late to the party, ship hand Anders.'

27

They Come

In which Josiah proves his worth

Moor steps into a lunge aimed at Anders. 'At least you've afforded me another chance to kill you!' He thrusts again as Anders dodges for a second time. 'How very generous.'

Anders has no sword – none of us is armed – but he does have the storm lamp still in his hand. He swings this and, ducking Moor's blade, smashes it into his face.

Moor wails, groping at his burning skin as flaming oil and shattered glass rain over him. His officers close in. 'Kill them! Kill them all!' Moor screams.

Josiah spies a thick length of rope, one end burned through and flaming with tar. He snatches it up from the deck to swing it overhead, encircling us in a ring of buzzing fire, while Anders wheels around with the remnant of the lamp, sweeping wildly at the nearest officer. The petty officer backs away. Jonathon and I search frantically for weapons of our own.

There's a stand-off between the fire-wielding Josiah and the sword-bearing officers, but it doesn't last long. One of the bolder men, the chief officer, strikes at the rope and breaks its momentum with his blade. I rush him, throwing him off balance, and try for his sword. We grapple, I slip and he brings the sword up, slicing open my hand. I stumble backwards and scramble a retreat, nursing my wound while dreading a killing blow.

A cloud of smoke descends upon the ship.

Again, Josiah swings his burning rope, this time clobbering the petty officer around the head, releasing a plume of sparks and a reek of burning hair. Moor recovers. Aiming for Josiah, he charges in and takes the whip of flame across his flank, unabated. Josiah brings the heavy rope back around in time to deflect a sword blow that snags the rope. The others tear in with deadly intent, rapiers poised to slash and stab.

Blood beads on my temples and brow.

What a wonderful moment to sweat blood.

There's so much of the slippery crimson fluid dripping down my face that my oncoming opponent pauses, his features wrinkling in disgust. Still, he descends, sword point closing on my empty hands and I retreat with desperation now, because I know something else is happening behind the whir of moving bodies, silvered blades and fire, the shouts of fire-fighting mariners, the gush of water from buckets, the hiss of flame, the crackle of burning timbers, the roll of the ship, the creep of smoke. I sense it more than see it because, in this elongated second as my life draws to a close, my vision is consumed with my approaching death. I picture Penney, the curve of her cheek, the embraces we shall never share, but there is no time.

What I know, through the blur of confusion, is that a new presence approaches the deck.

They come like the speeding shadows of an accelerated dawn, like the gush of brine falling from a broken wave.

They come.

They form.

They emerge.

They tower.

And *they* are gawpers.

28

The Splendour of the Moon

In which Banyard drinks rum

They come and, oh, how they come!

Smashing bodies aside, casting them screaming to the depths, slamming them like cudgels scattering twigs. The men at the rear are taken first and then the captain, followed swiftly by the chief officer. One by one the men fly from the ship, propelled by the gawpers' arms.

A gawper seeks out Philips and, one-handed, lifts him from the deck by a shoulder. Philips screams into the abyss of the gawper's face and all the while those white eyes burn into his. It searches him, frozen in time, before launching him with ease fifty feet out into the sea. His screams streak the sky until the waters receive him.

Our opponents are soon dealt with, leaving Moor, turning on his heels, facing first one looming form, then another and another. More of them close in.

I've tried, since that moment, to look back, to view again the scene and know their number, to glimpse their faces but, try as I may, I cannot say how many there were. It is as though there is a hole in my memory. All I can vouch is this. They appeared in the thickening mist of smoke with terrible speed and with a power that seemed to birth from some manner of vengeance.

White-eyed, they surround Moor and, as their forms close in to block him from view, he releases a scream like hot blood, a scream I wish I could forget.

It is the last sound he will ever make.

When it is done and Moor's lifeless shell lays crumpled on the deck, they turn to Josiah, to Anders, Jonathon and me. They steal close, their ragged forms but inches from ours. Their eyes burn into ours, their minds probing us like white flame. No, I cannot see their thoughts, and yet I feel them. We all do. And for heart-jolting moments, we are tested. We are read like books flung wide open, our minds laid bare to that pale flame, not one of us daring to twitch a finger beneath the intensity of their solemn gaze.

When they are finished and we have, apparently, passed the test – whatever that may be – they distance, dissolving back into the smoke, leaving us in a single laboured breath amid the pandemonium of a burning deck and smoke-bound fire-fighters.

Those mariners fight hard against the flames. Their lives depend on it.

We deliberate for a moment. Take a lifeboat for ourselves or join the fight? That is our choice. We join, hauling buckets, tearing down blazing sails to halt the spread of the flames, heaving ropes and tackle to bring all under control and, slowly, surely, it works. Small victories lead to larger ones. The fire succumbs to our hard labour. Flames die as water splashes and runs, and a vast area of ship that had blazed is salvaged, the inferno herded into three smaller fires. The smoke dissipates with the last of the flames and the survivors stand assessing the damaged galleon, wondering how we might go about navigating with such a wreck.

With further work, it becomes clearer. We take the few surviving sails and rig them in strategic positions to maximise our capture of the wind. We saw through what remains of the main mast – it is a liability, threatening to topple at any point –

and ditch it into the sea. We make good of a damaged craft, both officers and crew working in an unfamiliarly united way. It can be said that, to a fair degree, the usual rank and order has been purged with the flames. The officers' numbers were halved by the gawpers' attack, the high command among them, and those remaining seem leaderless and in no state to antagonise a hardened crew.

An experienced mariner named Oswald gets talking with Anders, who seems to be respected for his seafaring nous by both the officers and his fellows, and a working relationship blossoms. Their roles are never discussed or announced. It seems enough for all concerned that it works and that, beneath its capacity, we might all live to see land once more.

One of the first motions this pair instigate is to turn the ship and head for Dockside. The crew cheer and pass rum around, all thoughts of the trading voyage to Morracib, the Urthian port, abandoned. With what haste there is left to muster, we limp home beneath a crystal sky of numerous stars.

I stand leaning on the gunwale of the deck in my bloodstained shirt, my wounded hand bound, too restless to sleep, full of stew and rum. The salt wind is cold on my face. Anders joins me for a time, catching me gazing at the moon, which seems exceptionally large and bright, each crater, valley and shadow intricately carved in gleaming frosted glass. It hangs in the sky like a gargantuan lamp.

He brings more rum and two goblets, handing me one and filling it. 'For a moment there I didn't think I'd live to see another moon.'

'Me neither. Though we made well of things in the end.'

'We did, indeed, with a little help.'

Neither of us has the energy to mention the gawpers outright. It's too large a subject for this lulling moment and the lateness of the hour.

'You know, in all the confusion I've quite forgotten if I ever thanked you for your timely rescue,' I say.

'I wouldn't bother. I nearly doomed us all.'

'And yet here we are.'

Gazing at the splendour of the moon.

'So, you missed the trial. You would have enjoyed it.'

'I'm sure. I almost made it. Moor and two others were waiting, watching Court Road. They would have had me if it wasn't for Ebadiah. He was watching for them and warned me. I ran, as did the boy.'

'They caught up with Ebadiah, left him at death's door.'

Anders is quiet. He looks out to sea. 'I didn't know. I am truly sorry.'

'It wasn't your fault. You were saying, you ran from them.'

'They meant to kill me. I fled to Dockside, hoping to lose them among the shipyards, but they trapped me in a courtyard, forcing me to climb to escape. They followed me over rooftops, again cornering me. I fell from a chimney tower and they left me for dead. Fortunately, I had a soft landing.'

We sip rum.

After a pause, I ask, 'What will you do now? Moor is gone, but Cullins...'

'Yes, I'm aware. My life will continue to be complicated but, one day, Cullins will get his comeuppance. I swear it.'

'I'll drink to that.' I think of the beauty on the beach, the girl on the sand and the life cradled within.

We raise glasses and sip.

'Listen, Anders, I have a confession. I took a burned fragment of a letter from your fireplace back in Dockside. It bore Moor's name.'

He smiles. 'I did some sleuthing of my own. Stole the letter from under Cullins' nose – after he'd read it, unfortunately. I realised it would only endanger my life further if they found it in my possession, so I destroyed it. It was sent to Cullins with the sole intention of ensuring Jonathon Barrows' capture – sent by a man at Hunt and Slaker.'

29

The Widow's Hand

In which the voyagers return

It's days later and gone midnight when Josiah and I arrive back at 96 Bunson Street. The front door creaks loudly. We hurry into the warmth, trying to be quiet but clomping around like wounded aurochs. It's not surprising that we wake Mother. She rushes down the staircase, lantern swinging, to stare at us.

'Mother!'

'Michael! Thank goodness. I thought we were being robbed. Where on Earthoria have you been? You're pale. Are you sick?'

'I always look pale, Mother. I'm fine. A little weary, perhaps. We've not had much sleep these past days.'

'Josiah, you look well. Come in. Sit down.'

'I'm well. How are you?'

'I'd be better if I was left in peace to sleep the night, but oh, it's good to have you home. I feared you were dead.'

With trepidation, we enter the sitting room and are at once dismayed. Ebadiah's makeshift bed is gone and there's no sign of him. I'm too heart-heavy to ask, though Josiah steps up.

'What of Ebadiah? I guess the surgeon was right.'

Mother approaches the bottom of the stairs, not yet in the room. 'Ebadiah...' She pauses, sorrow flooding her lamplit features. She turns her head at the faintest of sounds. It's one we fail to hear at first, but then the lopsided footsteps grow louder overhead and a shadow hits the top of the stairs. It's followed closely by a boy in a loose-fitting nightshirt, limping with the aid of a crutch, one eye covered by a bandage wound around his head.

'What is it, Aunt Sarah?' Ebadiah stops at her side to peer at us with his good eye through the gloom. 'They're back!'

The next morning I find a white envelope addressed to M in a flowing script. The letter must have arrived while I was away and Mother has set it aside. Quickly, I slit it open and unfold the single page which carries but four lines.

> *Dear M,*
> *All is well. I wish to convey my heartfelt gratitude for your*
> *services.*
> *Forever in your debt,*
> *A*

Smiling to myself I strike a Sulphur and ignite a corner of the page, holding it up and watching it burn.

The threader Annabel Stafford is safe.

The widow carries a fragile smile, a secretive smile. It is mostly cradled in her eyes. She already knows much of what has taken place and I heavily suspect she understands the reason I have called her to the Mysteries Solved office for a meeting. Mother has taken care of that, through no direction of mine, I hasten to add.

Koslyne Blewett passes the windows and enters the front door, which jingles merrily with its shining new bell.

'Ah, dear Koslyne, do come in.' I usher her into the case room where Josiah, Mardon and Penney are already gathered. There is a hefty butter cake sliced and waiting on a plate alongside a carafe of steaming black bean soup. 'Do take a seat. I'll be with you in a moment.'

I dip out into reception to call Lizzy. 'Do join us. Flip the door sign to closed, if you will.'

Elizabeth turns the sign and follows me back into the case room.

'Well,' I begin, choosing to stand. This is a moment I've been looking forward to for some time and, for some time, I thought it may never come, so now that it's here it tastes all the sweeter. 'Thank you for attending, Koslyne. I've a proposition for you.' I rub my hands, partly for effect and partly in glee. 'It grieves me to inform you, though I'm sure you're already aware, that Mysteries Solved, failing catastrophically, has been unable to win your case against the honourable gentleman – by which I mean the most dubious of fellows – Jacob Cullins, and that we are unable to pursue the case any longer. However, it so happens that Mr Cullins recently suffered a dreadful calamity of his own, when a large amount of his savings was callously stolen from a deposit box in Yorkson's Bank. The thieves – curse their rotten hides, wherever they may be – have yet to be apprehended and the Drakers are sadly clueless as to their whereabouts. We can only assume the rogues made a clean getaway.'

'I was saddened to hear it,' says Koslyne, smiling candidly.

Josiah grins. Elizabeth and Penney glare at him with puzzled expressions and I clear my throat and throw him a frown until he stops.

'By sheer coincidence, around the same time, I happened to have received an inheritance, a considerable sum, I may add. My great-uncle Archie, long estranged and recently deceased, named me the sole heir to his fortune.'

'I didn't know you had a great-uncle Archie,' says Penney.

'Oh, yes.' I'm confidently in my stride now, lying like a professional. 'We Banyards have a vast and sprawling extended family. Members on every continent, you know. Old Archie is just one of many, many relatives with a penchant for travel. He moved from Tower End to Urthia so long ago there's no longer any trace of his ever being there. It's almost as if he never existed! He travelled about quite a bit after that. Spent some time in Amorphia, Acutane and even Zenziba. Very hard to keep track of a man like Archie. Anyway, the fact is it seems I was a bit of a favourite of his and now I have all this cash. I wish to put it to good use, which leads me to my proposition.

'The widow, here, has lost all her savings and, by sweet providence, I have gained some. I would therefore like to offer Koslyne a position at Mysteries Solved. The role will require light duties and will pay extremely well.' I address Koslyne. 'Please remain at the close of this meeting to discuss the finer details. I would also like to share my good fortune with the rest of the Mysteries Solved employees. You will each receive a significant bonus for sterling work on our recent cases. How does a hundred guineas a head sound?'

This is received with gleeful exclamations and the room smiles back at me.

'Very well, then. I shall see the arrangements are promptly made. Now, who's for a cup of black bean soup?'

When the others have gone, I sit quietly with Koslyne. There are suspicions from the others. Of course, Josiah knows everything and Mardon knows a fair deal. Penney likely suspects something dubious has gone down and let's hope Lizzy never finds out. But when it comes to Koslyne, I have a notion that not much escapes her grasp.

'It's strange that you came into this money at precisely the same time poor Mr Cullins lost his.' It's not an accusation, exactly. More of a commendation. She knows. She knows exactly who stole what from Yorkson's and she understands why. It's written in the gleam of her eyes.

'As I say, a most peculiar coincidence.'

'Well, I for one wish those thieves every bit of luck.'

'I'm sure they would appreciate the sentiment.'

'As for your offered role at Mysteries Solved – '

'Ah, stop right there. When I said I have a position for you, I was bending the truth, somewhat. In all honesty, there is no role, but we *must* make it appear so, or risk unwelcome enquiry.'

She offers a frail hand, her near-translucent skin cool and yet brimming with warmth. 'Indeed. Then with deep gratitude for your failed services, I accept.'

Next, we have unfinished business with Jonathon Barrows. He's kindly requested our presence at his reunion with his father, and Josiah and I have agreed. He has taken a few days to recuperate, eat, drink, rebuild his strength. He didn't want his father to see him in the state we found him.

But first, we're meeting him at Hunt and Slaker.

When we arrive, the shop is exactly as I remember it, except for one addition. Jennie Lowery is there, clinging to Gerard Monkfield's arm.

'Good day, Miss Lowery, Mr Monkfield.'

'Do call me Gerard, please.' He twitches nervously at our arrival, a movement that only augments his mole-like appearance. 'How may I help?'

'We're here to see Jonathon.'

'Jonathon?' He looks concerned and surprised.

'Yes, I'm sure he'll be along any moment now. We'll wait, if that's all right. Oh, here he is now.'

To Gerard's and Jennie's discomfort, Jonathon strides briskly into the shop, sharply dressed in a tail coat and topper, a lacquered cane in hand. His eyes are less sunken than the last time I saw him and I'm sure he has a way to go yet, but he looks much recovered.

'Jonathon?' Jennie gawks, at once releasing Gerard's arm.

Jonathon shakes my hand and then Josiah's. 'It's good to see you again, gentlemen, and under much improved circumstances.'

'Indeed. You're looking better.'

'I'm as well as can be expected.' He turns on Gerard and Jennie, his gaze heating. 'No thanks to you!' He points at Gerard with the cane.

'Me? Whatever do you mean?'

'I mean this.' He takes a diary from his pocket and opens it.

From between two pages he carefully plucks the burned corner of a page bearing small-lettered, meticulous handwriting. I think, if a mole could write, this is how its work would appear. He dangles the corner before Gerard's eyes.

'Uh...' Gerard is dumbstruck.

'Yes. I thought you'd say something like that.' Jonathon is bursting with suppressed rage. 'Recognise it, do you? *I* recognised it. Your hand is unmistakable.'

Gerard backs away. 'No, wait! There must be some mistake!'

'There's no mistake, Gerard. You wrote a letter to warn Cullins after Moor's visit. A letter betraying me, telling him he must act or I would see him gaoled. What was it you hoped to gain? Oh, I know you took a shine to Jennie, but was there something else? Did Moor pay you for information about me? My address? My route to work, perhaps? Of course, with me gone you were almost guaranteed to receive my share of the company, too.'

'I... He...' Gerard stutters.

'Save it, Monkfield. I don't care. Get out. We're finished.'

The mole-man summons courage. 'You can't. You can't do that. I have rights!'

'Not any more, you don't. I'll tell you what we're going to do. I'm going to buy you out. I'll buy your share of the business for half its market value and you'll be grateful for it. Now take your stuff and leave, or you can explain your actions to the Drakers.'

'The... the Drakers?' The thought clearly terrifies Gerard. I don't think he gets out much. He takes a last glance at Jennie before snatching his bag and leaving.

Jonathon watches him scurry from view. 'Jennie, I think you'd better go, too.'

'Me? But, Jonathon... Why?'

'Just go.'

Jennie leaves and in her wake remains an atmosphere that smells of new beginnings.

After a contemplative pause, Jonathon gestures to the door.

'After you, gentlemen.'

We leave the shop and he locks up. We walk to his father's house, quiet but content to be free and on solid land. We stretch out our legs and pace the length of Peak Street, climbing gradually higher over the city. Almost level with us, a Hinkley Air ship drones across the skyline. Today it is clear and blue.

As we approach the door to Mr Barrows' house Josiah and I slow, allowing Jonathon to go the last few yards alone. It feels only right that we are here to witness the event and yet we don't wish to intrude on a private moment. We simply watch as Jonathon knocks and knocks again, as a second of doubt passes and his father opens the door only to collapse on the spot, as the son collects his father in his arms, bears him up and helps him back into the house.

There are tears.

There is reunion.

And there is joy.

Epilogue

There are but two further elements to unravel before my account is done. The first concerns the longsuffering Jemima Gunn, in dire need of rescue.

Her papers arrive some two days after Jonathon's glorious reunion with his father, and I check them thoroughly to be sure everything's correct. One mistake, a single minor error, and not only will her escape be forfeit, but her life also. The papers must appear not too old and not too new, with just the right amount of wear and a believable patina of dirt. That's my speciality. I take pride in scuffing the corners to perfection, in achieving a spread of grime so even that time herself would be convinced of the documents' authenticity. I add a few well-placed creases here and there, and return to the corners and edges, working them until they bear a soft papery fluff.

By now, a serious conversation between Mardon and myself has taken place. It went something like this.

'Her name is Jemima Gunn. She's a hard worker, a good girl. You could do a lot worse, I promise you.'

'That's all very well, Michael, but I don't need another servant kicking around the place. Hobbs does just fine.' He tugs on his pipe and blows smoke rings into the air of the green room. The fire cackles at me and I feel I'm losing.

'Give her a go. You won't be sorry and, like I said, I'll pay her wages and all expenses.'

'Yes, you've said that three times now, but I just don't like the risk.'

I pour him another glass of port for I've nothing else to offer. No, wait. I don't, but Jemima *may*. I grab her documents and flip through them to the one with her imograph. Perhaps this'll sway him. 'Look. This is her.'

He takes the identity card and squints at it as though to humour me. He studies it longer than necessary before meeting my gaze and expelling a puff of air that says *you really know how to wear me down*. Through all his bravado I sense Jemima's raw beauty working its magic. 'She's easy on the eye, I'll say that much. All right. One month. A trial period for one month and beyond that I'm promising nothing.' He drains his glass.

'It's a deal.' We shake hands. I'm fairly confident Jemima can prove herself given the chance, and I know I can trust Mardon with her.

The next morning, I visit Jemima at the butcher's shop to brief her. She's as twitchy as a city fox but ready and, in a few hours, she'll be free of Maddox, the knowledge of which should be enough to pull her through.

While there, I remind her: 'Everything you're currently wearing. Don't keep a thing. Not a ring, nor shoe. Understand?'

'I understand,' she whispers across the meat counter.

'Mardon already has your papers. You'll receive them when you arrive.'

'Very well.'

'Your name is Ruby Shaw. Get used to it and forget that Jemima Gunn ever existed.'

'I will and I'll leave the bundle beneath the bridge. I won't let anyone see me, just as you say.'

She's good for her word, too. Soon after eleven that night, I find the bundle carefully wrapped in brown paper, propped against the arching underbelly of Rook's Bridge. If she's played her part well, Maddox is satisfied and unsuspecting, sleeping off his usual wine consumption while she has left and is on her way to freedom.

I unwrap the clothes and take my time laying them out on the bank of the Tynne. I perform a sort of victory dance as I work. It's only then that I notice the neatly folded dress is the one she bought to replace the dress Maddox tore. It seems appropriate somehow. Choosing a spot in the shadow of the bridge and in partial view of pedestrians above, I cast the dress onto the grassy bank hoping it looks like something discarded by a deranged soul and, pirouetting back to admire my handiwork, I murmur to the river.

'Goodbye, Jemima Gunn.'

The following evening I have Josiah pick up a copy of the *Camdon Herald*. He delivers it to me with his usual panache, lobbing it across the room before slumping into a chair opposite me and helping himself to a deep glass of port. I'd say he has his feet firmly under the table but they're actually resting on top of it. There are several dozen further bottles of port maturing in the cellar. We have no need to ration it, now. Not only are Cullins' golden Doleks sitting in my bank account, but Mr Barrows was so overwhelmed to have his son returned to him that he's paid us a substantial reward.

'What you looking for, if you don't mind me asking?'

'What *are* you looking for. *My* asking. *Me asking* doesn't make sense.'

'Course, sorry.'

'*Of course*. Not *course*. And take your feet off the table. We're not animals. And stop slouching. Silkers don't slouch.'

'Wow, you're touchy tonight.'

'Can you blame me?'

'I suppose not.' Josiah knows all about Jemima's escape from Maddox and that I won't relax until I know she's safe.

I turn the pages, hoping for a report on a local suicide by drowning. I know, it's not a congenial thing to hope for, but what can I say?

Before I find anything, I'm compelled to skip back to the front page, for the flash of an image sticks in my mind – a familiar urn, championed in the podgy hands of a museum official.

'I see the urn's back in the bank.' Josiah gulps port and nods towards the paper.

'Sip. Don't swig.'

He'll never get over this, you know, the latest in a long line of *excellent ideas*. And I'll never hear the last of it. I read the headlines through gritted teeth.

MYSTERIES SOLVED: CAMDON DETECTIVES RECOVER DOON'S BONES

Oh well. It's certainly put us on the map. Lizzy's run off her feet with all the new enquiries. It seems, all of a sudden, that almost everyone in Camdon needs a detective for some reason or other.

I continue to search the pages.

Ah, here it is. A small article towards the back of the paper. Jemima's threader existence was worth all four lines of an inch-wide column.

LOCAL BUTCHER'S GIRL: SUICIDE BY DROWNING

It doesn't matter that there's no imograph and few details and, of course, a body has yet to be found. What's important to me is that they believe she may be dead.

I smile and take a sip of port but, walking to view the world from the window, my celebration wanes. There are no stars tonight and the inky sky over Camdon is suitably dark even with the pale-blue glow from the city's watch-lamps. Out there are countless thousands of Jemima Gunns and Silus Garroways, all in desperate circumstances. And perhaps Mardon is right: I can't save them all.

But I can try.

A
Banyard & Mingle
Mystery

Volume II

THE GREEN INK
GHOST

B J Mears

instant
apostle

Prologue

Josiah's spade strikes wood around five feet down.

'That's it. Willard's coffin.' Standing at the edge, I peer into the pit.

'I think it *is*.' Josiah scoops soil from the lid, adding to the spoil heap. When he's cleared half of the lid, we swap places and I finish the job. The coffin is still intact and seems remarkably strong. Oak, presumably. Little else would survive as well, buried for so long. It even withstands Josiah's substantial weight. We clear the clinging earth from around the sides and gradually work the coffin up and out of the grave, laying it on the ground. It's awkward, slippery work.

Now for what is, perhaps, the grimmest part of the job.

We prise the lid off with the tips of our spades and look upon the withered remains of Willard Steeler. Josiah recoils at the sight. Steeler's skull leans, jaw yawning, hair fragmented and grey, falling to his pallid brow. He is little more than bones dressed in a gentleman's fine grey suit and black tie. All silk, of course. What flesh survives is dried out, the skin thin like parchment stretched tight.

There are superstitions surrounding the dead among the threader population, more so than with silkers. There are tales of witchcraft, of ghouls rising from the grave to haunt, drinking blood, preying on the living, but we silkers take a far more pragmatic view. The dead are dead. We observe a simple yet tempered respect for them.

Usually.

'It's all right, Josiah. There's nothing to fear.'

'But he looks so... alive!'

'Yes. He's half-mummified. But take it from me, he's thoroughly dead.'

Because the coffin is intact the interior is clean of dirt, except for the partial decay of the body, of course. This will make our job a little more bearable, for now we must search the corpse and the entire box. Unfortunately.

I take a half-crown from my pocket. 'Heads or tails?'

1

The Unwanted Letter

In which Banyard receives a letter and Mingle receives a clout

My father's death was a mystery from the start. He was well one minute. Dead the next. It all happened in such a trice that, before I knew it, at the age of fourteen, I'd become the master of the house, proprietor of the private investigations agency Mysteries Solved, and sole comforter to my bereft and ageing mother.

A Draker, one of our city watchmen, found Father's body one night at the end of an alley in Old Camdon, not ten minutes' walk from our home at 96 Bunson Street. Nothing suspicious about that – each of us ventured across Rook's Bridge into the old town on a regular basis – and, with no visible damage to his body, the mystery was passed directly to our city's hard-drinking but capable coroner, Myrah Orkney, who quickly labelled it death by failure of the vital organs. I mean, could there be a vaguer cause?

And why?

Why had his body upped and failed like that without warning? Yes, he had suffered illness some six years before, but he had fully recovered. I'm no pathologist but it seemed most peculiar.

Among my inheritance came Father's old tricorn, now my

favourite hat. I will not part with it for the world, though in a sea of toppers it is most unfashionable. It carries with it a sense of the man he was, as though all those years of use have imbued it with something of his nature.

Father's passing left his partner, Jeremiah Shrud, overwhelmed with work so we bought him out with some of Father's savings. He promptly wrapped up what cases he could before retiring from the business and moving away, leaving my mother and me to handle what remained.

In any case, that was five years ago, and I only mention it here to set the scene because, as I sit in the case room upon this sweltering summer's morning, my father's death becomes poignant once more, as you will see.

The office is humming today, a blur of activity. The air is stifling. We have many cases in progress and my operatives race around at a speed unusual for our dusty outfit. To be fair, it's become less dusty since we employed Elizabeth Fairweather as secretary – Lizzy for short. She sits primly at her desk, as shapely and smart as ever, dealing with a queue of clients. Mysteries Solved has never before been in such demand and we owe it all – well, most of it – to my esteemed partner, Josiah Mingle, and his inclination for *excellent ideas*.

Ridiculous ideas, more like.

Josiah, now rescued from his previous life as a threader, is gradually settling into the flow of silker ways and often lurches purposefully around the office, dictating, organising, reviewing, interviewing. With the sudden influx of cases, I saw fit to have him manage one – we'll see how that goes – and I fancy he carries his head all the higher because of it, which is a good thing because it might improve his muscle-bound stoop. He's still crowing over our successful recovery of Great King Doon's priceless remains and funerary urn.

Which he stole in the first place, by the way. Did I mention that?

But these new cases lose interest for me when I open the letter delivered to my desk this hour. It's an unsettling, unwelcome message.

The paper is crisp and creamy. The same flowing script of green ink forms my name on the pristine envelope and the words inside. I unfold it and read as time pauses, my associates dashing in a haze around me. For me, all is quiet, all is frozen, at least on the outside. Within, my heart rises to my throat, pounding like the jibes of a dilapidated steam truck.

> *Dearest Michael,*
> *My story is long and involved and so I shall strive to remove myself from the episode about which I will here divulge certain facts. I have other reasons for wishing to remain anonymous, reasons that I am not at liberty to share. However, it is imperative that you believe I know the following details to be true and without question.*
> *The first is this. Your father's death was unnatural.*
> *There are several other similar deaths you may also find of interest, each erroneously pronounced, those of Zacchaeus Mandon, Foster Keen and, lastly, Miss Martha Judd. Those responsible, a secret order of high social flyers, are long overdue their comeuppance.*
> *I cannot name the culprits outright as yet, and I fear I may never do so due to circumstances beyond my control. Yet, suffice to say, I believe a little digging would reveal much. You should begin at the grave of Willard Steeler.*
> *Yours truly,*
> *Demitri Valerio*

The moment passes. The world continues to turn as questions flood my mind. I raise the page to my nose and sniff. Foreseeably, it smells of ink and paper. No help there, then.

In our reception room I grab Lizzy's arm as she passes.

'This morning's letter – did you see who delivered it?'

'No, Mr Banyard. It was on the mat when I opened up. I simply placed it upon your desk.'

There's an explosion of glass at my side as a large mass enters the room from the street, shoulders first, via the windows to land before me on the floor. Shards rain and settle and, after the briefest silence, a voice of fury follows Josiah's trajectory.

'And let that be a lesson to you, sir! I've never been so insulted!'

Josiah picks himself up and dusts himself down as, outside, the hulking figure in the top hat and cloak slouches away. Pedestrians on the street stop to watch. Steam trucks and clockwork cars continue to hurtle by. And that's pretty much how Josiah first entered my life, too; exploding into my world with shattering consequences and heralding a new atmosphere. He's an expense I can ill afford. Most of the time he's a kind of idiot. And just occasionally, a genius.

'Good morning, Josiah.' I brush a glistening fragment from my shoulder. 'Who've you been insulting now?'

'It wasn't an insult. It was a compliment,' he replies.

Lizzy interjects with a shrewd guess at the truth. 'You complimented Mr Farringsgate's wife?'

Josiah nods. 'A little too highly, I fear. You can take the window out of my wages.'

'Was it worth it?' I ask. I've noticed that Lizzy has been watching Josiah frequently and, on the odd occasion, has flirted with him. She flashes him a killer smile.

'You haven't seen Mrs Farringsgate,' he says. 'You'd have complimented her, too.'

Lizzy slaps him lightly on the shoulder. 'Oh, Josiah…'

I *have* seen Mrs Farringsgate but I choose not to correct him. 'Perhaps. Sweep this up and get on to the glazier at once. We have the security of the office to maintain.'

At least the airflow has improved.

'Right away,' he grunts.

We're all good. In fact, we're as thick as thieves.

'And work on your client relational skills. I suppose Mr Farringsgate will disengage our services now.'

'Naugh. He'll come around. I'll visit this afternoon and grovel. Farringsgate loves a good groveller.'

'I'm sure – and you'll gain another glimpse of the formidable

Mrs Farringsgate, no doubt.'

'Why, Mr Banyard, whatever are you implying?' quips Josiah.

'You're bleeding,' says Lizzy, placing a hand on his shoulder. 'Sit down. I'll fetch a dressing.'

Josiah is one of those people who enjoys life to an irritating extent. He appears to relish Lizzy's attention as she brings dressings and scissors. She releases his tie, undoes several buttons and draws back his shirt to reveal the cut and several bulges of muscle before swiping the miniscule wound with iodine and taping a cotton wad in place.

'There. Good as new.'

He lunges to peck her cheek but she shoves him aside before he can strike. She slaps his arm again. 'Josiah Mingle, I'm not that sort of girl.'

Josiah closes his shirt and re-knots his tie, grinning. Lizzy smiles back at him. As he sweeps glass, my thoughts return to the letter and my father's mysterious death. Questions float to the surface.

Why has the writer waited until now to send a letter? Who is he? Can any of the information be trusted? If so, it is a report of four murders. Quite a claim, though it seems the author is for some reason unwilling to provide much assistance in naming the guilty.

Several phrases stand out upon a second reading.

Episode: A carefully selected term that conveys much. What this person experienced that led them to their conclusions must have happened over a reasonable period of time. It's safe to assume, then, that the conclusion was built upon a number of instances and is no mere whim. No reactionary cry, but a deliberated and calculated communication.

High social flyers: Perhaps this accounts for the lack of names as it implies people of influence and, therefore, great power. It follows that they might also be dangerous and fear has curtailed the writer's words.

Unnatural: The writer has gone to lengths to avoid the term *murder* and therefore to avoid an outright accusation. Perhaps again the threat of reprisal is the cause. They are not brave or able enough – for whatever reason – to name names.

Two further questions bother me.

Firstly, the author obviously knows more than he's saying. Is a second letter soon to follow?

Secondly, the message ends with a suggestion although, in keeping with the rest of the letter, an ambiguous one. More so, it's implied: exhume Willard Steeler's body from the grave. Is this truly what was meant?

For a while I'm too deeply entrenched to share this new development with anyone. I sit, attempting to digest it, recalling those last days of my father's life as I witnessed them. I remember him being insular at that time, constantly busy, always out in the field, following one lead or another. He went to work early each morning and came home late, exhausted and looking more haggard than ever before. Shrud, working an unconnected case, was unable to provide answers to the questions left behind. Even my father's case notes were of little help. It seemed nothing could be done and certainly nothing we could do would bring him back. To compound the general air of hopelessness, both Mother and the Drakers persuaded me to forget any thoughts of investigating. Our efforts soon waned in the overbearing shadow of Father's funeral and our grief.

This letter, however, has changed all that. One small page has quickly turned the whole thing on its head and now there's nothing left to do but investigate.

I make a cursory search for the casefile my father was working on when he died. Perhaps there is something in there that may help. From memory it is file number 2216 but the shelf by my desk only holds files as far back as 2300.

I lean through the doorway into reception. 'Lizzy, where are all the old files?'

Sitting at her desk, she looks up from a clipboard. 'They're boxed up, in the store room. Top shelf.'

'Right.' I enter the store and rummage until I have the file in hand. I pause, turning back to the boxes to root out a second file, this one fat and bearing no number but instead the word *Gawpers* written down the spine. It's an old file my father kept, holding records of every gawper encounter known to him.

Now, gawpers, in case you were unaware, are beings of legendary status. Many believe they exist. Probably more believe they don't. Gawpers come and go like the mist. No one knows how they do it or where they come from or where they go, but it is thought, by those who believe, that they come with ill intent. It is said that those who encounter a gawper are doomed; that if they do not perish immediately they will die soon after; that, if somehow, they manage not to die, some other tragedy will befall them. A loved one will collapse or become fatally ill with some terrible disease, for example.

Gawpers are tall beings with glowing white eyes of flame with which they probe your thoughts while you tremble, fixed to the spot like a statue. It is impossible to tell how the gawpers move. They appear to glide above the ground, or the water – wherever they happen to be.

You may be forgiven for thinking, 'My, my, Micky, you seem to know an awful lot about gawpers.' Well, there's a good reason for that.

I've seen them.

And each time it's happened, I have sweated blood.

I place the gawper file on the shelf over my desk before returning to my father's last casefile, wondering. Did he meet his end beneath the flaming white gaze of a gawper?

The file's rust-red cover is tatty, the edges worn. An elastic band holds it closed and a stamp in faded red ink on the front reads UNSOLVED. With my father's funeral and everything that followed, I can recall little more about the case other than the number and the general nature. It wasn't my case, after all. Father was investigating the death of a wealthy man of Highbridge. Even Shrud told me to let it go and, begrudgingly, I had done so.

Now my interest peaks and I can't help myself. The name on the spine reads Oliver Ingham. I open the cover and read.

Oliver first came to Mysteries Solved with fears for the safety of his daughter, Tillie, who had received several threats in the form of badly written letters. Flipping through the file I soon find them. The writing is as terrible as my father's notes suggest, the letters poorly constructed, the words irregular, misspelled and speckled with misplaced capitals.

Miss Tillie Ingham,
ShoRt is yoUre time Now. DeAth comeS fore You. OOh, thE wurms wil Taist your Flesh and Go murMur.
I wiL have JustiCe.
DWeria PhilShaw

Was the hand that shaped these words crippled in some way or perhaps that of a child in early schooling? I take a new sheet of paper and attempt to copy the style. It's almost impossible, the written formations being so unnaturally peculiar. My closest attempts come when I swap to write with my left hand. All of a sudden a word leaps out at me from the letter.

RUN.

The first three capitals that are misplaced. Was that the true meaning behind the letter? A clear message in a simplistic code? One has to wonder.

Perhaps not, though. I jot down the rest of the unnecessary capitals.

ASYOETFGMLJCWS

Surely meaningless. Checking back for my father's remarks on the letters, I find he recorded no relating comment. It's frustrating because I'm desperate to know what he made of all this.

I move on to the second letter.

Miss Tillie Ingham,
Die whore. Die. I'm comminG for your hEarT. Black is the cOlor. YoU Traitor! DArkness awaitS You. HOw yourE flesh wil fester wiTh ForGotten wurMs. I wiL have JustiCe.
DWeria PhilShaw

There it is again! Am I mistaken? The first unconventional capitals! The message is unmistakable.

GET OUT.

Wondering who this *Dweria Philshaw* is, I read and reread my father's notes but there's no mention of the threatening letters other than a basic description of their unusual style. It's so peculiar because I'm sure this is where anyone else would have started. I certainly would have. It's almost as if some of the notes are missing.

And then it strikes me.

Mother...